THE
SACRED
SORROW
of
SPARROWS

A COLLECTION OF LIVES

Siddharth Dasgupta

**NIYOGI
BOOKS**

Published by

NIYOGI BOOKS

D-78, Okhla Industrial Area, Phase-I
New Delhi-110 020, INDIA
Tel: 91-11-26816301, 49327000
Fax: 91-11-26810483, 26813830
email: niyogibooks@gmail.com
website: www.niyogibooksindia.com

Text © Siddharth Dasgupta

Editor: Jayalakshmi Sengupta
Cover Design: Siddharth Dasgupta
Cover Photograph (Front): Anna Ismagilova
Cover Photograph (Back): Excellent Collective
Layout: Shraboni Roy

ISBN: 978-93-85285-68-4
Publication: 2017

Printed at: Niyogi Offset Pvt. Ltd., New Delhi, India

For

The desires that consume,
the addictions that free,
and the sorrows that heal

～

Contents

Prelude

These aren't particularly sad stories. At least, they weren't meant to be.

It's just that sadness, the perpetual show-off, marks itself out like a pure flush of red in an otherwise clear liquid. You could have happiness, you could have penance, you could have silence, you could have ecstasy, but somehow it's the sadness that lingers the longest; often an unexpected arrival, many a time a quiet observer to relationships being played out in seemingly unblemished harmony.

And so happenstance decrees, the characters in these tales are either hopelessly or hopefully lost in the wilderness of their hearts, flailing for breath in the madness of their souls. You'll chance upon mirth in these narratives, some warmth, a touch of coincidence, and maybe even a few unexpected helpings of gratification, all tempered, of course, by a very human sadness. Nothing too potent, nothing too defeating, just the unassuming occurrence of lives being played out to their own silent music. Stripped to their cores, these fables tread something of a middle path, for the most part, as do our lives really, for the most part.

Irrespective of how extreme some of the characters may appear or how outlandish some of their actions may seem, one hopes that they resonate with you in some form or the other, as simple human beings trying to get on with living simple human lives while they flutter riotously across the canvas of their horizons like tiny sparrows. They cower, crippled by the fear of things not known;

they soar, freed from previously existing yokes; and they endure, their destinies and their desires directed by hope.

And what does a Sufi and his mystic navigation of the world, steeped in soil and anchored to the sky, have to do with any of this? Perhaps nothing, perhaps everything. Perhaps in his universal dissection of this most sacred of emotions, you'll unearth these words and these stories, tethered to the fabric of human skin and its fragile sins.

If at the end of it all, you find yourself suffused in the hushed kiss of sorrow, do accept this heartfelt apology. Because these aren't particularly sad stories. At least, they weren't meant to be.

The Baker from Kabul

awn; the haunting echoes of morning prayer lingered in the air. A large, disjointed colony of birds began to flutter with abandon, making their way excitedly to a designated address. They knew the man would soon be there.

Along the creek—the same ancient, meandering creek that had given birth to a city now bearing almost no resemblance to its older self—danced a row of small restaurants, bakeries, *shawarma* stalls, and decades-old family-run grocery stores, their reflections shimmering in the water as it swayed to the morning's silent song.

A very tiny number of them had been sleepily opening their eyes, their shutters being pulled up and their doors being unlocked by similarly sleepy owners. They weren't exactly at the water's edge but distanced from the to and fro by a slender sliver of pavement that circled its way all along the creek; a remarkable journey that managed to traverse two entirely different halves of the city, and with it a wealth of stories, immigrants, and reflections. And yet their identities—a pensive collage of hopes and fears and dreams that would neither be shaken nor easily fulfilled—managed to leap out with defiance and land into the water with a finality that seemed to say, *Hey look, this is who I am, you might as well get used to me.*

The streets were still, bereft almost entirely of human life. An ocean of mosques had begun dispelling a few faithful, their simultaneously cascading waves of dawn's *Fajr* having abated no more than a few moments ago. A few night-crawlers were stumbling out of the night's excesses—played out either in someone's home or a sufficiently exclusive, sufficiently secretive party. There were those who had succumbed to the lure of lust. The morning's rays having brought about a sudden realisation of the truth, they were now having to come to terms with the little matter of shame, followed by its more potent relative, atonement. All of them put together numbered none too many.

By the creek, the haphazardly functional flock of pigeons, seagulls, and the occasional lark were getting a touch restless.

Where could he be?

But Fateh Masood was in no hurry today. His mind was fresh, his heart was full, and he walked with a song in his steps; this despite a protracted limp on the left foot. Out on the intricate maze of roads in this neighbourhood of his adopted homeland in Dubai, out on the Creek Road leading up to where his bakery stood, and down near the water's edge where he could see his reflection bathed in radiance, he was taking his time to absorb everything.

As he neared the familiar green, white, and yellow signboard that read 'Afghan Bakery House', welcoming visitors within, he saw a woman standing outside and quickened his pace.

"Ah, Ms Fatima, have you been waiting very long?" he enquired, reaching into his pocket for a bunch of keys that circled around a locket carrying an inscription from the Quran.

"You're late," she admonished him, with a smile.

"Please accept my apologies. I was wrapped up in the beauty of it all."

"The beauty of what exactly?" she questioned him with a hint of mischief, much like an elder sister would.

"You know, I walk these streets every day, as I have for the past 25 years. Every single morning, sometimes during lunch, sometimes at dusk. But it's human nature—you just forget how beautiful everything is," he concluded, opening the door and ushering Ms Fatima inside with a gracious bow.

"Now you're just speaking in lyrics, Mr Masood," she admonished him again. "Why don't you tell me exactly what you saw?"

"Well that's just the thing, I didn't see anything special. I saw the same things I've been seeing every day. Today, I took some time to appreciate them." He stroked his long grey beard with intent, as though signifying a full stop to his answer.

"Well you must tell me some more, but first, I think you have some pretty impatient customers waiting out there," she gestured, pointing towards the back.

Fateh nodded and stepped behind the counter with urgency. Quickly, he took two large loaves of bread out from a cabinet and began slicing them into small pieces. Once he was done, he collected the pieces and the crumbs on a plate and opened the latch on the back door.

While his bakery faced the small lane that eventually merged into the larger Al Fahidi Street, it was the back door that opened out to an audience with the water and a faithful, if somewhat restless, group of patrons. Almost immediately he was surrounded by the impatient birds, who had been waiting long enough for their daily morning treat.

Stepping out from beneath the hastily constructed roof-covering and walking past an old bench, which had blended into the fabric of the bakery and served as the perfect outpost for cigarette breaks and contemplation alike, Fateh carried the plate over to the railing that separated him from the water. He flung a majority of the bread into the water, and scattered the remaining pieces on the ground. He watched as the birds swooped down from different directions, their unified cries reaching a calamitous crescendo of celebration. He watched them for a while, his long Pathan suit fluttering gently in Dubai's fresh December breeze

"You see, Ms Fatima," he continued his chain of thought as he stepped back inside, "the Sikh gentleman who runs the kebab shop at the corner of Bank Street and is up every morning even before I am; the old Pakistani tailor with the one blind eye, whom everyone on Meena Bazaar refers to as 'one-eye Salim'; the Hindu priest who begins preparing the temple here on Fahidi Street right from 4 in the morning; the Emirati security guards who take their place on the doors of Al Fahidi fort and the museum—everyone has so much beauty in their souls."

Ms Fatima looked at him and sighed. "Oh, go on, why don't you just admit it, you old fool…your son is arriving tomorrow."

Fateh laughed as he held his hands up in the air. "You know everything, Ms Fatima. We've been working together for what now? Thirteen years or so? There's no way I can hide my feelings from you."

"No you can't," she replied, smiling. "Now let me make sure everything's perfect for him," she motioned, making a sweeping gesture across the bakery.

In the short time that he'd taken with the birds, Ms Fatima had already whipped the bakery into working order, ready for the day's business. Fateh marvelled at her, but didn't mention it for fear of getting admonished again. He sat down on the old wooden chair behind the counter and observed everything.

The Afghan Bakery House was a small place, and if Fateh was being honest, 'Afghan Bakery Shed' might have been a more fitting name. But what it lacked in size, it made up in warmth, and that rare thing called 'character'.

It opened its doors every morning at 6:30 am, and as you entered from the small lane, there were two wooden counters immediately to your left, with glass panels showcasing a variety of Arabic *kuboos*, Afghan loaves, Indian *rotis*, and hearty brown breads.

Fateh would usually be behind the first counter, taking orders from a fiercely loyal customer base—many of whom had discovered him nearly three decades ago—and handling payments.

He sourced the *kuboos* and the *rotis* from Parvanah Ziad, the wife of his dear friend Mohammad Ziad, who came in every morning at 7 with a freshly-baked, aromatic batch in a large wicker basket. But he took care of the Afghan loaves and the brown bread himself, kneading them, pounding them, and making them from scratch, first thing in the morning. He repeated this once again in the afternoon while exchanging barbs and banter in his customary gravelly voice and a distinctly robust, if at times dry, Afghan sense of humour.

The entire bakery was painted in a dull green, pastel brown combination, save for the area that was used for actually baking the bread. This space that spanned the back of the bakery, leading towards the exit, was a dark red.

As Fateh looked all around him, it appeared to him that the rust and the scratches, the chipped wood and the tiny rivulets of cracks on the walls, had all become an integral part of the bakery. He stared intently at the minor decor and furnishings that he'd not bothered to change all these years: a worn sepia portrait of Mohammad Zahir Shah, the last king of Afghanistan, staring into the distance with a strange sadness; a morning prayer taken from the Quran, written with calligraphic splendour and framed with a touch of gold that had withered over the years, but not quite faded away; and finally, the most cherished of possessions, a simple black-and-white photograph that showed four people standing and smiling with soft awkwardness at the camera. He walked up to the photograph.

"I was quite handsome then, wasn't I?" he pointed out to Ms Fatima with a laugh. "But look at my Afsana, she was so beautiful..." His sentence lingered in the beautiful old air of the bakery, lost in the throes of memory.

He glided his fingers over the face of a strikingly attractive woman, with long black hair partially hidden by a headscarf. A descendant of the Pashtun tribe, her face glistened with still beauty. She held the hands of a small boy and a small girl, standing on either side of her.

"My Rukhsana," Fateh brought his finger over to the girl's face. "Look how pretty she is. One day, Ms Fatima, I'm going to surprise her and her husband in Germany," he bellowed, "and I'll take lots of gifts for my grandchild!" He duly brought his attentions on the little boy. "My Anjum, so handsome. You know this photograph was taken just before we left Afghanistan; just before the war with the Russians broke out. The children were only four and five years old, but one already knew that they would be beautiful, that they would be handsome." He smiled, a few tears settling comfortably in his eyes.

Ms Fatima came up to him and held his hands. "Memories are all we have, Mr Masood. Please make sure you make many more when your son arrives tomorrow."

Fateh smiled at her. "Yes, you speak the truth. He is 29 years old now, we have to create many more memories because we have lost so much time. But things are going to be different from now." He wiped the tears away from his eyes. "This is the first time he'll be here in almost 14 years. I've managed to bring him over only once, you know. But this time is going to be an important one; I'll make sure he stays for good."

Ms Fatima looked at him with surprise. "Really, what have you planned?"

He patted her hand with affection. "Don't worry, you will know when the time is right."

"Alright," she said, simply, and went about putting some finishing touches to her tasks.

The counter sparkled. The dough, other ingredients, and minor accoutrements were lined up in perfect order. The floor had been given a good scrubbing. The small but surprisingly cavernous wood-fire oven was cleaned thoroughly as was the tandoor kiln that stood next to it. The photographs on the wall were given a light dusting without disturbing them; the photograph of Fateh, Afsana, Rukhsana, and Anjum, especially so.

The faithful began streaming in—a few as early as 6:45, some on their way to work in plush corporate offices, some on their way to yet another futile day of job-hunting, some at the beginning of an arduous day, driving taxis for not much more than abuses from growling customers. Fateh spoke to each and every one of them, his gruff voice a startling contradiction to the kindness of the words or to the mischief, or to those moments of genuine happiness at meeting an old friend.

When it was time to close, at 6:30 in the evening, Ms Fatima came up to Fateh.

"Tomorrow I'm going to bake something special and bring it in for Anjum. It'll be better than anything you've ever baked," she said and left.

Fateh was left with her childlike laughter ringing in his ears. He stepped out of the bakery and watched her walk down the lane, towards her home that was just a five-minute stroll. He marvelled at this 68-year-old Afghan woman. And he ruminated on how the two of them, both having lost the love of their life, had managed to find friendship, support, comfort, and perhaps, even a strange sense of family with one another.

Fateh decided to take the metro that evening. He had various modes of transport to call upon each day. He would either take the metro, or be dropped and picked up from the bakery by a taxi-driver friend, or best of all, he would simply walk when the weather was nice, as it was now. But the walk took over an hour, and he wanted to get home early. A friend was dropping by that night.

As he locked the bakery and set off for the Al Fahidi Metro Station, his mind, full of happiness, was alert once more to every little sight and sensation. He walked past the Pashmina House and saw two foreign women arguing about the authenticity of the stoles with a hapless storeowner. At the Grand Mosque nearby, it was time for *Maghreb* prayer at dusk, and the shrillness of the crowd and the waywardness of the taxis and the clamour of the pedestrians on Ali Bin Abi Taleb Street were suddenly doused by the majesty of the holy verses rising into the air.

Fateh paused for a moment on the footpath, offering a silent prayer before continuing on his way. He walked past Kabul Textiles—a constant if not completely authentic reminder of home—so many memories of his homeland, both painful and joyful, were wrapped within the textures and fabrics of its carpets.

As he came on to Al Fahidi Street, he passed by the antique Bastakiya area, now home to chic galleries and cafés, all intent on cashing in on a vintage vibe and those much sought-after bohemian credentials. He'd never had the inclination or perhaps the courage to explore that quarter, but now he thought that perhaps he could take his son there, show his highly westernised Anjum that he too was capable of a bit of style.

He came on to Meena Bazaar, a thriving, heaving ode to subcontinental ingenuity and flavour, and walked past an aromatic, undeniably diverse parade of tea-stalls, jewellery shops, textile merchants, odds-and-ends brokers, stand-alone mechanics, fix-it experts, and the like.

He stopped for a bite at the delightfully straightforward Eatwell Cafeteria and grabbed himself a customary *shawarma*—its combination of meat, mayonnaise, pickles, and fries, just the tonic after a hard day's work. Soon, he had reached the station, and he shelled out six dirhams for his ride back home.

On the metro, he managed to use his broad shoulders and towering sense of presence, limp and all, into finding a seat and settled in for the 20-minute ride. Fateh wondered why he was feeling particularly nostalgic that day. His son was on his way; he would reach Dubai the following night. He had big plans to discuss with him. He had this large city to show him—this city with which he shared such a tumultuous relationship but had now come to be at peace.

The distance to his stop was not all that far, but there were two particularly crowded stations on the way, allowing Fateh enough time to drown himself in a wealth of memories from the past and hopes for the future. As the train took off, dusk's aftermath cast a wide net across the city, and from his elevated perch, atop the high overland metro, he could see the old homes on Al Mankhool Road, welcoming solitary lost souls or families who had finally attained their Dubai dream. Along with some of the oldest families of Dubai, these villas were a cauldron of authentic Emirati flavour in a city often lacking any. He saw his own reflection staring back at him from the window, the city and his identity having merged as one.

He thought about the time when he had first arrived there, two-and-a-half decades ago, fleeing a country soon to be decimated by war. He reminisced about how he had landed alone, a 35-year-old alien who wore his tribal Pashtun identity as a badge of pride, but one who found himself stripped bare naked in this strange new world. He stared at the horizon, and remembered how this entire land was bereft of anything worthwhile, and how he had seen fancy buildings being erected and gleaming skyscrapers being summoned, and lives being enriched and lives being crushed, nearly overnight, and how it had left him breathless, craving for home.

The announcer's call for Al Jafiliya Metro Station broke his stream of reflections. He got off and began walking towards his home, the limp casting an elegiac cadence to his steps. His home was in Satwa, one of Dubai's most vibrant neighbourhoods and one of the few showcasing any genuine sense of street spirit. Not so much a melting-pot of cultures, rather a loud, happy clash of lives and colour that played out to an ethnic Arab-Indian-Emirati beat.

The community's arterial Al Diyafah Street, packed to the rafters with Lebanese all-night eateries, ice-cream parlours, and Indian takeaways gave birth to several tiny tributaries, and Fateh's ramshackle home, charming in its own stubborn way, was in one of them. He shared this ground-level quasi-bungalow with two other men, an anomaly of sorts for an area where it was quite common for seven, eight, sometimes up to ten men to hole up together, reconciled to living claustrophobic lives where notions such as identity and space and boundaries simply ceased to exist.

Fateh himself was an anomaly of sorts in this subculture of indentured aliens. The bakery was doing fairly well. He had done fairly well. He could easily move out to somewhere nicer, possibly even take a home for himself. But his soul seemed at peace in Satwa's mad dance of lives, its rush of languages, ethnic essence, and recognisable din, a source of simple comfort. It seemed at peace with his two unobtrusive home-mates—Arshad, a 31-year-old Afghan, who handled the accounts for a large godown in the Thar-like Al Quoz area, but who secretly harboured hopes of striking it rich in Dubai's real estate market someday, and Afzal, a 38-year-old Bangladeshi who was office admin and a man Friday for a media agency in Dubai Media City. Most significantly, his soul seemed at peace with the reverberations of a homeland long lost, which it stumbled upon with regularity, whether in the loud conversations of the neighbouring Afghani taxi drivers here, or in the hearty kebabs of the small stands that sold them well into the night there.

✿

Late that night, Fateh Masood and Dalbir Singh sat down under the open skies in front of Fateh's home, sharing a meal of Lebanese pita-bread *arayes*, flatbread chicken, and cheese *manakeesh*.

"You know what I find funny every time I'm at Al Nafoorah, picking up dinner?" asked Dalbir.

"No, what?"

"That there will be taxi drivers, dirty from a long day's work, there will be receptionists and office boys, there will be me, who works at the docks, and then there will be these rich kids dressed in shiny, fancy clothes, off to the disco or to a party—we'll all be there, together, but we can't ever imagine living each other's lives, can we?" He paused as he took a large bite of his *manakeesh*. "We're all being served by the same guys, sometimes we're all sitting on the same red plastic chairs, and just for a second, you feel there's no difference." He laughed.

"Yes, Dubai is that sort of city," Fateh nodded. "Despite everything, I've come to look at it as home, maybe even treat it as home…" He faded away, consumed by what he had just said.

"You can't lie to me, brother," Dalbir replied. "This will never be home. That look in your eyes tells me it will never be home."

Fateh smiled. "But what can I do, my friend? Home is something that was lost so long ago. I remember that week before we left like it was yesterday. The fear, the rumours. The Soviets were coming, the Mujahideen were being raised. I had to make a decision you know, I knew we had to get out." He pointed towards his left leg, "Look at this, this happened two days before we were to leave. An explosion in the main marketplace. Everything changed that day. I couldn't move, but I had to, for my children…for my Afsana…" His eyes welled up with tears.

"I am very sorry, brother…"

"Don't be sorry," Fateh interjected. "Allah has a plan. Only he knows, only he decrees. I couldn't bring them to Dubai, of course.

There was nothing here; there was a lot of talk about there being lots of money and lots of oil and lots of gold, but who really knew? I decided to send Afsana and my daughter away to Germany to live with my uncle and his wife. And my son…" He paused, gathering his thoughts from a lifetime ago. "Well, him I had to send to Canada, to live with my childhood friend Syed and his family. I wanted the best possible life for him. For all of them, the best possible life."

Dalbir patted Fateh's hands with a sense of brotherly affection. "I've heard these stories before, don't you remember?"

"Yes, but these stories are all I have," he uttered. "I need to keep repeating them…otherwise I might forget."

Dalbir looked at his friend, intently. "You repeat them as many times as you like, brother. I will listen."

"You can never fool fate, can you?" Fateh continued. "I took my family out of Afghanistan so we could be safe, who would have known that my beautiful Afsana would perish to cancer…" his voice trembled with the past, his deep Pashtun eyes abounded with sadness. In that moment, everything about him—his six-foot frame, a generously flowing grey beard, long but thinned out strands of dark hair, bloodshot eyes, and that face marked with the scars and echoes of the past, appeared to Dalbir as childlike.

"That's all our lives are, a game of trying to understand fate," Dalbir said, finding reflections of so many of his own stories and experiences in the sorrows of this man who had come to be his brother over the past decade or so, just an Afghan and an Indian, just a Pashtun and a Punjabi, trying to make sense of their fortunes in a foreign land, trying to piece together their disparate journeys through a patched-up language of Hindi, Urdu, Punjabi, Pashto… whatever did the trick.

"But fate, she's treated me well, *mashallah*," Fateh spoke after a while. "My lovely Rukhsana is now married and very happy, as you know. I went to Germany for the wedding. There was so much happiness; I knew Afsana, up there in heaven, was looking down on everything. And as for Anjum…"

"I know, I know, he'll be here tomorrow night," Dalbir interjected, giving him a hearty slap on the back.

"Ah, but what you don't know my friend is that there are lots of big plans on the way, things are going to change, you mark my words."

"What are you on about?"

Fateh put his plate away and took a large gulp of water from a bottle. "I haven't told anyone this," he said, measuring his words as he went along. "You know the Elahi grocery store next to the bakery, the one that's been shut for the past four months?"

"Yes, what about it?"

"I've gone and bought it!" His eyes gleamed as he continued. "I'm going to merge it with the bakery and make one large bakery, I'm going to make this the best bakery in Dubai!" he exulted.

"That's incredible!" Dalbir shouted out.

"Isn't it? I'll hire more staff, maybe two more people, a large wood-fire oven, like you see in the cooking shows, a large traditional tandoor in which I'll bake *rotis, naans,* and Punjabi *kulchas*…you my brother will be very happy with this. And best of all, Anjum's going to own and take care of all of this."

"What?" Dalbir questioned him, taken aback by the revelation. "Have you told him about all of this?"

"No, I wanted to surprise him by showing him the place first. I haven't told anyone actually, except for Rukhsana. I blurted it out when we spoke on the phone last week. She always manages to draw things out of me. Anyway, this is my big dream, a big family bakery that I can pass on to my son." He stopped and stared at the distant high-rises and gleaming skyscrapers over on the perpetually plush Sheikh Zayed Road, casting their sheer richness into the skies. "This is home, Dalbir, this is all there is for now. Someday, all of us will return to Kabul, *inshallah*, but today, this is all there is."

Fateh went to bed that night restless with his dreams, the anxious energy of a child nibbling away at his heart. In his restiveness, he began to contemplate about his Indian friend, the closest thing he had to family in this city—a big, burly, bearded man who carried the fragrance of Punjab in his heart and the beauty of India in his enjoyment of life.

He thought about the time the Americans had turned on his land and how the Pakistanis had colluded with them, and reminisced over how he had discarded all his Pakistani taxi driver friends and the few of them working in small grocery stores, almost immediately. His wounds had seared too deep, his pride had loomed too large. His mind went back to witnessing Cricket World Cup games with Dalbir, when they would be part of the huge crowds gathered outside any of the stores with a television on Diyafah Street and celebrating riotously whenever India thrashed Pakistan. Were those games and those meals and those occasional visits to the illegal wrestling matches, played out in furtive corners of the discordant Deira neighbourhood, and the aimless strolls along Satwa's snaking alleyways the formidable reasons for the friendship they had forged in a largely alien environment?

He remembered the photographs Dalbir kept in his steel trunk, of his beautiful, shy wife and his two strapping young boys. He wondered whether all of them would ever meet, at the one place, and whether their children would go on to become great friends, and duly pass on this legacy to their kids, one unbreakable bond of friendship, across cultures, across generations…

Afzal awakened Fateh the next morning. In his wayward slumber from the night before, he had overslept a bit.

"Brother, there is a package for you at the door. The man refuses to give it to me."

Fateh arose and walked up groggily to the front door. He signed for his courier package and sat down on the steps. He opened it and found a letter. He began to read it under the pale light of post-dawn.

Dear Abba,

I hope this has reached you in time. I wanted to call and speak to you, but I knew you would be slightly disappointed, so I though a letter would be better. I will not be coming to Dubai. Some friends of mine are making a small trip to Vancouver, and I've decided to go with them instead. That part of Canada is very beautiful, so I don't want to miss this.

You'll be happy to know that I'm doing very well in my job. I have just been promoted to assistant executive at my consultancy firm. I wish I could explain my job to you, but it's really very complicated, and I don't want you to get confused. Canada feels just like home to me now. I don't think I'm ever going to leave. When you manage to take a break from baking and selling bread, you should come here for a short trip. That's all for now, I shall give you a call once I've returned, in six or seven days' time.

Oh, before I forget. Rukhsana called me a few days ago. She told me about the small grocery store you've bought and of your plans to create a larger bakery. Forgive her, I know it was supposed to be a secret, but you know how talkative she's always been. Anyway, I think it's a good plan. I wish you all the best. Just make sure you hire a couple of good, trustworthy people to help you with it. You don't want to be taking on too much by yourself. I'll speak to you later, Abba.

Anjum.

The sun had risen a fair distance, but its light, dwarfed by the unbroken chain of towers, cascading along Sheikh Zayed Road to the east, lay dim and scattered. Fateh stared at the letter for a long time. He stared at the envelope too, studying the Canadian stamps on it. He turned it over, and read his son's name aloud, repeatedly: "AJ Masood…"

I wonder how far it is from Toronto to this place, Van… Vankoover, he thought to himself. I wonder what makes it so special.

He folded the letter, put it back into its envelope, and placed the envelope back within the courier packet.

It was nearly 8:45 am. Out by the creek, the birds were frantic. Had he ever been this late? They circled and swooped the area behind the bakery, the flock of pigeons even hovered over the bakery a few times. But nothing. All they saw was an old lady wearing the long Muslim dress, a headscarf covering her hair, sitting on the small public bench near the front door. She must be waiting for someone as well, they thought, before circling back around and taking their places on the railing behind the Afghan Bakery House. They waited for a while longer, with full faith, until they couldn't anymore; until all you could make of them was a blurry haze of a speck, trying to reach for its own space in the sky.

The Train Rolled
Through the Night

As a child, I used to fall asleep to the sound of Indian local trains. The specificity is important here, because very few things in this world used to sound like these trains. Very few things still do, come to think of it. Theirs was an individual pattern, a certain rhythm, a distinctive cadence, if you will, that marked them apart from any other train in the world. Or any other object in the world, to be perfectly honest. I would hear the 10:30 local, rumbling in from some distance away, well past my decreed bedtime, its ominous approach punctuated by those startling whistles of objection. There were other trains of course, scattered right through the day, but the nightly 10:30 held a special pull over my imagination.

It appeared to hold the mysteries of the world within its burly iron frame, within those curiously rectangular cabins, framed edge-to-edge, within the yellow and maroon coloured bogeys, often reduced to rusted imitations of their former glories. Slowly gathering pace, slowly gathering sound. So much so, that by the time it had passed my window in a furious huff, it would have left everything shaking and rattling in its wake—my small window's partially and perpetually unhinged frame, which tilted to one side and always gave the impression that it was about to fly away at any moment, the bushes and young trees that were part of our compound, and along with them, a young boy's heart.

Needless to add, there was the sound, oh, the sound. It sounded like the noise made by the guns in those black-and-white gangster films that dad watched on Friday and Saturday nights. I was too young at the time to figure out names like Cagney and Bogart, but I understood the menace. And I identified the same in those trains. The same menace, the same momentum. Only, more poetic, with a decidedly melodic outlook towards life with the sceneries and homes they were passing by. That sound was my favourite song, my enduring lullaby…

Ra-ta-ta-tah
Ra-ta-ta-tah
Ra-ta-ta-tah
Ra-ta-ta-tah

You could count sheep to it, you could build castles in the sky with it; you could fumble your way through a couple of lines of poetry with it, you could aggregate some of the morning's complex arithmetic riddles through it. Always, a thrilling daily parade of life and its players, flashing by in a whiff—some absorbed within the paper, others dutifully engaged in a game of cards, and some, quite magically, standing at the edge of an open cabin door with their hair flying wild, beaming a smile and flinging a wave as they passed me by. These were the rebels, and they were the ones I felt drawn to the most.

Our home couldn't have been nearer to the tracks if it had tried, and it often worried me when the breeze was particularly fierce that we would be pulled out from the earth and dragged into the path of an oncoming local. But we never were. And my affair with the trains grew, much to the amusement of two fairly unobtrusive parents and the delight of a similarly afflicted elder brother. And so it was, come rain or shine, come stern reminders to go to bed or scary thunderstorms, sleep would never take me without the 10:30 having passed by...as it did, that one night, when the familiar rhythm engulfed and pulled me in, reluctantly, towards sleep...

Ra-ta-ta-tah
Ra-ta-ta-tah
Ra-ta-ta-tah
Ra-ta-ta-tah

The scream came out of nowhere, piercing the skies. I arose with a fright and looked across to see my brother in the exact same position as I, tense, upright. The train gradually passed us by, but the memory of the scream lingered.

We waited for a few minutes, but there didn't seem to be any activity or movement inside the house. This was surprising, since my father was always alert to the slightest intrusion, never mind that the intrusion was usually nothing more than a slightly confused looking mongoose. My brother Ankur, an unruffled seven to the fanciful five that I was, deduced that since our bedroom was closer to the tracks while our parents' bedroom was on the other side, they might have missed the scream altogether. Hmm, that argument seemed plausible enough.

"We're going out there," he declared.

What? Was he crazy?! "Umm, why?" I asked.

"Don't you want to see what it is?"

Hmm, fair point. I might be a bit scared, but I'm certainly no coward. "Okay. But if mom and dad woke up...?"

"They won't. Try not to bump into anything."

So, off we went, two raiders of the lost night, armed with the foolish curiosity of young boys and our trusty gumboots, the bright blue ones that lay caked with mud, even though it had been over a month since the rains had left. We felt and fumbled our way past the small passageway that connected our room to the main back door.

Ankur managed to open the latch with expert precision, and out we were—into the thrill of the night! Once we had navigated the perfectly manicured lawn, mom's outer circle of gladioli, and a somewhat marshy cluster of land that seemed abuzz with dragonflies and a curiously potent smell of turpentine all year round, we saw her. *Her.*

There she was, *on* the tracks. In the blackness of night, we could make out only a few elements—a basic form and shape, the long loose structure of the dress she was wearing, and a dark shawl that must have been draped over her shoulders at one point, but had carelessly slipped across her shoulder and lay sprawled on the mud.

Who was this woman? How did she get here? Was she still alive? As we ventured right up to her to get a closer look, we saw it. The blood. An endless pool of blood that lay exposed in the unforgettable night; a swirly trail of black that appeared to glisten even under the night sky, seemingly nourished by a few distant stars and an occasional moon. The moon appeared to be an accomplice in the crime, playing a sly game of hide-and-seek with a fluffy bouquet of clouds, giving us an unexpected glimpse of the woman, and then, just as suddenly, bathing her in darkness

At first numb with horror, attracted and repelled alike by the serpentine flow of liquid, we soon mustered enough courage to sit on the edge of the rails, right beside her. We sat in silence. I wanted to be strong, I wanted to be brave. But the drama was too much for me, and I began to sob, softly. Ankur moved over to me and held an elder brother's arm of assurance across my shoulder.

"Don't worry," he murmured, his own voice shaking just a touch.

I wanted to believe him and looked straight at him. But the look on my brother's face now was one of pure horror.

"Look," he gasped, pointing at the vast emptiness behind me. As I swerved around in a flash, I already knew what to expect. It was a train. It was the night's 11:30 delivery. You could make out its foreboding outline, framed as it was against the harsh brightness of its headlamps that were slowly coming into view. The loud whistle signalled its intent, and we knew it wouldn't take more than a couple of minutes for its dark presence to bear down upon us.

We looked at her. Though she wasn't exactly on the tracks, she was close enough to them to be swept along in the monster's wake, or so we felt. We knew her body would most likely be crushed, or worse. We knew we had to act fast. We got up and began to pull her by her feet with all the might and fervour our young bodies could muster. We didn't know if she was even alive. We had no idea what we were getting ourselves into. But we knew we had to pull.

As the train approached, closer and closer, its light began to illuminate her face, till almost all of it lay revealed under the curious gaze of a mischievous moon and an unforgiving train. I was entranced, unable to tear my eyes away from her long dark hair as it fell across her face on one side, unable to remember if I'd ever seen skin so porcelain-like. And her eyes? They were the eyes that really did it; oval almond-shaped gems that were lined thick with kohl. I was entranced by the fact that they lay open, even though she might well have been dead, glistening under the distant stars and the unearthly light.

"Snap out of it!" Ankur hissed, sensing we were nearly out of time.

With one last breath and one final piece of effort, we pulled, desperately. That dramatic exertion dragged her hair over the tracks, and we yanked her by her dress, leaving her a good couple of feet outside harm's way, even as the train thundered by in a deafening roar of derision, its whistle silencing whatever else lay of the night. As we sat by the dirt and watched it pull away, a curious thought swept over me. I thought about how lucky she was, in a way, to have the sound of the train as her eternal lullaby, to have its dreamy cacophony as the thing that put her to sleep on her last night...to have its echoes stirring in the wind, night after night...

Ra-ta-ta-tah
Ra-ta-ta-tah
Ra-ta-ta-tah
Ra-ta-ta-tah

We eventually got around to waking up the parents that night. We didn't go into the details of our adventure of course, only telling them that we had been awoken by a scream and had no idea what it was.

It was dad who 'discovered' the body, and it was dad who informed the police. By dawn, our sleepy neighbourhood and the long-forgotten space of land that separated our home from the tracks was a hive of activity. Evidence was gathered, details were taken, questions were asked, answers were given. No one seemed to have any idea who she was. Just a beautiful stranger, tossed out from the train, left to the cruelties of this complicated world. Or a troubled woman, perhaps, having no other recourse than to bring her life to a sudden, crushing end?

Lots of enquiries were made, and the night's 10:30 was traced all the way from its origins to its final stop. I heard later that many passengers were questioned and a pair of seedy-looking characters were marked out as possible culprits.

Her entire body was eventually covered in white cloth and hoisted on to a strange, makeshift stretcher of sorts. It was carried away by two men from the local hospital. They were dressed in those clinically depressing white shorts that most of the hospital service staff wear. They heaved her into the ambulance, which had to trample over some our plants to get to where she lay. I looked at their legs and winced. They were dotted with dragonflies.

The job was done. Just like that, she was gone. It was all so clinical. The commotion duly died down, as did the questions, and finally, this woman who no one had any clue of, disappeared gently from memory, as she had from that night.

I found it hard to sleep for weeks after that. My fascination with the train, though intact, now carried a certain foreboding element to it. I would lie on the bed at night and keep my eyes open with my fingers, trying to keep sleep at bay through force. I had this lingering sensation that if they were to close, *she* would come flooding back in.

Eventually though, unencumbered by the weight of wisdom and age, I began to let go of the memory. My fondness for the trains came flooding back in, as did my strange thought from that night that she was in a better place, that she was in a fortunate space, even at peace, in the arms of the train's moving lullaby, free to call upon that familiar sound at her beck and call…

Ra-ta-ta-tah
Ra-ta-ta-tah
Ra-ta-ta-tah
Ra-ta-ta-tah

He arrived at my front door a week or so ago. He had, apparently, managed to secure my address after making quite a few inquiries from scattered family and friends. He was quite nondescript, in that peculiar way door-to-door salesmen tend to be. He said his name was Paresh, and I immediately felt sad for him, thought I don't really know why.

"Are you Akshat Kannan?" he wanted to know.

Yes, I was.

"Are you the son of Mihir and Kamla Kannan?" he wanted to know.

Yes, I was.

"The brother of Ankur Kannan?"

Right again.

"Was your father a part of the defence establishment and did you once live in Bungalow 33B, Appleby Road, off the old railway track in the south Indian town of Wellington?"

In a way, yes, he was a sports administrator hired by the National Defence College, but he wasn't an integral member of the army. And yes, that was the home I was born and grew up in.

As I replied, it struck me that neither my brother nor I had had the heart to go back there since our parents had died. Ankur had moved to Bangalore, and after earning his chops with the Marriott Group, had broken away to set up a small café of his own. It wasn't doing spectacularly well, but it kept him happy most days, and there's a lot to be said for that. I had moved north to Delhi, flirting between a job in publishing and weekend dalliances with an experimental heritage tour company.

"Is there something I can help you with?" I finally asked him, mildly annoyed with the stream of questions.

"Actually, I think I can help you with something," he replied, with a somewhat smug expression on his face.

Without much explanation, he rose and walked out the front door, returning with a square, not-too-large carton.

"What is this?" I asked, fearing that my salesman speculation might have been right after all.

"This is yours, I believe," he replied. "You see, Mr Akshat," he continued, "only last week I moved into my new address, at 14, Mission Street, Pondicherry."

Seeing no recognition on my face with regard to the address, he continued.

"I'm a government employee, you see, and this house has been fixed for us when I moved to Pondicherry last month. I have a small family, you see, just my daughter, my wife, and me, so this bungalow is very much suited for us. Actually, you see, it is where the whole of the United Petrochemical Engineering team has been shifted to, we all are living in only five to ten minutes from each other."

Beginning to find the 'you see' and his pidgin English slightly tedious, I almost asked him whether he would be more comfortable speaking in Hindi, so that we could get on with it. I held back though, sensing he was nearing his grand revelation anyway.

"But how is all this connected with me?" I asked him, trying to push things along.

"Ah, but you see, I had the whole of the house cleaned before we moved in. And they did a okay-okay job, actually you must come and visit us sometime," he grinned, widely.

I nodded, sagely, still having no clue where this was headed.

"But those stupid cleaners, they did not bother to clean the attic, you see," he persisted. "I was up there myself, 12 or 13 days ago, so much dust, oof! Anyway, I didn't want to bother with those men again, so I began to clean the small attic myself. That is when I found this."

As he pointed towards the carton, I felt relieved that we were finally nearing the end of this decidedly odd conversation and the intrusion of this decidedly peculiar fellow.

"Mr Paresh," I uttered gently, "why should all this be important to me?"

"Because it is yours!" he beamed, pushing the carton towards me. "Well, it must have some connection anyway, from what I have understood. What I mean, you see, is that it belonged to the people who lived in the bungalow a long time before us and the only type of contact I could find in the things inside..." He paused,

as though preparing himself for the final revelation. "The name...
Anyway, I think you see it for yourself."

The rest of Mr Paresh's explanations and 'you-sees' and travails
in trying to locate either me or my brother and the fact that he got
called up to Delhi for a meeting that week, so he decided to bring
the carton along with him, you see, instead of just calling me and
informing me about it, and the strange slanted look he gave me as
he spoke, all of it just faded away into the background, relegated to
a dull, irrelevant monotone when held up against the curiosity of
what that carton actually contained.

I began sifting through its contents, and in my mind, it almost
appeared as though I had been taken back in time, back to a place
accented in sepia and framed with poignancy. There were a few
ancient papers, which were nothing more than official documents
of some sort. There were three old volumes of Charles Dickens, and
I marvelled at the state they were in, age not having withered either
their hard-bound veneer or their sense of literary crispness. Then
came a photograph of a woman.

Which is when I froze.

It was her.

Her.

Over two decades had passed since that fateful night on the
tracks, but her face had been etched into my consciousness ever
since. I couldn't be mistaken about it. Those eyes, dusted with
colour, that beautiful porcelain skin, a sense of, I don't know what
it was, distant sadness perhaps? It was her. I held the photograph
in my hands as though it were a national treasure, afraid to either
tear it apart or disturb its sense of frozen perfection. Even through
the frayed edges of the photograph and the marks and scratches
that had invited themselves in and the large sway of sepia that
washed over the image, there was something about her that was,
I don't know, ethereal almost. I turned the photograph around, and

next to 'Victoria Photos, Arts College Road, Pondicherry' I saw a name that had almost faded away from existence. Flora Fleming. I repeated it out loud to myself. Flora Fleming. I tried to picture her presumably Anglo-Indian existence, her life in Pondicherry, her life in a home that now lay occupied by a hard-working man, his wife, and his daughter, neither of whom had any notion or any perceivable interest in who she might have been.

I suddenly realised that Paresh was still in my house. I quickly regained a bit of composure and offered him some coffee, which he happily accepted. As he sat and drank his coffee in my living room and continued to make polite chit-chat about his new life, about the fact that arranged marriages can be a 55 proposition and how he'd struck gold in that regard, and about his daughter who was showing early signs of becoming a bit of a chess whiz, my mind was far away. It was in Pondicherry, yes, but not in the town he was recounting to me, rather, a few decades into the past. I didn't quite know what I was feeling or how I was going to engage in any sort of meaningful conversation with this fellow who, though extremely kind and remarkably industrious, held absolutely no interest in the thoughts of a man inundated with a million questions. I was relieved when he thanked me for the coffee and left.

The carton's only remaining contents were some letters, rolled together and fastened by a black string. With a wildly beating heart, I unfurled the first one and began to read. It was from sometime in the late 1970s. It contained words like 'love', 'attracted', 'distance', and 'together'. It spoke of a woman's thoughts being consumed day and night, it spoke of an attachment that was more than her heart could bear. It spoke of happiness that lingered in the air, it spoke of memories that accosted her everywhere. I read another, and then another. There was a stray envelope in there too, the catalyst for Paresh's committed investigations, no doubt. A silent tremor began to invade my body. Before I knew it, I had gone through the entire pile. The latter ones began to reveal words like 'regret', 'longing', and 'unfulfilled', but the 'love' and the 'together' never ever faltered. Irrespective of mood and tone, regardless of date and year, the letters had one similar constant. They were all addressed to Mihir Kannan. They were all written for my father.

※

Ankur and I sat on the tracks, taking turns to swig from a bottle of Jack Daniel's. It had been well over a decade now since we'd been back here, a couple of decades since that scream, and nothing appeared to have changed, save for the fact that we were there in the evening, under a shocking blue sky and the impending burst of dusk. We looked out along the tracks, as it stretched a mile or so beyond our house and then curved its way to oblivion. We looked out at our house. It was still our house, of course. It was the family home, just a family home bereft of family. Neither Ankur nor I had had any interest to stay on here, or stay on in Wellington, and without our parents, of course, the house was nothing more than a collection of childhood dreams...a largish treasure-chest to be dipped into from time to time.

We thought of the woman who had lain there, not more than a foot away from where we sat. We knew her name now. But still, we knew nothing of Flora. Between long quaffs of dry whiskey and extended drags of a local *beedi*, between loud laughter of two drunken brothers and the occasional tears of two orphaned children, we tried to make sense of the past.

"It's strange how things come around, don't they?" Ankur began.

"Yeah," I agreed, taking a long drag from the local cigarette. "This place is always with me, though there's not a damn thing that's remarkable about it."

Ankur laughed, as he spoke, "I know. But things don't have to be remarkable, they just have to be...there," he trailed off, trying to spot our parents through a haze of memories.

"You doing well?" I asked, trying to bring the flavour of another city into our present circumstances.

"Yeah, when you coming on over to have a taste of authentic south Indian appam and stew, done with an oriental twist?"

"God, that sounds terrible," I replied, laughing loudly. "Nah, I'm just kidding man." I took another large swig of whiskey, its dry, dark flavour just the tonic for the anxiousness within me. "Since we're both down here anyway, we could just head there together after this," I suggested.

"Sure thing."

He played with a few strands of grass near him, while I tried to fling pebbles along the course of the tracks, doing our best, clearly, to avoid bringing things out into the open, before Ankur eventually did.

"What happened that night?" he asked me, point-blank.

I'd been waiting for the question, but the directness of it still hit me. "I don't know, man. I've been imagining every damn possibility since I received the carton, I just don't know."

"Do you think, dad...?"

"I just don't know."

"But wouldn't he have..."

"I just don't know."

We knew it was a futile task, trying to make sense of the past. But we spoke, because there was nothing else to do. We spoke of our parents, with love and kindness. We spoke of Flora, with something resembling reverence. The wind picked up, and the large row of eucalyptus trees on the other side of the tracks began to sway in somewhat drunkenly fashion, mocking us gently, as it were. The overgrown shrubs, sprinkled weeds, age-old trees, and long grass that now populated our garden began to do the same. The tiny patch of marshland was still there, as was its potent smell, all turpentine and dragonflies, and the wind gradually picked up those remembrances entrapped in youth. We played that night out, over and over again. We played out the irony of the cops and the townsfolk hunting for an imaginary perpetrator from the train, when the actual act might well have been committed from the ground. We considered Flora and her state of mind, and whether she might not have, in a final act of tragic love, timed things to perfection. With anguish weighing down on our hearts, we dissected our father and what sway this love might have held over him all those years, and whether a man whose firm hand and inner kindness had set the template for our lives early on would ever have had it in him to execute an act so dissonant from himself. We thought of love in a time gone by, and how emotions left unsaid and stories without a sense of closure, or worse, how love that lies unrequited, can end up dissolving souls in blood. We discussed those letters, and I read from a couple of them I was carrying in my pocket. My voice trembled, just as a train appeared on the distant horizon. We arose and let it pass us by. A couple of red-blooded youth on the roof of one of the cabins waved out wildly at us, and we did the same, happy in the knowledge that they had found a way to get to where they needed to be. We went back to the letters, and wondered whether dad had also kept a bundle of letters at home, maybe hidden away somewhere in the attic at one point, and whether they'd been letters from her, letters that had been returned…or simply, letters he'd been meaning to send and just couldn't summon the courage to. We tried to remember his handwriting and how the curves reared up proudly, and whether those same proud curves had graced the 'F' in her beautiful name.

That night we slept in our old room. It was more a symbolic gesture than anything really, since we knew we were never going to return to that house. We were going to have to let go of it. We talked for a while, drank some more whiskey, trying to pinpoint a few cherished stories from our childhood that the house had harboured.

"Hey, remember when we were playing cricket in the garden with that shiny new bat dad had brought from Chandigarh?"

"How could I forget," replied Ankur, with a grin.

"Man, you smashed the first ball I threw at you right through the kitchen window."

"Yeah, and do you remember what you asked father as you tiptoed in to fetch the ball?"

"Umm, excuse me Dad, but did you hear a thud?"

We burst out laughing, recalling the look of incredulity on dad's face at the time. Ankur recollected another little nugget from the past...

"How about that time you decided to try your hand at making them breakfast?"

"Thanks buddy for bringing that one up," I grinned. "Now let's see how good your memory is. What did I ask them when things went wrong?"

"How could I forget? You dragged me along for moral support, remember? And then that timid—sorry Mum, but is it a good thing if the kitchen's filled with smoke?"

We burst out laughing again, and Ankur fell on the floor in a heap, liquor and laughter having done the trick. Through the darkness of the room, with all the lights turned out, through the darkness of the moment, betrothed as it was to a warm Wellington night, I thought I saw a faint glimmer in his eyes, the faintest sparkle of a tear.

The 10:30 local duly came along. My heart began to beat a little faster. Like clockwork, the window-frame, by now reduced to hanging on to its very last vestige of dignity, rattled and shook with fierce seizures. Announcing its intent through those haunting whistles and that thunderous gallop, the train soon rushed past our window in a fierce temper, gradually allowing my heart to rest a little easier. The 11:30 pm came and went as well.

Ankur must have fallen asleep by then. I lay awake for a long while, looking out of our room, across to the tracks, and further into the blank canvas of the night. I lay awake, intent on keeping memories at bay. I don't know what time I finally dozed off, but just before I did, I remember thinking that our lives would always, in a sense, be attached to those tracks. And that no matter how hard I tried, I would never ever be able to fall asleep without a certain momentum echoing in my mind, without a certain rhythm resonating through my dreams. It was the sound we were destined to be attached to forever, an aching lullaby that whistled as it went along on its merry way. And, just like that, I must've fallen asleep as well, strangely comforted by the cadence of an innocence lost. Strangely comforted by the lingering soundtrack of our lives, its rising passions a proportionate music to the frailties of our hearts…

Ra-ta-ta-tah
Ra-ta-ta-tah
Ra-ta-ta-tah
Ra-ta-ta-tah

A version of this story, entitled *Trains and Other Childhood Curiosities*, first appeared in *Cha: The Asian Literary Journal*, Issue 32.

Gulmohar Drive

The Smell of Earth

A word flashed before Shenaz Wadia's eyes where it lingered for a while, each letter flailing as though it were written in shapeless smoke, before drifting away forever. It was a word her grandma had taught her—the grandma whose warmth, enduring Parsi eccentricity, and unencumbered laughter were her most vivid memories of days gone by. Even after it had floated off, the word and its essence lingered.

Petrichor. The smell of the earth after the first rains. When everything is fresh with hope, when cities are pregnant with the possibility of beauty.

She remembered making a strange face when she first heard it as a child, the word striking her as ugly and none too appetising. But it had stayed with her nonetheless—slowly becoming an unobtrusive part of her travel dictionary as she began tiptoeing into places strange and new, becoming a part of her belongings as she moved away and made another city her home, becoming a part of the larger lens with which she'd begun to view the world. Most pertinently perhaps, becoming a part of the city she had grown up with...its memories, its smells, its regrets.

So much so that together with 'ocean', 'magenta', and 'serendipitous', *petrichor* had gradually gone on to become one of her favourites, a quick summation of everything the monsoons stood for. *Petrichor* played around with her thoughts as she drove under the curious sway of yesterday, right into the arms of Mayo Road. Back to a childhood home, whose most cherished occupant, Grandma Tania, had now passed away.

Once on Mayo, Shenaz felt as though the past 10 years had never even happened. She began to take stock of things, her mind able to recall people and homes and addresses and sequences by memory, not needing sight to validate its claims

There was the old Khosla bungalow, a haunting postcard from the past. She could almost see the twins, Ravi and Mehak, bounding through the gate on their way to school; the sparkle on their spotless yellow schoolbags somewhat diffused by the strange dissonance of time.

Next up were the Thimmaiahs, whose red-bricked roof still bore that scar from when it had been assaulted by an errant cricket ball struck by the Mehta kid from across the road, and whose living-room still seemed to echo with the remnants of endless laughter from those Diwali parties that used to drag on till dawn.

On to the Qureshis, and Shenaz closed her eyes for an instant to take in the whiff of *haleem* and traditional Hyderabadi biryani, being slow-cooked for days in clay pots, and those huge cauldrons that used to rise above her head.

Moving on to where the Ahluwalias and the Sens had once lived, across from each other, bringing with them vivid images of her college days—of scaling walls after breaking late-night curfews, of running through wet next-door lawns in order to catch those great bands from Bombay. Shenaz opened her eyes. She sighed.

Next up, the Wadias. Shenaz turned off the ignition and waited at the gate. The burly wooden guardian to their home had turned old and a few chinks were showing in its armour. She got out of the car and walked up to it, allowing her fingers to caress its cracks and crevices, trying to find some answers to the questions she had played with over the years within those marks of a life long-lived.

"Shenaz Baby!"

She was shaken out of her reminisces, as much by the suddenness of the yell as by the fact that she was being addressed as 'baby'. She peered through the gate's pillars and saw an old man hurrying towards her from the caretaker's quarters that were at the far left corner of their compound. Ah, Mistry Bhaiyya! Shenaz waited till the old man unlocked the gate, and immediately took his hands into hers.

"*Bhaiyya*," she spoke softly, addressing him in that endearing Indian word that could traverse friend, elder brother, stranger, and caretaker, based on situation and context, with simple ease. "It is so good to see you after all these many years. I'm surprised you could recognise me this easily."

She could see that it had taken no time for the old man's eyes to well up with tears.

"You think people ever forget the ones closest to their hearts? We have waited so long to see you. You've kept us waiting for ten long years." Mistry Bhaiyya waited for his tears to abate. "Your Parvati Didi is in Indore visiting her family, otherwise she would be drowning in tears right now."

"And your kids?" Shenaz enquired.

Mistry smiled. "Well just like you, they are not kids anymore. Radhika got married a few years ago and she lives in Baroda with her husband. She blessed us with a grandchild two years ago. While Ramesh lives in Nashik. He's working on one of those big farms out there. We have found a girl for him, and soon I will have more good news to share."

Shenaz beamed. "That is lovely news. It makes me very happy that the entire family is doing well. You have never left my thoughts, any of you."

Mistry looked into her eyes. "I remember how all of you used to play together—you, Mehr Baby, Pheroz Baba, my Radhika and Ramesh…time just flies by."

Shenaz gave his hands, which were still in hers, a tight squeeze. "I better get my car inside and park it in the garage."

"But it's so early in the morning," commented Mistry. "Where have you driven from, surely not all the way from Delhi?"

Shenaz laughed. "No, no *bhaiyya*. I just wouldn't have had the patience or the skills to navigate myself over such a long distance. I actually flew into Bombay yesterday morning and spent the day with Pheroz and his family. I was planning on taking a cab to Poona, but Pheroz suggested that I take their car instead. He has a much large one now, this is his old and neglected car."

"And how was Pheroz Baba?" Mistry wanted to know. "I mean I hope things were well between the two of you. Was he upset that you did not come for…"

"He understood," Shenaz interceded. "I'm sure the people who matter to me will understand."

Mistry's eyes welled up with tears all over again. "I had known Tania Madam for nearly 40 years and had been a part of this family ever since. It was so sad, it just doesn't feel the same anymore."

Shenaz patted his arm gently. "As long as we keep remembering the people we have loved, they never really go away…"

Shenaz walked towards the car, suddenly aware that her own eyes were glistening under the influence of tears. As she drove her brother's small, well-worn car into the garage, she noticed that nothing much had changed: that same musty smell, those same cracks in exactly the same places, that large pile of files, letters, photographs, and documents accumulated over the decades, those wooden cartons filled with God-knows-what, nothing much had changed at all. As she took the house keys from Mistry, a thought struck her.

"*Bhaiyya*, is the house—the furniture, the rooms—all covered up?"

"Oh no, baby," he replied. "The house is ready for you. The family was here only a month ago, no? I suppose they knew you would return sooner or later."

Mistry left to tend to a few things in the garden, leaving Shenaz at the covered front-door entrance framed with that familiar smell of bougainvillea creepers and memories.

❧

That Which Dissipates; That Which Lingers

The sun's coy early morning rays, suffused with a misty diffusion, bred from laziness and the pervading presence of the monsoons, bathed the Wadia home in a ripened glow of poignancy.

As Shenaz wheeled her two suitcases inside the front door, she realised that Mistry Bhaiyya was right. The house *was* ready for her. When Grandma Tania passed away over a month ago, most of the family had trooped in from various parts of India, some from abroad. Shenaz had been fairly certain that they would've covered the house in sheets and blankets upon their departure, unsure when its doors would be opened again. But perhaps Mistry Bhaiyya was right; her appearance must've been anticipated at some point in time.

Shenaz began to walk through the only home she'd known for 21 years of her life. She felt a small shiver run down her spine at the eerie familiarity of everything in front of her eyes: the simple yet beautiful wooden furniture that populated the large living-room and each of the four large bedrooms; the framed, fraught photographs of three generations of Parsi ancestors, looking down upon her in black-and-white gazes or sepia stares etched in time; the classic European bentwood chairs and large circular table that formed the focal point of a kitchen draped in dew; the verandah where a thin rectangular table and a long divan welcomed visitors to tea and *naan khatai* from Kayani Bakery at any time of the day; a back porch framed with flowers, looking out on to the lawn that lay pristine if silently overgrown green; those steel boxes and cases that were home to strange instances of ancestral affluence; family photographs on various walls that showed Shenaz, her sister Mehr, and her brother Pheroz with their parents Delnaz and Cyrus at various points in their lives, in different stages of togetherness and moodiness; those richly eccentric curios that lay sprinkled on shelves, cupboard tops, and wooden cabinets alike; those ancestral keepsakes that had lived in this house for so long they had almost seeped into the fabric of the walls; that evocative Camp smell that managed to seep through every portion of the house, a distinctive fragrance of the city of Poona and this particular neighbourhood, an old yet comforting smell, bred from the confluence of memories, childhoods, and those ubiquitous gulmohar flowers; everything lay spread out before Shenaz's eyes, as it once had, as it always had.

Shenaz paused for an instant and took a deep breath. She was standing at the door to Grandma Tania's room. Gradually, she walked in. Bathed in a mellow mood of sunshine, the room reminded her of a scene from some classic noir film, even in the present, somehow destined to always be viewed through a veneer of mystery-laden sepia.

There were Grandpa Mirzad's two fairly undemonstrative portraits that stood side by side on the wall to the left—one showing him as a handsome young man of 28, hair slicked back with élan and that thin figment of a moustache that could only be described as Clarke Gable-esque; and the other, of the same dimensions, showing Mirzad as a 78-year-old, fragility not having dimmed that gleam in his eyes.

These stared at the two portraits of Grandma Tania on the opposite side of the room—similarly, one as a young woman, the other as the woman Shenaz had always known. Her grandma had never been a very pretty woman, but there was something about the sense of mischief brewing in her eyes and the generous mounds of curly hair and the petite nose accentuated by little dabs of freckles that somehow made you linger on that face.

The bedroom was an encomium to her tastes and her treasures—two towering wooden cupboards filled with family records and favourite dresses and what have you, a few scattered watercolours by a dear friend, a large window-dresser packed with a messy, though abundant, collection of creams and lotions and lipsticks, and small, unremarkable traces of her family, cherished only by her.

Shenaz walked around the room for a while, overcome by her grandma's overpowering presence that permeated its spaces. It smelled like her. It *felt* like her. It held the curious confluence of that slight trace of sandalwood whose origins had always been a mystery, her dab of Christian Dior that was destined to linger in the air forever, and, as always, the mystic fragrance of the gulmohar flowers whose trees lined their avenue from beginning to end, draping their street in a canopy of flourishing leaves and the excitable sparkles of those graceful red blossoms, only in full bloom every time the monsoons came around.

Shenaz ran her fingers over the plump queen-size bed. Its mattress and the lavish bed sheet spread over it billowed like a singular cloud overfilled with pride. Every square inch of the bed echoed with memories of the matriarch. This was where she had slept when she had first gotten married, reclusive at first and then drawn irretrievably towards the man she would come to regard as her soulmate; this was where Shenaz's mother had been conceived; this was where parties thrown in those early days would sometimes converge late at night, either pulled in by a game of cards or the even more licentious matter of neighbourhood gossip; this was where she had regaled family, friends, and guests alike with riotous tales of Bombay from the '50s when jazz, drugs, films, and art were at the threshold of something new and something wild; this was where she had cradled, cursed, and cherished her three grandchildren, bestowing special attention on the little one, whose one exaggerated curl across the side of her forehead reminded her of a photograph of Marilyn Monroe's she'd seen, once upon a time; this was where Mirzad had passed away, silently with grace, leaving this world much as he'd lived when in it; this was where she had laid down alone in the afternoon and at night for 13 years, nursing a glass of whiskey with soda, together with remembrances from when they'd both been young and in love; and this was where she had uttered a last silent goodbye, to her Bombay, to her Poona, to her family, fractured yet not quite forsaken, to her daughter and her husband, to her grandchildren and her home, and to that one grandchild with the curly locks, the one whom she had been unable to lay eyes on for close to a decade.

Shenaz felt a strange weight descend upon her shoulders. She knew it wasn't something as well-defined as guilt or something as sharply-etched as remorse, yet it carried some of the same characteristics. She lay down on the bed, on Grandma Tania's pillows, and allowed her tears to pull her towards sleep. Exhausted by her journey to Poona and all the emotional anguish that had come with it, she slept where her grandma had once slept…deeply, peacefully, regretfully.

IRANI CHAI AND ITS CONSEQUENCES

Damn you Poona, you beautiful sad song, Shenaz thought to herself as she settled into one of the old bentwood chairs at Café Yezdan and peered out through its large brick-lined windows at a monsoon on the verge of making up its mind.

"Did you say something?" Susan asked.

"No, just thinking to myself," Shenaz replied. "Thanks for dragging me out of bed at 7 in the morning, by the way. It's not like I could have done with some rest after five hours of driving yesterday morning. Remind me again why I informed you I had arrived?"

"Because you felt guilty about abandoning me all those years ago and not really seeing me in, oh, about 10 years?"

Shenaz smiled as she looked towards the young men judiciously kneading, heating, and fluffing the mounds of dough in Yezdan's open kitchen cum bake-house. As their *brun-maska* duly made its way from the bakery, Shenaz wondered how many millions of these Parsi-styled buns lathered with butter the storied Parsi café had served in its 150-year-old history.

"Cheers!" Susan welcomed her out of her thought, raising the three-quarters filled glass of hot, sweet chai that accompanied their breakfast. Shenaz clinked her glass with Susan's.

"I can't believe you missed Grandma Tania's funeral," Susan said, without any discernible hint of emotion in her voice.

The immediateness of the accusation took Shenaz by surprise. She took a sip of her hot chai and looked at her friend.

"I was shaken when I'd heard. Mehr had called me from Singapore. In a haze, I'd thrown some stuff into a bag. As I was about to leave for the airport, it suddenly came to me. I remembered Grandma Tania telling me once: 'I want my death to be a lively affair, no *rona-dhona* please. If I catch any of you crying or making a scene, I'll give the lot of you one tight slap!' I realised that I wouldn't be able to do justice to her wishes; I would've been a wreck. Besides, with everyone being there at the same time, I felt it would've been a recipe for disaster. I knew she would understand. Anyway, I'm here now, aren't I? When I can say goodbye to her in peace…" Shenaz looked towards a flock of birds shooting across the overcast sky in wayward formation. "I think it's a nicer way to say goodbye."

Susan smiled at her friend. "This place hasn't changed in nearly 200 years now," she mentioned, sipping her chai. "It's like a stubborn, cantankerous old Parsi uncle; weird and wonderful in its own bloody way."

Shenaz let out a laugh. "Yeah, old photographs of Yezdan look like they could have been taken this morning, don't they?" she averred. "Like a portrait time forgot. That's why I chose this place when you called up this morning, I guess I wanted to be frozen in time for a while."

As they sat eating their breakfast and drinking another round of chai, Shenaz studied Yezdan through the ways of its characters: the band of Muslim brothers, heavily bearded and elegant in their white *kurta-pyjamas*, engrossed with matters of family pride and national politics; the waiter boys in their bright red T-shirts, some with resignation etched profoundly within their eyes, for a life not having worked out quite the way they had planned; the heavily-set owner who sat at the front of the café, casting an idle eye over the affairs of an ancestral heirloom that had passed hands across probably three or four generations before reaching him; the young, much-in-love couple going through their meal of fluffy cheese omelettes and scrambled eggs with toast by feeding each other bites from each other's plate; and on the table next to theirs, the old Parsi gentleman with the bright shock of thick grey hair, seemingly suspended in a fragment of time, the faraway look in his deeply-set eyes hinting at a love affair having met a cruel end decades ago, or a cherished love having forsaken his side in the twilight of his now-pointless life...

"What happened back then?" Susan blurted out, as matter-of-factly as her previous accusation.

"Huh?" Shenaz wondered, coming out of her character dissections.

"Ten years ago, what happened? I mean, to an extent I know. It's not like we've never spoken since then or haven't kept in touch. But still, I'd like to hear it from you."

Shenaz sighed, causing Susan to laugh. "I'm sorry, I don't mean to put you on the spot. But it was like having a loved one snatched away from your life without warning or much explanation."

Shenaz had known the questions would flow thick and fast here in Poona, some from inquisitive sorts, some from dear friends. She warmed to her task with a large sip of her hot chai.

"I was deeply in love with Akshay, as you know. We were young, I realise that, but the love was genuine and deep. It wasn't just that my parents were against it, but it was the manner in which they began to shun me that stunned me. You don't know how sensitive this thing is for Parsis, marrying outside the community and all. To marry within the community, to keep the flame alive—that's the mantra that's fed into you. It's different for you. I mean, sure, you're Catholic but there's still more than 20 million of you in our land. How does that constitute a minority in any way? But for Parsis, the fact that we're just a handful of us spread around the world, it's a perpetual sense of paranoia about one day simply... disappearing. And here I was, ready to get married and have children with a Hindu boy. Such blasphemy! Never mind that our archaic Parsi laws still refuse to consider a child born from such a union as Parsi." Shenaz paused to take in the weight of those tumultuous days that had torn her life apart and scarred the Wadia family forever.

"They were brutal with me at times," she continued, in that soft voice of hers. "Just with their words and their harshness...brutal. And it was relentless. It took Akshay away from me, it tore our dreams apart, it even shook my connection with my brother and sister for a while, nothing made sense anymore. I simply had to leave this city, else I would have ended up killing myself. Delhi seemed far enough away." She wiped away a slowly-forming group of tears from her eyes, even as Susan's hand reached across the table and comforted her. "Well, that was 10 years ago and here we are now. Two reunited friends, bonding over *brun-maska* and a game of fill-in-the-blanks." Shenaz laughed as she wiped away most of the tears.

"I guess I hadn't realised the extent to which your parents had turned their backs on you," Susan spoke finally. "But didn't your grandma…"

"Oh, it was difficult," Shenaz cut her short. "I mean she spoke to mom and dad a few times, she tried to bring us all together to talk things out, but I guess it was beyond her too. You know how she adored me, right, and I know that she liked Akshay and that she supported us being together. But somehow, I really don't know what it was, I always felt a strange, what's the word, reluctance on her part to come out in strong vocal support of the two of us. Given how headstrong and opinionated she always was, that surprised me. In a small way, I think that even disappointed me; I could never quite figure it out. Anyway, grandpa had died a couple of years ago…or was it three…anyway, that spark of hers had started to dim. She was still Grandma Tania, but maybe a slightly more, I don't know, mellow version I suppose you could call it."

"And Mehr and Pheroz, what's your equation with them now?"

"As it's always been, warm at times, cordial at others, heated at times, lovey-dovey at others…basically, your typical Parsi sibling relationship," she laughed. "Mehr's gone on to be the quintessential Parsi girl—marrying a rich Parsi businessman. Having a couple of kids with Boman, she's nicely sorted. We try and meet once a year or so." She signalled to the waiter to bring over another round of 'cutting-chai'. "Pheroz and I are closer, his family's wonderful. He's married a Punjabi girl. But of course, his children get to be Parsi, you see, so everything's hunky-dory with the folks," she laughed again.

"And…and your parents?" Susan ventured, with some hesitation.

Shenaz thought about the question for a while. "There's too much bitter water that's flown under that bridge. I've reconciled myself to the fact that family for me is my brother, my sister, my lovely little nieces and nephews, and my memories of my grandmother. Anything else is unnecessary. That's all there is to it."

As early morning gave way to the working crowd coming in for their breakfast at Yezdan, the two women caught up at length about each other's lives and the strange emptiness of a decade lost. They spoke of Poona, they spoke of Delhi; they spoke of childhood fights and of having turned 30; they spoke of silly childhood crushes and of adult love affairs gone awry; they spoke of their own fractured relationships and how time, eventually, does manage to tide over things.

"I'm having a party tonight," Susan mentioned, as she was about to leave. "It's not in honour of you or anything, so don't get a big head over it. Just some friends and some great food, it'll give you a chance to feel as though you're part of this city once again."

"Maybe it'll give us a chance to feel as though we're back together once again..." Shenaz offered.

Susan smiled. "You've never really left, either physically or emotionally." She rose and hugged Shenaz warmly before giving her a kiss on the forehead. "It's lovely having you back. The party's at the old KP bungalow, you must've forgotten the address by now. I'll text it to you."

After her friend had left, Shenaz remained at the café for a while longer. Her memories of Yezdan came doused in generous flakes of dough and the smell of sweet biscuits. She thought about the no-frills café and its magnetic hold over a strong faithful; she ruminated on the Camp quarter of the city she was in, and how the rich aura of its cantonment had remained intact all these years; she reminisced about the other Irani cafés and Parsi bakeries that were as much a staple of Poona as its leafy by-lanes and eternally beautiful weather; she contemplated about growing up as Parsi in a city with such a strong ethnic confluence and such rich weaves of diversity; she lingered over the memories of a Hindu Akshay, now happily ensconced in the arms of a Parsi wife whose parents had been less concerned about the fate of their dwindling tribe.

She roamed happily through the silent roads and the majestic oak trees and the large bungalows, belonging either to retired army personnel or to some of the city's entrenched families, and the enduring essence of gulmohar that were collectively the heart and soul of the neighbourhood she'd grown up in. She danced her way through her thoughts of Poona, a city she loved by heart, three hours removed from Bombay, in the heart of western India, silently creating a collage of life in its own languid style...each thought merging into another as though they were disparate segments of a singular dream. Her recollections nicely sated, Shenaz arose with a strange gladness in her heart. She felt she was home. And yet, that weight...

CRADLED BY THE BYGONE

The mammoth banyan tree's imposing trunk and penetrative roots had been part of the soil for so long, that they had burrowed deep within the earth and established themselves as an unshakeable, never to be uprooted guardian of the plot and its forgotten acres. The incumbent held guard, with an air of old-world majesty, right in the heart of the long-standing Richards Bungalow in Koregaon Park. Its companions were other banyans and oaks of similar if slightly less impressive vintage, a multitude of smaller trees and shrubs, and grass that had grown wild over the years, left free to run riot all across the compound. It was just past 9 at night, and even through the veils of darkness, Shenaz could make out each and every element of this 'forest', marked out as they were in silhouettes, dark frames, and whispers.

She tried to trace all the misadventures and wild experiences that she'd had in Koregaon Park, innocent at first when she was a child, much more rebellious in her late teens and early twenties when those first flushes of falling in love with Akshay had hit her with a surge that wouldn't be suppressed. She silently acknowledged how this neighbourhood had always been a central character in her life. Koregaon Park was Poona's bohemian quarter, a nicely charming confluence of greenery and hedonism. While it played home to a large assortment of bars, cafés, clubs, and live music venues, each catering to a suitably eclectic collage of bohemians, travellers, students, expats, and the spiritual set, its network of seven narrow, parallel-running side-streets also played home to some of the city's oldest and wealthiest, safely ensconced in their extravagant homes.

These were sprawling affairs. Some were palatial mansions with vast acres of gardens and anonymity surrounding them. Some contained entire families, others were forebodingly large, silent and decrepit.

It was the latter that had always fascinated Shenaz. She was absorbed by their dark sorrows and their fragile emptiness, brought on by a combination of warring families, deceased occupants, or simply, happenstance. Their large plots would be overrun with weeds and shrubs and the lilting regrets of forgotten bougainvillea, their roofs would be wilting under the ominous severity of the large banyan trees, and their walls would have given way to the austerities of time. Some had been paeans to debauchery in their heyday, back when the mystic savant Osho Rajneesh and his ashram brimming with a global sect of pleasure and wisdom seekers had been at their most powerful. These very bungalows had witnessed, and in some cases continued to do so, dramas including Bollywood love affairs fringed with notes of desire and loss, unfettered spiritual orgies, drug-addled rave parties, and the like. Shenaz thought about the Roberts home she was in, once a family-home filled with warmth, now simply a sparse, neglected behemoth that occasionally opened its doors out over the weekend to the family's children, Susan included.

"Eerie isn't it?"

The question turned Shenaz's gaze away from the darkened fauna and towards a man carrying two glasses of wine.

"Gosh, you're thirsty, aren't you!" she commented.

He smiled. "While it's true that I have a severe alcohol problem, this one's for you."

Shenaz smiled back and accepted her glass graciously. "Eerie, yes, but beautifully so," she remarked, pointing towards the darkness.

"I agree," the man concurred. "Like a nicely creepy Tim Burton film, or one of those beautiful film sets from black-and-white Bollywood."

They were out on the elevated porch of the bungalow, once an untouched white, and fairly smug in the beauty of its curved pillars and decorative elements. But that had been decades ago. Now it resembled an alcoholic diva, crippled by the ravages of regret; still beautiful, yes, but in a crumbling, decrepit sort of way.

"I'm Shaunak," the man offered, extending his hand.

"Hi, I'm Shenaz."

"Shall we take the royal swing?"

"Why, I suppose we must."

"This used to be a beautiful swing once, Susan tells me. Now it's just, well a bit sad."

"Oh, it *was* beautiful. I remember swinging on it with abandon as a child—Susan pushing me, then me pushing her. Old lady's still got a bit of charm though."

As they got up on the swing, Shaunak took Shenaz by surprise.

"You've been out here most of the evening, away from the party going on inside. Are you sad?"

"Why would I be sad?"

"Susan mentioned your grandmother. I'm so sorry."

"Oh she did, did she? Hmm, yes, I guess a large crowd wouldn't have been my choice for tonight. I couldn't say no to Susan though."

Shaunak tinkered with his glass, and its red wine mingled with the fragile paper lamps on each corner of the porch, casting playful shadows on the swing.

"Is it strange being back in Poona? I mean, you do live in Delhi now, don't you?"

"I'm slowly easing into it. The only thing strange is being here without my grandma."

"Do you miss her very much?"

Shenaz watched the shadows leap at each other to the music of the swing's movements. "I do," she spoke finally. "It's a strange mixture of loneliness and a sharp tinge of regret over things that happened a long time ago; it's a pretty heavy feeling," she articulated herself and stared off into the darkness.

"I hope both—the loneliness and the regret—fade away quietly, without you even realising that they have," Shaunak said, his words going well with the nearly imperceptible rhythm of the swing.

Shenaz felt a strange attraction towards Shaunak. He was tall and dressed in her favourite combination of a good-looking pair of jeans and a white shirt. He had a nonchalance about him that didn't appear forced. And a warmth about him that felt real. But as she examined him intermittently between sips of her wine and instances of conversation, she realised it was his face—a simple, handsome face filled with the vulnerability of a nomad, tempered by the coarseness of moderately rebellious week-long facial hair—that drew him to her. He was, she decided, a very good-looking man.

Between his sips of wine and talking about the gravity of loss before moving on to their respective childhoods in Poona, albeit in different circles, Shaunak was coming to much the same conclusion as Shenaz—that he too was attracted to her. He noticed how a few mischievous strands of her just-beyond shoulder-length hair, including one pretty, exaggerated curl, fell endearingly across her face from time to time, he noticed her eyes fill with a soft and distant sparkle, he noticed that rather comely speck of a mole right in the heart of her face, he noticed a profound, poetic sadness brewing within her, and he noticed that whenever she smiled, she lit up the darkness of the porch. She was, he decided, an extremely pretty woman.

"Getting along well, are we?" Susan stepped on to the porch carrying a tray filled with snacks.

"You do realise that the party's inside, don't you?"

"I came out for a breather," Shenaz replied. "I wanted to stare at the garden for a while."

"Then I came along and accosted her," Shaunak confessed. "I do believe there's space for three on this swing."

Susan happily squeezed herself into one end of the swing, by Shenaz's side.

"Do you remember playing games on this thing?"

"Yeah, I was just telling him."

"And have you asked him what he does for a living?"

"Well?" Shenaz intoned.

"Oh I'm a struggling actor," Shaunak replied. "Though I don't know if there's much of a living to be made from it."

"Oh, you live in Bombay?" inquired Shenaz.

"No, I'm a Poona boy. I only head to Bombay when there's an audition around, which isn't very often."

"The other thing, I meant the other thing," commanded Susan.

"The other thing?"

"Oh," Shaunak caught on. "I was hoping to surprise her and sweep her off her feet with it. I'm also a poet."

At this, Susan burst out into laughter. "The worst kind Shenaz, the worst kind. He'll inflict these one or two liners on you at any given time, at all given times. Soon, you'll be begging for mercy."

"Oh I think I can take care of myself," Shenaz replied.

Shaunak cleared his throat and took on the possessed veneer of a poet from the ancient Mughal courts of India. "Roses are red, violets are blue...wait, that's for someone else," he stopped himself. "Right, here goes: 'Ah, serendipity, she sighed. When things appear serene, and then suddenly start to go dippity, he murmured. And so they parted.'"

"Ah, this is more spiritual haiku than poetry," Shenaz opined with a smile.

"A haiku, she said. "Seventeen syllables, no less." I laid down my pen, distraught. "Would 140 characters suffice instead?" I asked.

Shenaz and Susan both burst out laughing.

"Well I'm headed back inside," Susan interceded. "I do wish you'd come and join us."

Before leaving, she offered her friend one last bit of information. "Actually, he's not that bad a poet; he does have his moments."

As she left, Shenaz handed Shaunak her glass. "For you, my lovely poet. From one longing heart to another, *shukriya*."

Shaunak accepted her glass and downed its last sip. As he watched her leave, he sighed under his breath: "An ocean of words, submerged under the weight of profundity. Before a few break free, with an urgent cry, 'Pick me! Pick me!'"

Stepping inside the sparse, warmly lit lounge-room of the bungalow, Shenaz made a bit more effort to mingle. She had wanted to continue talking to Shaunak, even share her silences with him. But she had stopped herself. She knew she must. At the party, Shenaz found no one from her past—everyone from her previous life in Poona had either been scattered or had left or had simply lost touch.

Susan's current bunch of friends was an interesting lot: a restaurateur, who carried a cigar with him but never actually lit it; a nightlife impresario, whose loud laughter reverberated across the empty corridors of the bungalow; a couple of struggling artists, who spoke energetically with their hands; a mini faction bearing vague creative credentials who had converted one of the smaller side rooms into a de facto drug den, and so forth.

The music was lively, so was the atmosphere. But try as she might, Shenaz just couldn't get into the swing of things. Her mind was mired in memories. She smiled when she caught Susan ducking into drug central on a couple of occasions, remembering how they'd stolen away to share that first exhilarating joint together, or how they'd been lulled into doing some coke during that weekend away with the girls during the summer of '97. Shenaz thought about joining her for a drag or two, but her mind was restless. Caught somewhere between a deepening melancholy over all those yesterdays and a strange urgency on meeting Shaunak, she finally relented. She sought him out and took him aside.

"Everything good?" he inquired.

"Yeah, but I just needed someone…to be still with, for a while."

"What's on your mind?"

"Nothing much. Trying to find my place in Poona. Thinking, I'm going to have to get back to Delhi by the end of this week. Thinking about my grandma." She paused to take in the softly-lit room, filled with shadows and hidden spaces and cracked walls and happy conversations. "Do you think I think too much?" she completed her chain of thought.

Shaunak burst out laughing. "Yeah, well there's a thought. Give yourself some time in Poona, maybe that's what you need to get over your grandma. I wish I had something more substantial to offer you."

Shenaz looked into his darkly-set eyes, pools of blackness within the room of guarded lights. "You've actually been more helpful than you might imagine."

Shaunak took a moment to consider his rhythmic reply. "That you might imagine / That you might perceive / In the end, we're broken mirrors / One part you, one part me."

Shenaz sighed for effect. "Ah, now that's a bit of Urdu *shayari* sensibility, Mr Shaunak. Oh, I'm sorry. Would you give me a second?"

As Shaunak stepped away to catch up with a couple of friends, Shenaz took out the phone that was ringing in her bag. Susan caught sight of her from the other end of the room, first trying to hear the other person's voice through the music, and then speaking for a while. By the time the call was done with, Susan could see that Shenaz had turned pale. She rushed across the room to see what the matter was.

"What's wrong baby?" she whispered. "Shenaz!"

"That was Akshay on the other end of the line," Shenaz replied, before submitting herself to the rest of her wine.

Catching glances of her between trying to concentrate on the conversation around him, another small verse reared itself in Shaunak's mind... "The tender crush of fragile hearts / The pieces of a cherished past / The music in her kohl-rich eyes / The refrain of it was you, not I..."

Yesterday's Aftermath

The sky was a rolling canvas of greys and the occasional sparks of silver. That's the way it had been since early morning, stretching over now to late afternoon. Shenaz could smell the giddy essence of gulmohar flowers all around her. Instigated by the overcast skies and facilitated by the pure breeze in the air, they had been spreading their red-infused fragrance with élan. Shenaz's street in particular was heady in its bouquet of rare red romance. Sitting out on her front porch, pouring another cup of hot chai for Susan and herself, Shenaz was in the process of relating all that had taken place earlier that morning.

"He's looking even better now, the handsome bastard."

"Men lucked out when it came to age."

"Yeah, especially the good-looking ones."

"So that's it, he just wanted to meet up and say hello?"

"Pretty much. You know how this place is a village, right? Someone must've told him I was back in town. For all we know, it might've been a common contact from your party last night. Anyway, we met up around 11, at Marz-O-Rin. He remembered my addiction to their cold coffees. We took one of those tables on the balcony that looks out on the road and all the greenery surrounding the place. Goddamn city, sometimes I tend to forget how pretty it can be. It sneaks up on you, no?"

"Was it awkward?"

"It started off a little bit like that, we hadn't set eyes on each other since we were 21. But then a strange thing happened; our adult halves took over. I know how surprising that must sound. It was just two friends catching up after a long time. In a way, it was a really healing moment for me." Shenaz gently bit into her lips, trying to articulate her own thoughts on the morning, as much as answer Susan's queries. "Every time I look at him, every time I hear his voice, there's naturally this big book of memories that comes with it. There is that deep attraction from the past, all the scars that came with it, and all the hurt that came on top of it. But this morning took care of a lot of things."

"What do you mean?"

"I think any guilt or regret that may have hung in the air, simply flowed away. That period had been as painful for Akshay as it had been for me." Shenaz looked up at the brisk rolling clouds, playing curious spectators to their conversation. "Aside from all the pain and the sadness and the blame, deep down I knew it was me and my irrational parents who had brought all the madness into his life.

To see him now, content, without any bitterness, I immediately felt my sadness over the past step away from me," she concluded.

"Were there any sparks, what about the attraction?" Susan asked, reaching for a *naan khatai*, the same biscuits from Kayani Bakery that Shenaz's grandma used to put out for all her guests.

"I can't deny that. I felt overwhelmed at first. I wanted to grab him and drag him back to when we were young. I mean I'll always have this space in my heart that's filled with Akshay. But the minute he showed me the photograph of his two little kids, the minute he showed me Sanober's photograph, the minute we began to talk about our journeys and about what's been happening this past decade, I knew it was just two friends catching up with each other's lives…not two lovers trying to bring back the past."

"That's a good space to be in, baby."

"I feel lighter. I don't know what to call it—closure, relief, humility—I just feel lighter. Well, about Akshay anyway," Shenaz surmised, wrapping her arms around herself. In the familiar surroundings of home, in the lap of the monsoon she used to know so well, her thoughts had moved quite seamlessly from Akshay towards Grandma Tania, and what she would've made of her granddaughter's life right now—her choices, her relationships, her sadness, of her being back in this home that still bristled with the persistent presence of someone she missed with heartbreaking finality. Susan cosied up to Shenaz and slid her arms around her, attentive to many of the silent repentances swirling around in her friend's heart.

"Do you remember Farah Aunty?" Shenaz asked after a while.

"She was part of your grandma's card-pack, wasn't she? The same one?" Susan enquired.

"Yeah," Shenaz laughed at the memory of those high-pitched card-games that nearly always ended in someone or the other being branded a 'cheatercock'! "I'm heading over to see her this evening.

I came across this small box of her things that grandma had marked 'Farah'. I hope she's still in the same house a few minutes from here. I don't know what she'll make of this, of seeing me out of the blue."

"Oh don't you worry," Susan assuaged her fears. "All her friends loved you to bits, as much as she did. Listen, I've got to run."

As she got ready to leave a little later, Shenaz pursed her lips again and came out with it.

"Susan?"

"Yeah?"

"Shaunak, was he alright last night?"

Susan stopped and went back to the divan.

"I think he was shaken a bit. Actually, concerned is more like it. I mean you just upped and left, and I think he was left holding on to the conversation you two had been having."

"Yes, I feel really bad about that." Shenaz replied. "Could you give me his number, I'd like to call and apologise."

As Susan gave Shaunak's number to Shenaz and walked up to her car, she stopped once again on the driveway and turned back towards Shenaz. "I'm not going to mess around with your life, that's not what friends are for...well, recently rediscovered friends anyway. But I want you to take it a little bit easy with this guy. I mean he's really lovely, and these last couple of months we've gotten to know each other, he's shown himself to be really quite different from the rest. But the place you're in, I don't want you to rush into anything you might not be prepared for," she concluded, and sent Shenaz a kiss through the moisture-laden air.

As Shenaz watched Susan pull away from her driveway and out of the main gate, as she watched Mistry Bhaiyya shut the gate and beam a large smile in her direction, as she wrapped her arms around herself at the advent of a fresh gust of breeze, her heart was suddenly assaulted by that same haunting sadness, that same inexplicable cloudiness that infiltrated every thought of her grandma. She went back to her favourite room and lay down on the bed populated with memories.

She hummed a song she remembered from those days. She tried to coax a few answers out from the shadows that lurked in the corners. She fell asleep, unsure whether coming back home after all these years to say goodbye held within it a secret direction to the rest of her life, unsure whether a tugging sense of melancholy would be her constant companion in the only city she had known as home.

❀

An Audience with Osho

Nearly all the leaves, flowers, and sharp-edged pieces of bark glistened under the remembrance of the previous night's downpour. To Shenaz it felt as though they had been kissed by someone the previous night, but had then awoken in the morning to find their lover gone, left behind with only those fresh, translucent dewdrop of memories...

Shenaz walked along the entire three acres of one half of the garden, in silence. The Osho Teerth Garden had changed its shape and dimensions several times over the years, but had never lost its spiritual essence. In the Zen Buddhism tradition, mini rock formations, water features that sprang up unexpectedly, narrow pathways lined with flowers, statues carved out of stone, and an abundance of old trees filled its spaces. The garden had once been the address for a sewage stream that flowed through the area. The vestiges of that stream had been cleaned, purified, and incorporated into the garden's flow. It now resembled a small mountain stream making its way through a sacred Himalayan point of pilgrimage, not a once-neglected piece of filth in the heart of Koregaon Park.

Shenaz sighed. She remembered the place well. She remembered some of its bending bamboo shoots and old oaks and towering banyans by heart; the ones who arched themselves with the grace of a ballerina, the ones who cemented their roots with a near karmic finality, and the ones who spread their flourishing arms with the strength of a protective entity. She felt at home.

When she'd entered the garden at the break of dawn, she'd stopped for a few moments in front of the dark statue of Osho and had sent a few prayers up into the sky. The holy man's fierce gaze had seemed as hypnotic when engraved in stone as it did in photographs or in real life. The Zen Garden was his work of art, brought to life by his hordes of followers and members of his ashram—some unfailingly fanatical, others on a more sound spiritual footing. But what they'd ended up creating was something close to perfection—a green oasis of light and hope in the heart of a bustling metropolis.

Shenaz walked along the garden's pathways, now left muddied by the previous night's rain, and skipped gingerly over its bridges and rock formations, now left slippery for the same reason. As she walked, she reached over for some of the bamboo shoots that had been curved to form arches, and shivered under the glistening mini-showers they predictably poured on her body. When she'd traversed one half of the garden and back, she crossed the road over to the other half. At the entrance gate to the other side, she found Shaunak waiting for her.

"Well hello there," she expressed brightly.

"Hey you," Shaunak replied. "I was trying to make up my mind—this half or that half of the garden. Good you came along. A bit early in the day, isn't it?"

Shenaz smiled. "Sorry about that, but the gardens only make sense early in the morning. Shall we walk? I've done all of this, could we go the other way?"

"Yeah, I don't mind," Shaunak replied and they stepped on to the mud trail that negotiated the garden's second half. They had the vast expanse all to themselves, save an early morning jogger or two and an odd unobtrusive meditator absorbed in the yogic breathing practice of *pranayama*.

"I'm sorry about the way I left a couple of nights ago," Shenaz uttered. From the moment she'd awoken that morning, thoughts of how this conversation was going to go had played out in her mind. "I got a call from someone I used to love a long time ago," she resumed. "We were engaged and going to get married before circumstances broke us apart quite horribly."

Shaunak was silent for a while. "I'm sorry for both of you. So, did you have an emotional reunion?"

"Oh, it isn't that. Yes, we met yesterday morning but it was nice. We met as friends. I think we managed to wipe away much of the prolonged bitterness and random guilt there was between us. It was cathartic and healing at the same time." She brushed her palm against a row of flowers they had come upon, and her skin tingled at the ice-cold sensation of their dewdrops. "He's married now. We've both moved on."

Shaunak didn't say a word. The desolate beauty of the garden suited him just fine.

"This guy, he's Hindu and my hardcore Parsi folks had had a proper meltdown over it. My greatest doubt was whether I had ended up disappointing my grandma as well in that whole episode. With her passing away, with my not being there by her side, that guilt had grown so large I could barely breathe at times."

"Does it feel any better?" Shaunak asked.

Shenaz felt the first drops of a light drizzle sprinkle on to her face. "As if that one meeting yesterday in the morning wasn't enough, in the evening I dropped by to meet an old friend of my grandma's. Farah Aunty and she used to be great card buddies back in the day, I'd taken over a box that belonged to her."

"She must've been happy to see you?"

"Oh, she was. I remember how she always spoiled me with her home-baked cookies, back when I was a child. Farah Aunty to me will always be this smell of cinnamon, apples, sugar, and dough," Shenaz said, smiling at the thought of those childhood memories. "We got to talking about a lot of things—about my leaving, about my life in Delhi, about my not being there for grandma's funeral, all of it. Then I found out something I had had absolutely no clue about."

"What was it?"

"Farah Aunty told me that back when they were in college, Grandma Tania had fallen in love—this was before she met my nana. And he was a Hindu boy. She told me how her parents had been opposed to it as well, just as mine were. And how her family had nearly been torn apart. When the same thing happened with me, it must have felt as though there was some kind of karma at play. No wonder she hadn't come out in absolutely full support of me back then—she didn't want to see me keep getting hurt, she didn't want to see me dragged through what she'd gone through. But Farah Aunty also told me that they would talk a lot during those days, spend whole afternoons together. She says grandma told her that she was proud of me and that she loved me no matter what. Even after I'd left for Delhi, she never stopped thinking about me or loving me." Shenaz paused for a bit as they traversed another of those slippery mini-bridges. "And here's the other thing," she continued. "Farah Aunty told me that grandma had left our Poona bungalow for me in her Will. Can you imagine? I mean, my parents didn't bother to tell me, but naturally. And I guess my brother and sister hadn't known about it. It...I don't know...something so strange in having this home, here in a city that I left so long ago..."

Shenaz nursed her eyes, glad that her infant tears had merged seamlessly with the fresh raindrops on her face.

"Let's sit there," Shaunak suggested, pointing towards a stone bench that sat in silence, a whisper removed from a beautiful stone statue of the Buddha that stood almost entirely submerged by wild lotus leaves. Its haunting gaze protruded through the thick foliage. Surrounded by the flourishing sea of green, its sacred veneer cut through every fear and illusion of the city that hung in the morning air.

Shaunak and Shenaz stared at it for a while, each lost in the wordings of their silent prayers. When Shaunak turned to face Shenaz, he had a smile on his face.

"You do know she left that box behind on purpose, don't you?"

Shenaz was struck by how the thought had never crossed her mind. Before she could reply, Shaunak had a simple question for her.

"Does *this* Hindu boy pose problems for your new-found Parsi serenity?"

Shenaz was taken aback by his question. She smiled shyly. "I wouldn't say he poses a problem. I'd say he poses a challenge. The last few days have turned out so strangely, it's been all about me. Quite selfish when you think about it. I wonder what his story is…"

It was Shaunak's turn to smile. "Hmm, well let's see. I was born in Poona, but from the age of seven, have flitted between this city and Bombay. Poona for my dad, Bombay for my mum. That was how old I was when they got divorced. So you could say my family got fairly torn apart even earlier than yours. I dropped out of college early and joined a theatre group and then a touring troupe, so life got even more nomadic. I soon began to write plays—nothing major, just small, experimental stuff. I think it's fair to say that it was theatre that both recognised and nurtured my love for both writing as well as acting."

Shenaz watched as an errant raindrop perched itself precariously just beneath Shaunak's left eye. She was seized by the urge to kiss it away, but she held herself back. In that garden, filled as it was with monsoon's premature touch and early morning's poetic charms, his face looked even more tinged with vulnerability—rugged and handsome as it was—than it had that first night.

"It's been that way since," Shaunak went on, after wiping away the raindrop. "A bit of theatre, a bit of writing, and baby steps at trying to forge an acting career. Bombay has this ability to chew up and spit out the best of us. Thank God I have Poona to balance things out," he smiled as he finished the mini-capsule of his life. But he wasn't quite done yet.

"And then a couple of nights ago, I crashed into this beautiful Parsi woman—all elegance and distance and mystery. She's come with a lot of history and sadness to her, and the small fact that she's headed back to Delhi in a few days. So now, I'm just sitting here in this drizzle, trying to figure out the signs…"

Shenaz sat still, silent. She felt a wild storm brewing within her. "I'm not all that distant," she replied finally. She got up and walked towards the Buddha. "My parents have no sway over my life anymore. And the more I think about it, perhaps neither does Delhi." She focussed her gaze on the statue and all around it, its neighbours, flourishing with recklessness.

"They'll be gone soon," she mused absentmindedly.

"Who will?" Shaunak asked.

"The gulmohars. They'll all be gone soon."

"Yes, I suppose it's that time of year."

"This cycle used to fascinate me when I was a child. Come late April and early May, our street would almost magically be transformed into this proud parade of red, with the odd misfit speck of yellow. I used to stand in front of my house and take a deep breath. It felt like heaven." She held her arms out aloft as she completed her thought, urged on by the strange pull towards that old smell. "I remember the fragrance most of all, this overpowering sensation of something wild yet graceful...I wanted to grow up and be like that someday, like that smell, like how it made me feel."

Shaunak arose too and wrapped an arm around her. It was beginning to come down more strongly now. Shenaz didn't shy away, the mark of warmth on her shoulders felt nice against the cold tendencies of the raindrops. She drew herself closer to his body.

"They would withstand those first early spells of rain, even blossoming in larger numbers, abundant and eager. And there they would stay, making me feel as though they were going to prosper there forever on my street. But then the rains would begin proper, as they have now, and our ocean of red would instantly begin to wither—the leaves would shrivel, the colour would fade, their essence would disappear...before, one day, poof! It would be as though they had never ever been a part of my life, had never ever been a part of that first rush of summer...had never ever been that lasting memory of the smell of rain..."

Shaunak allowed Shenaz to immerse herself in her memories. There was something deeper being cleansed along the way. When they got back to the garden gate, he handed her a piece of paper. As she reached out to accept it, he pulled her gently towards him and kissed her. The kiss lasted for a while, carried along by the sum total of unspoken desires. When he turned to walk away, Shenaz opened up the crumpled piece and began to read it.

Been so many years now since you've been back home in Poona. A heady cocktail of memories and tomorrows, held under the sway of a strong westerly. Acquaintances, passers-by, strangers in the night keep playing the jokers in the pack. Everything is aflutter, everything is a flutter. I crave this, I crush this, I adore this, I abhor this. But transience is as transience does, and everything finds its way. Everyone finds his or her way. An ocean for every wake. A dusk for every drape. And you keep your heart open, and you keep your soul pure, for the skies are wild...and the road is life...

She watched him walk away, and held her heart to quench the intoxication within. It was pouring heavily by now. She looked at the piece of paper. Its ink had melted and much of it had flown, leaving behind an indigo-infused collage of drifting shapes. She watched Shaunak blend bit by bit into the monsoon's illusionary mist as he turned the corner and gradually disappeared into the air…

An Essence That Never Left

The fluffy bed felt as warm and poignant as it always had. Except today, it didn't carry much of the gnawing weight it had since the day she'd returned to Poona. Shenaz sat on Grandma Tania's bed and stared into her eyes courtesy the twin portraits that hung on the wall across from her. She reached for her bag and turned it upside down, emptying all its contents on the bed. Gradually, the bed was filled with a large cluster of red flowers whose fragrance soon had the room won over.

She caressed the gulmohar flowers she had collected with care while on her way back home. She wiped some of the rain and mildew off their petals, she brought them closer to her and inhaled their essence. They felt and smelt the way they always had— wild, abundant. She gathered all of them and placed them on the windowsill just alongside the portraits of Grandma Tania.

Just as it had when she'd first driven into Poona a few days ago, another word flashed before her eyes. As earlier, it came scrawled in shapeless smoke, on the verge of disappearing without a moment's notice. It was a word she'd noticed while reading an excerpt from a novel a few days earlier. Not knowing what it had meant, she had looked it up in a dictionary. The word was 'Ineffable'—that which is too great to be expressed in words, that which is too elusive to be captured in letters. She looked at the gulmohar flowers. The window lay open. Soon, the smoky, hazy word drifted towards the open window, before its letters written in smoke dissipated into the air, leaving behind a fragrant trail of an essence that had never really left.

Reversal and Its Residues

I am slowly, regretfully, crushing her heart to the words of an old Neil Young song. *Like a Hurricane*. We're back in the same café where we'd first met. Same French windows. Same record player. Same glasses of wine. In a sense, I think we realise the symbolism of things having come around full circle, a lifetime lived out in three days. None of which makes what I'm about to say any easier.

"You should leave Bombay," I tell her, and immediately look away, hoping that the little boy on the street will be there once again, keeping my heart entertained with his sublime sense of freedom. I turn my eyes back towards her, and see that tears have infiltrated hers, their dark rims already having given birth to small streams of black.

"I, I don't know what to say," she utters, and then immediately holds my hands, as though *I'm* the one deserving of compassionate care at this moment.

"I saw you last night, when you were dancing with Aamir. It was a beautiful moment. But the moment was mine, that's all I could think of, that that moment was meant to be mine."

She appears shaken. "There was absolutely…"

"Oh, I know nothing was going on there. But the pain and the sharp flood of jealousy were all too real. I don't want to have to keep guarding myself against life."

"I'm so sorr…"

"Don't be," I intercept her, sliding my hands over so that mine are now on top of hers—caressing, empathising. "Please, don't be." I take a long sip from my wine. "I don't want to be the man you end up hating, the man who ends up forcing you to be someone you're not…or the one who ends up throwing his idea of love on you. I felt things so purely, that first time we talked. Everything seemed clear, everything seemed certain."

We sit silently, allowing Neil Young to frame our thoughts, as the vinyl record tries to contain the madness in his voice …

Once I thought I saw you
In a crowded hazy bar
Dancing on the light from star to star…

Savannah finally breaks the silence. "I fear I may have lost my capacity to love when my father came home that day and told me he had had enough, and I knew by the way he said it that he wasn't talking about the weather or the government."

Far across the moonbeam
I know just who you are
I thought I saw your brown eyes turn at once to fire

"I know you'll make peace with it, I mean, I really hope you do, someday." I don't know whether I'm imposing this on her, that isn't the intention. "I know you'll open yourself up to the possibility of maybe finding…I don't know, finding…"

She leans across the table and puts her hand against my cheek, cradling my face. "I know you're right. But at this point in time, I don't want to end up destroying both our lives. I will not." She looks away towards the window, and I know that she's looking for the young boy as well, hoping he'll come around and save her from the inevitability of all this. "It was pure, I won't forget this, your face, your skin, your eyes, the love we made, the skies we touched…they will never leave me, and I have all these photographs that I…"

"I don't want to think of you in photographs," I intrude on her chain of thought, "or even as a physical shape or as a human body, framed by hair and skin and beauty." I draw circles on the tablecloth, absentmindedly, trying to figure out where I'm going with this. "I want to think of you in lyrics floating around me as I walk, the curves of each letter making up the best of you; a new language known only to me, a floating parade of stanzas that remind me of who we once were."

She gets up and walks over to me. She hugs me, with everything she has. I'm too numb to move, so I just hold on to her. She leans down further and kisses me, and as she does, her hair falls across my face, shielding us from the few other people in this café, who are by now amused by the quiet drama unfolding at table 7. Within this kiss, I remember her Mediterranean skin, rebelling and swaying to the incessant pulse of love; I remember her eyes, crystal pure in bliss at what Bombay had gifted her with; I remember her lips, forlorn at the inconsequence of their own hungry charms; I remember her breasts, luscious odes to the fragrance of desire; I remember her eyelashes, patiently demure in their own melancholic world…

You are like a hurricane
There's harm in your eyes
And I'm getting blown away
To somewhere safer where the feeling stays
I want to love but I'm getting
Blown away…

She's been kissing me, for the longest time. But this too must end. Her short summer dress and large folkloric purse can't stay here forever. I think back to the Jeff Buckley song, and the promises it held. I think back to Cantabria and Santillana del Mar, to a young girl hiding in sandstone churches, waiting endlessly for her prince to arrive.

Young is wailing away on his guitar, the way only he can, and just in this moment, it feels as though he's channelling my thoughts, filtering them through six frenzied strings of something nearing ecstatic sorrow. I walk up to the windows and stare outside. Savannah has gone. I peer out further. The young boy is nowhere to be seen either.

This is Bombay. This is Mumbai. And I couldn't be sadder. Because Bombay is bliss, and Mumbai is mist, and never the twain shall kiss; yet, and yet…

My bedroom is swept in dull grey. I rub my eyes and try to find my bearings with the day. It's overcast, but not the sort that cues impending rain. This faint light has come flooding in through the silk blinds, washing everything in a single shade, Savannah included. She's asleep next to me, her arms lying across my waist, some of her hair intruding into my eyes. We've slept in this morning, and it's nearly noon. I nudge her gently, then once again, and she begins to stir.

"Wow, did we sleep all day?" she asks me.

"Well, it's not that bad. It's just past 12, those clouds outside make it look like much later."

"Can I make you some coffee?"

"You barely know my apartment."

"That's okay, apartments everywhere in the world, they're all the same in a way."

We're having coffee in bed a few minutes later, with a packet of dark chocolate-chip biscuits for company.

"Would you like me to whip us up some eggs?" I offer.

"Oh no, we ate so much yesterday! Maybe we can go out later and have a really, really late lunch."

We're at ease with one another, enjoying this sudden spell of overcast weather.

"Did you enjoy yesterday?" I ask her.

"I wanted to thank you for that," she tells me, her lilting Spanish accent adding a sense of mystique to the most trivial of words. "It was beautiful, I've fallen in love with Bombay. There is something very Spanish here, you know."

"I don't understand."

"Just this madness for life—both our countries, really—they're hot-blooded, they love food…there is a pure sense of life."

She sips her coffee and stares at the clouds.

"Last night after we left the mosque and took a taxi and came to Marine Road…"

"Marine Drive," I correct her.

"Sorry, Marine Drive, it was so beautiful to just lie down under the lights and the stars. It was a really magical moment for me. I was in love with this city, I was in love with…well, it was just perfect, that's all. I can't tell which was more special—when the sun set when we were at the mosque and the sky had changed everything into this gold-red colour, or on Marine Drive, feeling like I'm a part of this city."

"This is Bombay," I whisper. *"This is Mumbai,"* even more softly. *"And I couldn't be happier. Because Bombay is bliss, and Mumbai is mist, and never the twain shall kiss; yet everyone gets along like a house on fire."*

She laughs. "Where did you get that from?"

"Oh it's mine, something I keep making up as I go along."

She looks out of the window, and I know there's no coming back from this.

We head to Ritu's place that night. She's invited us for dinner, along with a whole bunch of other people, many of whom I don't know. Ritu seems excited about Savannah, and that my emotions actually seem invested this time. But I try and temper her enthusiasm.

"I'm afraid thoughts of love and relationships might not be her favourite things at the moment," I tell her, knowing it to be true.

Fiza comes up to us with a couple of drinks in her hand. "I have two," she announces. "Who wants one?"

I take a large sip from a Long Island, and hand the glass to Ritu, and with our arms, we form a small circle of three.

"I don't want to force anything with her," I betray to them. "Let me enjoy this purely, for as long as it lasts, however long that may be..."

Savannah loves Ritu's place and she's enjoying herself. She keeps flitting between the living room and the balcony and all the Indian art Ritu has up on her walls, enjoying the company of the people who are here, endearing herself easily with that unforced charm. It's a nice bunch in here, and I'm involved in quite a few scattered conversations.

I step out on the balcony for some fresh air a while later, and together with the Arabian Sea's distant promises, U2's *Stay* comes on the speakers, fed through a not-quite-so-romantic iPod. I hurry back in. I need to dance to this song. I need her in my arms right now.

As I step back in, I see Savannah in a quiet corner of the living-room, with her arms wrapped around Aamir. They're dancing, slowly. There's nothing going on here, this much I know. Aamir's a friend. But this pain I suddenly feel is unbearable. As his hands drift on to her lower waist, he has, unconsciously, consumed a moment that was meant, undoubtedly, for me.

You say when he hits you, you don't mind, sings Bono.
Because when he hurts you, you feel alive
Hey babe, is that what it is?

There's nothing going on here. They're just dancing. I don't know a lot of things right now, but I know that this sharp stab in my heart will be a constant with Savannah, a perpetual gate-crasher in whatever's been written for us moving ahead.

And if you look, you look through me
And when you talk, you talk at me
And when I touch you, you don't feel a thing

A hum, a blur, a gentle aftermath. A hum, a blur, a piercing stab…

If I could stay
Then the night would give you up
Stay…and the day would keep its trust
Stay…and the night would be enough

In a Bombay minute, hearts lie in flames, prisoners to their own strange parade. And I begin to sing along, softly, so that no one else hears me…

Three o'clock in the morning
It's quiet and there's no one around
Just the bang and the clatter
As an angel runs to ground
Just the bang
And the clatter
As an angel
Hits the ground

"How long do you plan to stay on here?" Ritu asks Savannah.

"Yeah, I was wondering about that as well," Aamir chimes in.

"A day, a week, a month, a year, forever?" goads Fiza. "I guess we're trying to find out how much time we have to make you fall in love with Bombay."

We're all seated around a small circular table at Café Mondegar for a late breakfast. My motives behind inviting my friends over to meet her are two-fold—first, I want some of the lingering sadness from last night to be dispelled in the face of laughter and conversation; and second, I'm hoping that she begins to find a sense of comfort here, a nice familiarity that might want to make her stay for a while longer.

"I don't know," she smiles, her arm entwined with mine. "I don't think I can stay much longer. From here, I'll be off to Goa and then to Kerala. I've booked my return ticket to Spain for the end of this month."

"We have some time," I say, stroking her hand, trying to assure myself more than anyone else.

"This guy was supposed to be here for just a month," Aamir mentions, nodding towards me. "And now look, it's been seven months. So we still have hope for you."

I smile. It's the first time they're meeting her. They've already taken a liking to her, and why wouldn't they? "It's this project of mine," I remind Aamir. "The client's had a lot of design changes, it's kept evolving from one thing to another. I'll probably leave by the end of this year."

"Sit back and stay still, you're not going anywhere," Fiza informs me. She turns her attentions to Savannah.

"What do you do?" she asks, brightly.

"I'm a freelance journalist back in Valencia, I write for quite a few publications in Spain, many of them in Barcelona."

"I love how you say that."

"Say what?"

"Barcelona."

"It's good you like that, because that's how it's actually pronounced," I pipe in.

"What?"

"Bar-the-lona, that's how the Spanish go about it, and I guess they would know a thing or two."

"Actually," Savannah corrects me, "hardcore Catalans call it Bar-sah-lona. Valencia doesn't really know where it stands," she concludes, with a shrug.

"That's fascinating," Fiza responds.

"You find everything fascinating," Aamir says. "Probably because you're 'th-oo-pid'."

Ritu and Fiza both fling their napkins at Aamir, who ducks with expert ease. Savannah is smiling, and that makes me smile as well. I excuse myself and walk up to the resplendent old jukebox that's been as much a staple at 'Mondy's' as its omelettes, pepper steak, and cheap beers for over a 150 years now. I've made my selection. I wait for of a couple of minutes. *A Night in Tunisia* comes wafting through the café's compact, nostalgic spaces. A couple of its patrons give me an approving nod. Savannah herself turns around, smiles, and walks over to me.

"Ah, Miles Davis," she sighs, squeezing my arms.

"Written by Dizzy Gillespie," I remind her. "And Charlie Parker's on this particular version as well. Phew!"

We sway in front of the jukebox for a while, its golden afterglow bathing her cream and crimson ruffled skirt in a kiss of sunset.

"Let me show you around," I tell her, and take her by the hand.

Mondy's is fairly full at this hour of the morning, but we have enough breathing room to manoeuvre its spaces. I tell her about the Iranian immigrants who created this little gem and how it has been passed down over the generations, I tell her about the Regal Cinema next door, and how its majestic history is such an integral part of a city so immersed in the velvet crush of Bollywood, I tell her about the legions of stories and tragedies and romances associated with Regal, and how the fragrance of films filters through every pore of every citizen in this city.

This is Bombay. This is Mumbai. And I couldn't be happier. Because Bombay is bliss, and Mumbai is mist, and never the twain shall kiss; yet everyone gets along like a house on fire.

I don't want to stop. Her hand in mine feels right. I take her along the walls, and speak to her of Mario Miranda, one of Bombay's favourite adopted sons, and how his love for life and talent for detail gave birth to the unforgettable caricatures that adorn every single square space of the café's walls—the bow-tied waiter merrily holding on to two large jugs of beer, the Indian cowboy with a large 'Salaam Bombay' written across his T-shirt, the slightly giddy girl at the piano accompanied by her dog yapping along, a rowdy cat eyeing a fish twice its size, Parsis, Maharashtrians, Bengalis, Punjabis, Goans—the entire gamut of this high-definition, surround-sound, ambient-abstract country.

We chase after this same feeling of lust and rush, all day hoping that Bombay's wild horizons will heal the highly visible cracks in this affair. We're in it together this morning, all five of us. As we stream by Café Leopold, I take Savannah's hand, and guide her fingers over bullet holes from the past, when it stood firm against the spectre of evil and laughed in the face of cowardly terror, making sure it stood tall until the malevolent were deposited back to hell.

"Nothing can break this city," Aamir attests, with the conviction of a pastor firmly invested in his own truth. "Cowards, terrorists, assholes, wankers—they don't know that Bombay is invincible, its destiny merged with the souls of the gods. Nothing breaks this city. Those who've tried have found out the hard way."

"What doesn't kill us only makes us purer," says Ritu.

"These bullet holes are badges of pride, proud tattoos of a city that wears its heart on its sleeve and its passion in its eyes," I say, softly, as I stare around me at the wealth of Parsi photographs, memorabilia, traveller's diaries, and the trusty wood furniture, each a priceless treasure-trove of conversation, each a haunting testament to the simple powers of nostalgia.

Today, like yesterday, is all about South Bombay and Colaba. We don't have the heart to brave traffic and cross over to the other halves, in this city shared by seven different sisters, a few of which Savannah has already been acquainted with. We thrive amidst the mad rush of thieves and charlatans in Chor Bazaar, Savannah dipping herself in some Indian antiques and vintage signatures along this street market that looks as old as it actually is. We take in the Jehangir Art Gallery and its two showings of contemporary-Indian mixed- media artists with a separate, smaller collection from those crazy jazz *baba*s that made up the Bombay Progressive Artists' Group in the early '50s. It isn't too hot to walk outside today, and Colaba's wealth of colonial architecture, framed by old trees almost as majestic as the buildings they harbour, its wide open spaces, its smell of the sea, and its invitation to what may be, they're just the right tonics for our visibly swaying hearts.

I want to make sure that Savannah gets to meet a few of the city's legends, and so I'm orchestrating mini pit-stops as we engage with this day. We've dropped into the Yazdani Bakery in Fort, where Savannah is being treated to her first *brun-maska* and masala chai; we've stopped by Jimmy Boy's for a Mango Fanta and for photographs with that instant feel of the by-gone, no filters needed; we're taking a breather at Nutcracker, where the yellow upside down stools are staring at our square wedges of 'Seven

Layer Cookies' with envy. We've walked a fair bit today, through Kala Ghoda, past Causeway, into Ballard, back and forth, which is why we keep replenishing ourselves so regularly. And anyway, isn't a city's soul to be found in its food, in the aromas of its streets, in the fragrances of its concealed spaces? It's time for lunch now, and Fiza and I both agree that nothing else than mutton berry *pulav* at Britannia will do, so we walk inside its doors and are swept away instantly to a world of stories, and Parsi folklore, and the reflections of immigrants, each suffused with the right amounts of warmth, annoyance, and curiosity courtesy Mr Kohinoor at the helm.

I can sense she's thrilled by all this, I can feel it in her nails as they burrow into me lightly from time to time as we unearth Colaba's lost stories. She's taking photographs, she's laughing, she's getting to know the other three. There's genuine happiness in those dark eyes. And yet, we know we're going to have to resolve this, find a way to rescue ourselves from the finality of everything.

It's nearly dusk now, and I desperately need her to feel a particular experience. I take her to Haji Ali Dargah, where the sacred tomb of Pir Haji Ali Shah Bukhari lies in pious stillness, presided over by the Masjid. We see it from a long distance away, and Savannah's eyes are aglow with passion, this remarkable sentinel to Bombay's shores has consumed her with its white domes, its Mughal minarets, its Indo-Islamic flourishes, its patronage filled with all creeds, religions, and colours...all laid out for her in the middle of the Arabian Sea. As we begin to walk on the long bridge that links the shore to the mosque, evening prayer reverberates through the air. Fiza and Aamir stand in silence to offer their prayers, unable to kneel amidst this flood of humanity. In this medley, Savannah and I hold on to each other, tight, our bodies wildly redolent of the love we'd made the night before.

We make love to the city's frenzied rush for life, our bodies keeping pace with an incessant beat that refuses to slow down, urged on by the madness of youth and the silent desperation of two hearts adrift, in limbo. We rise and sway to the rhythmic clamour of traffic far below us and the silent melodies of the Arabian Sea out beyond us.

"I was born in a small town called Santillana del Mar," she tells me later, as we lie in each other's arms on a chair that looks out with wonder at the lights emanating from 19 million lives and at the equally arresting penumbra of the seas.

"I haven't heard of it," I tell her, stroking her thick, dark locks of rich brown and summer.

"It's a tiny village," she continues, "so I can't really blame you. There are barely five thousand people in there, so it's not the sort of place you can mess with your neighbour's wife and get away with it."

We laugh, and in our dark room with the lights all turned off, her skin glistens like diamonds, little drops of sweat forming an unspoken geography to the secrets within, her body laying claim to its own quietness.

"I'd love to visit someday," I sigh, after a while.

"It's a medieval town, so you always have the past right beside you, breathing down on you. It could get claustrophobic; sometimes you don't know where to turn." She isn't looking at me as she says this, but I know there's sadness in her eyes. "I had so many hiding places as a child," she reveals, all of a sudden. "The Old Quarter was filled with these dark places, they were scary, but you couldn't resist them. I would pretend I was a princess, trapped in one of the beautiful sandstone churches, or in my ancestral home, built of stone, waiting for a prince to come riding through Cantabria—through the rolling hills, through the farms, through the fields, through the cobblestone streets—and take me away."

There is a sudden departure in her voice, as though she has, in an instant, moved away from me to a place a million miles away.

"Why are you so sad?" I ask her, overcome by an urgent need to quell this feeling.

"Am I?" she questions me, softly. We stay in silence for a long while, our hot bodies drenched in the aftermath of love. She soon breaks the silence. "My parents got divorced this summer, after 32 years of marriage. It shouldn't affect me, I'm not a child anymore. But somehow…"

I hold on to her, just a little bit tighter.

"I think it was everything else that came crashing down with the news," she continues, "my thoughts on family, on relationships, on fidelity…on happiness itself, actually."

"I'm sorry," I tell her. I'm shaken too, by the realisation of how vulnerable we are to the frailties of familial relationships, even as adults, as we would've been as children. "Is this journey to India a direct result of that?"

"In a way, yes. I needed to get away. I don't live in Santillana anymore. We moved when I was 19. We moved to Valencia. We live in the same city now, the whole family, but in different parts. There is space now, a sense of distance. But still, I don't know why the news left me so crushed."

"Did it make you question your ideas about love?" I ask her, genuinely invested in what she might have to say.

She looks straight at me, and the startling purity of her eyes hits me hard. "Yes. Nothing lasts forever, this much is true. We can't fall in love, do you hear me? Even my time in India won't last forever, do you have any idea where we go from here?"

I have no answer. I lift her lightly, off my body, and arise from the chair.

"Where are you going?"

Where I'm going is to my broken down turntable, a faithful companion if ever there was one. I switch on the bedside lamp, and the room is tinged with the essence of mellow dawn. She instantly moans and covers her breasts with her hands, protesting against the intrusion, forgetting for an instant that we're high up in the sky and that the only thing in front of us is a vast carpet of darkness, framed by the underflow of a million different lights.

"I have no idea where we go from here," I tell her. "But right now, all I want to be is here."

Slowly, with its customary crackle, *Bésame Mucho* begins to play. Thoughts of *Great Expectations* and its two young lovers destined never to truly meet, framed by the camera's filtered kiss, enraptured by each other's movements as they dance slowly, come flooding into the room.

I look at her, and her eyes are moist with memories. She holds out her hand and draws me into her. We make love again, this time to a softer, slower cadence, guided by the truth in our stars, guided by Consuelo Velázquez's words that linger in the air like crushed butterflies…

Bésame, bésame mucho
Como si fuera esta noche
La última vez
Bésame, bésame mucho
Que tengo miedo a perderte
Perderte después

We smile in the throes of a bliss bathed in notes, aware of the lyrics and what they mean, aware of what each word holds for us in this moment. "Why did you tell me we were going to fall in love?" she asks me, her words sounding anguished under the spell of desire and its many predilections. "I, I…had to," I reply, breathless.

"Earlier this morning...the wine, that song, that conversation... you know that..." She hushes my lips, as the song takes over once more...

Kiss me more, kiss me many more times
as if this beautiful night is
the very last time
Kiss me more, kiss me many more times
because I fear I will lose you
I'll lose you sometime

She rises and falls back on me, time after time, her hair crashing against my body like ravenous waves having their way with rocks. The song gradually subsides, but our passions only rise, fed by a hunger that only loneliness knows, anchored to this earth by sweat, tears, cries, and the other sharp remnants of fatal human touch.

I've fallen in love with her to the sound of an old Jeff Buckley song. *Everybody Here Wants You.* As beautiful as the song no doubt is, the fact that it's being played on vinyl, through the rough and tumble ways of a moody record player, might be helping in accentuating the moment. The song is going to last for all of 4 minutes 45 seconds, and within that precious period, there will be just enough time for her to enter the café, examine her new surroundings, brush past me with an 'excuse me', and find her place in the general scheme of things. She will then order a glass of wine, Rosé, and proceed to crush my heart.

We watch each other between readings of the menu and a perfectly cultivated disenchantment of the people around us, our glances shy but our eyes wild. There is a gentle pallor to the skies, which, when filtered through the large French windows of the intentionally ambiguous persona of this bistro, is bathing everyone in a soft glow of gossamer and angel dust.

This is Bombay. This is Mumbai. And I couldn't be happier. Because Bombay is bliss, and Mumbai is mist, and never the twain shall kiss; yet everyone gets along like a house on fire.

I am, momentarily, distracted by the fact that Jeff Buckley now constitutes the past, a bit of a relic, classic in every sense, to be accorded the venerated vinyl treatment, no less. As the needle on the burnt red player coughs every once in a while, trembles in its own skin, and skips its own beat in the midst of those meditative black swirls, Buckley's voice, an anguished collage of heartbroken fragility and a mad lover's frenzy on the best of days, appears even more textured...even more vulnerable to the cruelties of a woman's memories.

Twenty-nine pearls in your kiss, a singing smile
Coffee smell and lilac skin
Your flames in me
Twenty-nine pearls in your kiss, a singing smile
Coffee smell and lilac skin
Your flames in me
I'm only here for this moment...

I think I might have identified a small pattern; she tends to bite into her lip every time the chorus comes around. Nothing brutal, you understand, just a delicate note of remembrance, dutifully embellished on her skin.

As she sips her wine and stares out of the window, her attentions and mine both collide on a little boy out on the street. He's been washing cars all day, both of us can tell. He has the dishevelled appeal of a mini movie star, all roguish charm and wickedly impish smile. He's crooning a song out loud, but silenced by the windows, I make believe that it is an old Bollywood classic. I want to invite him in and exchange stories with him all through the day, and I know it will be the best conversation I'll have all week. But I don't, because she's here, and I have to concentrate. I have to treat this with importance. This might never come around again, and I don't want to be sitting around in a bar somewhere 10, maybe 15 years down the line, telling a small group of close friends about the time I saw her, and then allowed her to gently slip away.

Hmm, such a thing of wonder in this crowd
I'm a stranger in this town
You're free with me
And our eyes locked in down cast love
I sit here proud
Even now you're undressed in your dreams with me…

It terrifies me, you see, in moments when I'm not pretending or lying or deflecting, that perhaps, just perhaps, not everyone is destined for true love, epic love even, the sort that ravages hearts and tears lives asunder and dispels all notions of God and bliss and destiny; it burns beautiful holes through my soul and I have to sit down, breathe, be still, breathe…I'm alive to this, fully aware, and it thrills me. We flirt through the language of bodies.

Her skin, wrapped in the kiss of a Mediterranean sun, her eyes, lined with the blood of a rebellious eyeliner, her lips, the blossoming of wine and dusk; her address, as ambiguous as this café, not wanting to be tied down to time or place, skipping away daintily from any boxes or safe descriptions. And then we get to my skin, dark, bruised, and hot-blooded; my eyes, the sort that always carry a hint of sadness in them, or so people say; my thoughts, consumed by this moment, infiltrated by its possibilities…

Love can taste like the wine of the ages, oh babe
And I know they all look so good from a distance
But, I tell you, I'm the one.

I walk up to her with my glass of wine, blood red.

"Would you mind if I joined you in a spot of window-gazing?"

She looks distraught, and just for a moment, I'm fearful I've interrupted her in a moment of deep solitary fulfilment, of a mind game wherein the two of us are always meant to be mysterious strangers, never actually crossing paths, never actually giving fate even the slightest chance of dissolving any potential perfection into smoke.

"I…I just thought I would…"

"You do realise we're the only two people in here drinking wine at 12:15 in the morning, don't you?" I interject.

She smiles, and I'm relieved that the moment of initial hesitation has passed.

"I'm Savannah," she offers. "From the open plains, I guess it has something to do with where I was born."

"I'm Sparsh," I reciprocate. "'Touch', for lack of a better word."

"I'm not from this city," she tells me, almost by way of apology.

"I'm not either," I reply.

"I'm not from this country either," she confesses further, "though I'm often mistaken for an Indian."

"You have Indian eyes," I tell her. "And I think it's nice that you can blend into another country, and another, and another, so simply. Some people struggle all their lives to blend into even one."

"You're right, I think," she smiles. "You're much the same, I get the feeling—that you're attached with India, but also attached with other places that you've known, places you've maybe even lived in."

We speak of horizons and circumstances; we speak of journeys and lost romances. I tell her that the Kala Ghoda district we're in is the catalyst for art in this city.

This is Bombay. This is Mumbai. And I couldn't be happier. Because Bombay is bliss, and Mumbai is mist, and never the twain shall kiss; yet everyone gets along like a house on fire.

I tell her about some of the fabled galleries; I tell her about some of the cool-as-blow bars dripping with stories and urban desire; I tell her about the sense of heritage that colours the district in haphazard shades of sepia and magenta and blush, and how centuries-old colonial buildings and old Parsi cafés and legendary music dives and boutique boulevards filled with a certain air of nonchalance all came to collide in this finite square space of infinite dreams and promises.

I know everybody here wants you
I know everybody here thinks he needs you
I'll be waiting right here just to show you
How our love will blow it all away...

"We're going to fall in love," I promise her, with a suddenness so pure, it leaves even me breathless. "It might take a moment, it might take a few more minutes, it might take the rest of the day, but you need to mark my words. You need to write it down on a piece of paper. Years from now, we'll look back, on this place and its walls adorned with charcoal flourishes and ethnic Indian signatures, on that boy and his intensely sacred eyes, on this wine and its secret languages shrouded in red, we'll remember all of it. And we'll know, beyond any shadow of doubt, that we were meant to collide and collapse into each other, and...and that it all started right here. By a window. In a café. To this song. With these words."

Dawn's Fatal Betrayal

'Whoa, what's going on here?' a disbelieving Fardeen wondered aloud, more to himself than anyone around. He rubbed his eyes and sat upright, his five-year-old body a study in curiosity.

He'd been awakened by a constant salvo of words drifting in the crisp, early morning *Lucknawi* air—the sound of which had come and settled beside him on his first floor perch. It couldn't have been later than 6:30 in the morning, as northern India's December mists still hung low like a coy veil.

Fardeen looked to his right. His younger sister Farzana, a feisty yet precocious four-and-a-half, was fast asleep, her blanket tucked away with expert precision behind and beneath her toes and ears alike. To his left lay…hmm, this was curious. Where was Fazal?

Bhaijaan, a masterly seven, was nowhere to be seen. Up to no good, no doubt, mused Fardeen, undecided on whether a foray into the neighbouring mango orchard or a secret early morning game of cricket was behind his elder brother's no-show. No, no. Wait. He corrected himself. Maybe he was at the old stone well, climbing up and down its steep, crumbling array of steps. Cricket seemed like the strongest bet, though.

The three Ali Khan children, through a strong mix of nagging, wailing, and the odd histrionic tantrum, had managed to score this first floor verandah all to themselves as their sleeping quarters. The room that came with the verandah was actually their designated address, with just about enough space for their flourishing personalities. But when it came to sleep time, the troika of adventurers had unanimously agreed that a life within the confines of four walls was certainly not for them. No, it was the freedom of the skies and a direct, even if somewhat diagonal, path to the sparkling stars that were far better suited to their predilections.

This came at a price, of course. Not only were they tasked with dragging out their own mattresses each night and lining them in a somewhat neat row, but worse, they were also the ones responsible for taking said mattresses to by-now unused beds and placing them back in an orderly fashion, irrespective of how sleepy they were. Also, late at night, long past the hour they were meant to be asleep, their talks on life and Virat Kohli and Salman Khan would often be interrupted by the rude, boisterous chatter of those pesky old uncles who sometimes came to stay on the space directly above theirs. They occupied a large room that had by now grown accustomed to the good-for-nothing cohort's long-standing dramas.

The two old ruffians would step out into the balcony for their nightly smoke and accost the unseen children below with their customary intake of strong-smelling *Lucknawi paan*, their conversations interspersed with flamboyant swearing, villainous filmy laughter, and an odd disgusting spray of *paan* spit. Eeks!

Despite these few hardships, the siblings would not have traded their nightly date with the skies for anything. Here, with the nocturnal breeze ruffling their hair, with winter's chill wrapping them in a sweet embrace, and with the promise of tomorrow spelt out in the mystifying patterns of stars in the late-night sky, they were at their happiest. In his heart, Fardeen held the firm conviction that the strongest element in their happiness was their parents' room, across the verandah, on the opposite side. Sometimes, the soft laughter of Afreen Ali Khan would come drifting by, and the astonishingly beautiful face of their mother would appear right before their eyes. At other times, Feroz Ali Khan would step out into the balcony for a smoke, and though they were meant to be fast asleep by then, they knew that their father knew otherwise. Ever so often, they could swear, he would give them a quick wink before finishing his cigarette.

Fardeen finally got out of the large blanket enveloping him. He trudged over to the balcony's railing and peered through its opening, down into the courtyard below. Hmm, this seemed odd. Was this another Eid celebration, one he hadn't been told about? There had already been two of them this year, hadn't there? Or had he lost count? Well anyway, everything about this scene looked like one of those Eid festivities. There were lots of people gathered in the Ali Khan family courtyard below, Fardeen recognised quite a few of them who belonged to their neighbourhood. They were speaking, chatting, and discussing things of great importance and with much merriment, no doubt. Yes, yes, this was definitely an Eid-type of a thing…some of them were crying those tears of joy that he and his siblings could never quite fathom. To cry when you're happy? What madness! Oh, oh, wait a minute, what was this? Food? Aha! No wonder no one had bothered to wake them up that morning. They obviously feared that the children would have had it wiped off within minutes! Such a blissful smell, almost teasing its way right from the family kitchen through the crowd and up into their haveli's upper rooms, coaxing everyone into its aroma. Was there some biryani in there? He couldn't quite tell. Some kebabs and *sheer khurma*, surely? Right, Fardeen decided. This was an occasion that demanded that the Ali Khan siblings show some solidarity. But where on earth was Fazal Bhai? Well, not to worry. He would, at least, wake Farzana up, and begin discovering what lay in store for the day.

❧

In Lucknow's old quarter of Nakhas, even amidst a cluster of similar-looking structures, the Ali Khan haveli stood out. There were several of these old mansions in the city of nawabs, many of them lost to the ravages of centuries, cut from the same architectural fabric that bore identical marks.

There would be a large, tall gate guarding the entrance, for instance, almost blanking out the home entirely from anyone out on the street and from prying eyes in general. This gate would have a small door carved within its boundaries, through which people entered and exited the house. Anyone knocking on the door using its large metal clasp would be duly scrutinised through the sliding opening of a slit above the door, to ascertain the identity of the guest. Once inside, you stepped into a central courtyard flanked by rooms on three sides, which went up to three floors. This large quadrangle space was left open to the elements of nature, bequeathed completely to the skies and the winds. A medieval mansion in many ways, crafted in a distinctively Indian architectural style, its legacy well preserved.

What immediately set the Ali Khan home apart was that their large wood-and-iron gate stood a stunning blue. Some of that blue had given way to the dark tone of the wood beneath. The smaller door was of a predictable grey, but right in its heart stood a resplendent, entirely unpredictable peacock, draped in a brilliant shade of pink. This confounding colour scheme was the children's brainchild, one that their parents had eventually given in to. But playful entrances aside, there was an air about the Ali Khan family that instigated an atmosphere of mystery and its ensuing speculation.

Some speculated that Feroz Ali Khan could trace his lineage all the way back to the nawabs of Awadh, the rulers of a once princely kingdom mired in rich tones of romance and regret. Was he a direct descendant of Nawab Asaf-ud-Daula, the ruler responsible for moving the capital of Awadh from Faizabad to Lucknow, thereby consigning the city to a perpetual veil of romantic lyricism and sublime sorrows? Was Feroz Ali Khan, thus, the unshakable link to Lucknow's most cherished monument, the Bara Imambara? Were the family blood cousins to Sadat Ali Khan, whose architectural proclivity had given rise to Dilkusha, Farhat Baksh, and Lal Baradari? And didn't Feroz himself bear striking resemblance to Muhammad Ali, son of Sadat Ali, under whom Lucknow had enjoyed a cultural and social renaissance in the early 1800s?

But the myth about the Ali Khan family that persevered the strongest was that they were linked, either through blood or history or happenstance, to Lucknow's most fabled denizen, Wajid Ali Shah. If Lucknow itself was inexplicably linked with a sense of beauty, with a sense of romance, with a certain gracious *tehzeeb*, then Wajid Ali Shah was the man chiefly responsible for it. A character torn out of history's most cherished pages, Shah had been a ruler, a troubadour, a poet-rebel, and a renaissance man, all rolled into one, far more concerned with the pleasures of the flesh and the passions of the arts than with such trivial concerns as governance and ruling over an empire. Under him, though the city may not have been in the most responsible of hands, it certainly witnessed a flourishing of the arts and a blossoming of the soul. His love for the city ran pure and deep, his love for amorous dalliances much the same. He sang, he drank, he loved, he returned for more. And as befitting a man of such wandering desires, his fall from grace was excessively savage, a bitter exile and an anonymous demise in distant Rangoon bringing down a sad curtain on a particularly colourful life.

Feroz Ali Khan did little to refute any of the rumours floating around him and his family. Whether of noble lineage, rich patronage, or wealthy forefathers, he chose to keep his cards close to his heart. He held the staunch belief that his personal life was his alone. The truth about his origins probably lay somewhere in between all the speculation. What was more certain was that unlike several other wealthy families, which had witnessed a remarkable drop in fortunes, consigned to living in dilapidated havelis and holding on desperately to crumbling vestiges of the past, the Ali Khan family had emerged from the throes of yesteryears in much better shape. On the surface, none of them appeared to harbour any resentment over the dissolution of their privileges.

The children in particular were a cheerful lot, going about their young lives in a moderately carefree environment of parental guidance that veered between strictness and leniency; a school life packed with friends from all religions and walks of life; and a comfortable existence in a home that though no longer luxurious, afforded a vastly nurturing environment filled with love. While Afreen ran the home and its ever-revolving coterie of guests and relations with ease, assisted in her cause by two old matronly women, Feroz had managed to shake the curse of many of his now-defunct *nawabi* neighbours by rising to the ranks of a branch manager at the Nizamgarh branch of the Bank of Lucknow.

If the Ali Khans were ever to have any doubt or regret over their present lot in life, they would only have had to look next door to have those regrets dispelled. Their immediate neighbours, distanced by a 100 metres or so, were the Khurshids. This family's storied history had been one of insurmountable tragedy. Amjad Khurshid, the family scion and a contemporary of Feroz's father, came from a royal Awadhi lineage that was far less shrouded in mystery. Unable to endure the sudden dissolution of the family title and its royal privileges after India's independence, he had succumbed to depression and the lure of the bottle, eventually dying a silent death in the arms of his favourite mistress. His brood of three sons had fought bitterly over his estate, each demanding his majority share in the large mansion that they once called home, until the haveli and their own family name was all but wiped away from memory, a mere footnote in the forgotten pages of the old Lucknow chronicles. After the haveli passed into the hands of the government, it was subjected to even more apathy and a predictably lackadaisical approach towards its maintenance. Grand plans of converting the mansion into a swish heritage hotel lay buried in the dust, together with any sense of dignity and grandeur that it once owned. A decrepit, haunting ode to the excesses of yore and the futility of greed, the mansion's solitary claim to fame these days lay in its centuries-old well, a broodingly cavernous structure of immovable old stones that reached deep into the earth. The well was an ominous creature whose oneness with the earth made it nigh impossible for it to be demolished.

The neighbourhood kids had discovered it, nurtured it, and brought it back to some semblance of life. They would gather around it fairly regularly and play marbles, or better still, would engage in a daring game of 'who goes down furthest'—an imaginary bounty of fame awaiting the one who eventually would, though such a possibility looked quite remote.

It was the stone well and its hidden location deep within the overgrown, eerie gardens of the haveli that now held Fardeen's attention as he tried to awaken his little sister, Farzana, from her deep sleep filled with butterflies and balloons. He was wondering whether they should sneak away there and try and locate Fazal Bhai, who would, no doubt, be in the company of local boys, similarly charming and roguish. As an indignant Farzana began to protest her way out of sleep, Fardeen decided that the makeshift cricket pitch at the end of their road was certainly a much more suitable address for his brother's location, and that they would duly escape there after having investigated the goings-on below.

❦

Once down in the courtyard, dressed in their pristine white *kurta-pyjamas* now somewhat crumpled from sleep, the siblings came to a unanimous agreement that Eid was upon them, yet again. Hurrah! They tiptoed their way around the proceedings and through the many hidden crevices of their home. They were by now conditioned, through an occasional beating and several admonishments, to making themselves scarce in the presence of company.

As they passed through the congregation below, Fardeen thought how he and his little sister were blessed to be of just the perfect height, one from which it was so much easier to understand the world. Whenever he was picked up by his father or flung across the shoulders by some uncle or the other, the initial thrill of height would quickly give way to a sense of boredom, of even annoyance, at not really being able to control or even identify life from that height. But from down below, close to the earth, he felt he was at the perfect vantage point to observe and examine grown-ups and their surprisingly childish parade of concerns. He loved watching *abba* and *ammi*, lost in deep conversation, or welcoming guests in their quiet charming manner, or in that peculiar state of teasing one another, which he had no way of knowing was something called flirtation; he loved watching the large collection of relations, guests, acquaintances, and friendships where each had something that no one else had. This is what he'd come to learn. No, Fardeen was just fine at this height. And as far as he was concerned, he wished he could stay here forev…

The heaving bosom of a particularly affectionate *mausi* quashed his thought process quite suddenly. Fardeen knew from his parents' idle chitchat that Aunty Afroz Akhtar had been quite the doyen of Lucknow's theatre scene in her youth, having been part of both the *Ada* and the *Roomani* troupes in their heydays. While her days of donning the greasepaint and regaling the audience with her sharp wit and a mesmerising smile might have become things of the past, Madam Akhtar certainly carried a sense of theatricality in all that she did. Whether inquiring about the price of tomatoes from the local grocer or shunning yet another suitor, her flailing arms, extended gestures, and bewitchingly sad eyes made every act seem like a piece right out of Vivaldi. She was 50 now, and had never been married, and in many ways, you sensed that such a woman never would. She appeared too consumed by the pleasures of this world and by the upkeep of her own self to ever bequeath herself entirely to any man. As she let go of her hug, Fardeen uttered an embarrassed hello, and then followed it up with a pleasant 'Eid Mubarak' greeting. Afroz didn't say anything and just stroked his hair with a lot of affection. Well, I wonder why she's not really putting much into it? pondered Fardeen. Afroz then transferred her affection on to Farzana, before moving on to join the others in that blissful diva glide of hers.

As the children made their way without too much fuss across the courtyard, they were greeted with an occasional warm hug, the usual tousling of hair, and the quiet murmur of adults getting on, undoubtedly, with their oh-so-serious conversations about life, jobs, the weather, and other oddities. They caught fleeting glimpses of several relatives through the crowd at different moments, but knew better than to disturb them in the middle of their conversations.

When they finally had enough of the social merry-go-round, they decided to retire towards a place closest to their hearts— the kitchen. The Ali Khans' kitchen was an ancient marvel of stone, brick, and memories—the last, probably, holding the most influence over its identity. It was on the ground level, naturally, and was separated from the open courtyard by a sliver of verandah that snaked all around the square. Despite being in a remote corner where it could easily go unnoticed, the kitchen was clearly the most cherished place in the morning's scheme of things.

When the children entered, they saw Khan Chacha at the helm of affairs, as he had been for nearly half a century, assisted ably, though rather frantically, by the two young Mirza boys whom he had taken under his wing. Shaan and Shaukat Mirza were 17-year-old twins whose family, mired in an unfortunate spell of unemployment, had been only too happy to send their children off to work at a respectable home, under the tutelage of a much-respected head cook.

Fardeen and Farzana were greeted with a large smile by Khan Chacha, which surprised them no end. They knew their patronal cook to be a man of hidden warmth and a compassionate heart, but openly affectionate he never was. When the smile was followed by a louder-than-usual morning greeting and an enquiry about their well-being, Fardeen whispered to his sister, "*Everyone's* nicer during Eid."

The kids were then taken to a large wooden table that stood in rather regal posture at the centre of the kitchen. This table had been both witness to, and central character in, many a festive celebration, family feud, and furtive romance over the years. But this morning, it was only a bearer of gifts. As Khan Chacha took them along the length of the table, the kids took their pick of the offerings on display: a couple of *keema samosas*, but naturally; some wonderfully fragrant *haleem*, rich in its sublime textures of mutton, gravy, lentils, and spices; a mental note of that saffron-scented *halwah* with its dense blend of honey, pine nuts, flour, and dates for later; and a small pink-coloured cup each, filled with a rose petal-like liquid that at once took their minds away to a place of happiness. The children took their little paper plates out of the kitchen and sat down at the edge of the verandah, with a fairly clear view of the goings-on in the courtyard. Shaan and Shaukat followed closely behind, carrying their cups and placing them on the stone floor.

The brothers politely inquired after them before leaving them to get on with their morning meal.

"I really wish it was Eid every day," chuckled Fardeen.

"Me too!" Farzana nodded in agreement.

"This is yummy! And can you believe how nice Khan Chacha is being? Don't you remember what happened last year, during *bhaijaan's* birthday?"

Farzana shook her head.

"*Arre*, when I'd sneaked into the kitchen and tried to grab us a couple of slices of the cake. He caught me and gave me a nice little whack on the head. Ouch!" Fardeen massaged the top of his head, more from the memory than any real pain.

Farzana giggled, munching away rather happily.

"Come to think of it, we had the exact same food that day as well," he reminisced.

"Where do you think mum and dad are?" his sister interrupted him, taking a small break from her eating schedule.

"Oh, upstairs I suppose," he answered. "Either they're getting ready, or they must be showing some of the guests around the house." After further thought, he corrected himself. "Wait, it's Eid, so they're surely in the prayer-room with a few people. They'll be out soon."

Farzana nodded.

Fardeen thought of something. He hesitated for a while, unsure whether his little sister would be able to grasp the profundity of his thought processes.

"Hey, you know something?"

"What?"

"Umm, I'm not sure you'll understand."

"Tell me *na*, *bhai*. I'm very old now, I understand everything."

"Well okay then. You know, even when dad's not here, like when he's in some other room, I can feel him watching over us."

"What, like making sure we don't get into trouble?"

"No, no, like making sure that nothing bad happens to us or that we don't get lost or something."

Farzana was silent.

"Like that time in Bara Imambara, when I got lost," Fardeen pointed out to her.

"Oh, I remember!" she responded with enthusiasm, glad that this hadn't turned out to be yet another story that she needed to be reminded of.

The Bara Imambara saga was now part of Ali Khan family folklore. The large Shia shrine complex had been built by Asaf-ud-Daula, the fourth Nawab Wazir of Awadh, over two centuries ago. The destination is a Mughal treasure and one of Lucknow's endearing favourites. Due to its ingenious architectural style, it contains the world's largest arched ceiling that stands tall without a single supporting pillar. Within the complex, the Bhool Bhulaiya is the intricate labyrinth of narrow stairway passages that lies above the Imambara. And this mysterious maze was where Fardeen had vanished.

In their illusions and inter-connectedness, the mazes are a severe challenge for adults, leave alone children. On their very first visit here, their father had warned the children about the obvious perils and how one mustn't fool around or venture too far on one's own. Predictably, Fardeen had begun fooling around immediately upon landing at the Bhool Bhulaiya. In the flash of an instant, in the muddled convergence of people inside the labyrinth, he had gotten separated from the rest. After both he and the family had managed to gain their bearings amidst the crowd, the realisation had dawned on them. Naturally, panic ensued. Hard as it may be to imagine, just one wrong turn or a moment of forgetfulness can lead to a torturous experience at the mazes. Gripped by fright, Fardeen had begun to scream out for his father. The entire Ali Khan family in turn had begun to scream back, each able to hear the other and make out which direction the voices were coming from, but still they were no closer to bridging the distances.

Within the labyrinth's seemingly identical assortment of stairs, tracks, openings, and hollowed corridors, Fardeen had been helpless. Some of the passageways he took led him to dead ends, while a few stopped abruptly at precipitous drops—now thankfully secured with grills. This was a structure built with the intention of bewildering enemy intruders, what chance did a child have? Its narrow lanes seemed to close in on him as he fumbled through its three storeys, surrounded by 400 and 89 door-less galleries, confronted by its thousand passageways, weakened by the continuous climbing of its unending staircases.

Despite the fright at being lost, Fardeen had known that things would be all right. He knew that as long as he kept hearing his father's voice, he wasn't lost. He didn't even need to hear that voice, as long as he felt that presence of someone watching out for him, watching over him. He would be all right.

After a 45-minute game of call-and-answer, the lad had been reunited with his family, amidst much merriment from the other children and a relieved slap or two from the parents. As a small gift, Feroz had led him by hand up the steep chain of stairs that led to the roof of the monument. And there, father and son had marvelled at the beauty of Lucknow—the Islamic minarets, the domes, the Rumi Darwaza, the Asifi Mosque, the distant flow of the river Gomti—spread out before them as a just reward. The experience had mattered to Fardeen and it came flooding back to him now as he sat on the kitchen's outer verandah, trying to explain this inexplicable bond to a somewhat preoccupied younger sister.

"Oh, there he is!" exclaimed Farzana, between a small mouthful of samosa and her brother's story ringing in her ear.

"And there she is," smiled Fardeen, putting aside his plate.

Their parents had emerged from the large prayer room on the second level and were walking down the steps. Feroz Ali Khan was dressed in a crisp *kurta-pyjama* made from Lucknow's fabled *chikan* fabric, his prominent countenance a firm rejoinder to the playful wind. Beside him, adjusting her stunning green *dupatta* over her head and shoulders as she walked, Afreen Ali Khan was a beautiful vision in white; her similarly pristine *salwar-kameez* rendered whiter against the sudden whims and swirls of the fluttering *dupatta*.

Both husband and wife bore a cosmic sense of unison through two similar scars surrounding their eyes. Feroz carried a diagonal wound just above his left eyebrow, one that had transformed from being a fairly scary-looking cut to a somewhat stylish badge of youth, a permanent remnant of a hunting trip gone wrong due to a young man's early mishandling of a shooting rifle. Otherwise, he bore stately features, with a broad face, framed well by a now-ashen beard, an angular nose, and dark, brooding eyes that spoke in the language of soft sadness. His hair, a handsome mound of jet black till he was well into his forties, had now receded into a slightly rebellious flow of charcoal grey. Afreen's mark was just below her right eye, the result of an enthusiastic playmate from her childhood accidentally scratching her across the face with a pencil. To cover the mark, she always applied a thick double-coat of dark kohl, leaving her beautiful eyes a playground of hidden mysteries.

The children watched as their parents went around greeting their guests.

"See?" Fardeen nudged his sister. "I told you they would be up in the prayer-room."

Farzana nodded sagely. "But *bhai*, will we also have to go and pray now?"

"I don't think so," Fardeen uttered, none too convincingly.

The children had yet to wrap their heads around the customs of prayer and the cycles of devotion that went with Muslim holidays, remembrances, and celebrations. But they needn't have worried. From the time of their great grandfather, their family had begun to loosen the vice-like grip of inflexible moral strictures. It was an ethos that had grown stronger with every passing year, with the children being the fortunate recipients of the most relaxed code of prayer and conduct than any of the family before them. While their parents prayed five times a day, their father had decided that his children would not be subjected to a religious regime and would be allowed to explore and exercise their choice when the time came. He knew in his heart that being a good human being, a compassionate father, a loving child, and a decent soul went hand in hand with being a good Muslim. Both Afreen and he would be strict whenever it was required, would be demanding when they felt it was right, and would colour their dealings with their children in an overall atmosphere of moderation and liberalism.

Fardeen watched intently as Afreen and Feroz welcomed their guests gathered in the courtyard with varying degrees of warmth, love, courtesy, or slight indifference, based on who was at the other end. He had already begun catching on to these things, and in some ways, had begun mirroring their interactions whenever he met the same people. The courtyard was filled with embraces, smiles, and tears, and the young lad would've been quite happy to just sit and watch the adults go about their exchanges. His intuitive mind was keen on observing how they dealt with one another; these grown-up beings not quite fortunate enough to see the world from his angles. Farzana had other ideas though.

"Hey," she tugged at his *kurta*'s slightly oversized sleeve. "*Abba* and *ammi* are down here, no?"

"Well yeah," Fardeen replied, a tad irritated in being distracted from his people-watching through an inane question.

"Then can we go up to their room?" she inquired further, clearly going somewhere with this.

"Ah," her brother caught on to her chain of though. "You're thinking of the sweet box, aren't you?"

The wide grin on his sister's face told him he had been right with his guess. The sweet box had acquired a cult-like status in the children's minds. It was a beautiful circular box made out of dark teak, enveloped entirely by a dark pink fabric that had shiny jewels embedded onto it in a star-like pattern. It contained a large assortment of sweets and chocolates, courtesy whoever dropped in with the offerings. In recent times, the box held a small packet of chocolate-covered dates, gifted by one of the cousins who had returned from Dubai. There were two small packets of 5-Star, an Indian staple that was little Farzana's all-time favourite, its chewy nougat texture allowing her to derive endless, noisy enjoyment out of each bite. There was Afreen's favourite too—long bars of Lindt dark chocolate, brought in by her sister only a couple of weeks ago. Finally, there was an assorted collection of mini M&Ms, Toblerone, and Snickers to keep the men of the house sufficiently engaged.

A small game their mother played with them was to hide the box in different places each time, forcing them to use their wits and slog for their reward. It was just a tiny, playful thing really, but the kids had let their zeal for the search get the better of them on a couple of occasions, and had ended up intruding on some spaces that were strictly off-limits for them. They had been spanked on those occasions, so they knew not to stretch their luck too far. More to keep his sister appeased than for any urgent sweet craving, Fardeen took Farzana by the hand and they leapt up the stairs, before slipping stealthily into the bedroom above.

Their parents' bedroom was, quite naturally, the most beautiful room in the entire haveli. It bore no real signs of major ostentatiousness, but Afreen had poured much of her heart into its details. There was a lot of love that had gone into each space. There were three-layered drapes on each of the three windows, every single one a thin, silk fabric of white, sober cream, and dull gold. These drapes were such delicate creatures that the sun was allowed to flow in with aplomb, despite their unity. And flow in it did, taking full advantage of the room facing eastward, bathing Afreen's decor and antique trappings in a remarkable mellow gold, palpable to those influenced by romance and its sensory immersions.

There were dark shelves and old cupboards that had been handed down over the generations, with many frames and curios of dull silver that Afreen had brought along as family heirlooms. There were portraits of both her and Feroz's ancestors, frozen in a timeless tint of monochrome that seemed to retain its dusty charm, no matter how regularly the prints and photographs were dusted and restored.

It wasn't a cluttered room; it had a certain richness. There was an ambience of profundity. There were stories and myths, and the unmistakable yoke of heritage, tugging gently at all its spaces. Right at the heart of things was a king-sized bed made of dark teak that Feroz had inherited from his father. It bore an exaggerated headrest, with the wood carved into many a swirl. The bed was particularly dear to him. It somehow felt like home; as did Afreen's mirror table, to her. A constant source of comfort, the warmth of the past more than anything, really.

The children set about trying to find what they'd come for, first going through a roster of the hiding places where they'd previously tasted success. They peeked under the bed, tried to squeeze themselves in between the bed and the wall, flicked through the large drawer of the bedside table, and even had a good look around some of the things placed outside in the balcony. But nothing. They then set about trying a few new places, taking care not to breach any rules of privacy. After a good 20 minutes of searching, they were tired and about to concede defeat, when a thought struck Fardeen.

When he'd rushed into the room the previous evening, bogged down by a dreary math problem, he had found his mother putting away a few old boxes and knick-knacks in the closet, the one that always smelt like granddad. He'd caught her off guard, and she'd hurriedly hidden something before turning back to reprimand him for sneaking up on her like that. Now, he headed for the closet.

Farzana tried to be the voice of reason, for a change. "*Bhai*, no."

"No what?"

"I don't think we're supposed to go in there."

"Oh, it's nothing like that. We're just not supposed to look inside things and try and open any of the boxes."

"Oh, okay. Are you sure?"

"Yes, I am. Come on now, let's have a quick look."

The storage room was a room by name only, barely having enough space for two adults to fit inside without stumbling over one another. The kids were just fine in there though. It held the perfect amount of space and just the right amount of mystery for their imaginations to fly. Farzana began counting the number of boxes, large and small, and assigning them made-up names. Fardeen, meanwhile, set about trying to find the sweet box, focussing his attention on the spot he'd seen his mother in the previous night. He climbed on to the lower shelf and peered into the shelf above him. He stood on his toes, trying to scan every dark recess of its spaces. Aha! Wait a second, what was that? He spotted a shock of pink at the far corner of the shelf. Readjusting himself on the shelf, he moved a couple of boxes towards the left, and reached out. He managed to clutch the outer edges of the pink fabric and dragged the box out towards him, but bumped one of the smaller boxes in the process. As it fell on the floor, the siblings stood speechless in fear, but seeing that it was unharmed, quickly regained their sense of purpose. Farzana opened the sweet box and grabbed a 5-Star for herself, breaking half of it and putting the rest of the chocolate neatly back into its wrapper. Knowing her brother's preference, she grabbed a mini Snickers for Fardeen, who accepted it rather absent-mindedly. His mind was on something else.

The little box lay on the ground with its lid snapped open. One of the contents had popped out. Munching away on his Snickers, Fardeen examined the object: a letter. It was written on a plain off-white paper, the kind on which, he had once seen, a hero wrote to his heroine in a film. He found it odd that a paper shouldn't have any lines. How on earth were you to keep your writing straight? He wanted to keep the letter back into the box and put it away immediately, but curiosity gnawed at him. It lay half-open on the ground, and its open, upper half revealed a single, simple enough statement that he could read quite easily: *My Dear Afreen…* As he flicked the bottom half open, his eyes instinctively ran towards the end of the letter, which carried another easily read sentence: *All my love, Vikas.*

Chewing his chocolate slowly, Fardeen began to think about the letter and the words he had chanced upon. His thoughts began to swirl around his mother. He thought about this person he'd never met before, Vikas. And then he thought of how he and his sister risked a proper beating if they stayed there much longer. Carefully sliding the letter back in and closing the lid, Fardeen placed the pink box back where it had been on the shelf and shoved the other boxes in front of it. Their minor adventure having been navigated quite successfully, the children ran out of the room, the pure taste of sweetness lingering in their minds.

Down in the courtyard, things appeared to be just as they'd left them—people, conversation, tears, laughter, embraces, the usual

Eid fare, pretty much. After leaving their parents' room, the children decided to go over to the opposite side on the second level and watch proceedings from a slightly different vantage point. Once on the second level though, their thoughts immediately turned towards the slow, melodic chants emanating out of the prayer room. Outside the room, they stopped for a while and listened.

"Sometimes, I like it," Farzana confessed.

"What?" inquired Fardeen.

"The prayers. Sometimes I like them very much."

"Me too."

"But sometimes, I don't like them at all," she opined further.

"Me too," Fardeen concurred, as he smiled and gave his sister a small squeeze.

They sat down on the floor in front of the room, listening to the prayers for a while. Fardeen remembered how the whole family had risen for early morning *namaz* during one of the Eids the previous years, and in the partaking of the morning feast during the month of fasting. Their parents had risen due to a deep conviction in their faith, and had observed the holy month with an unshakeable sense of reverence and fulfilment. The children had been awakened by the noises and sounds of preparation from the prayer room and the kitchen downstairs, but their initial annoyance had soon given way to a sleepy sort of excitement at the prevailing atmosphere around the house. That was the time Fardeen's parents had also encouraged his elder brother, Fazal, to undertake the fasting with them. He didn't last long though; he had given up after five days. They didn't persist. "I'm not going to force any of them," Feroz Ali Khan had averred. "I won't force them either," Afreen had said. "If they're meant to embrace their faith, they will."

Listening to the soft murmur of prayers from within the room, Fardeen was reminded of the muezzins and their calls to prayer during Eid, from both the previous year as well as earlier that same year. Their neighbourhood of Nakhas was filled with mosques, and the near simultaneous calls to prayer were like pebbles being thrown into a river, each small ripple leading to another, and then another, so much so that within a few moments, this silently rising, majestically unfurling cascade of prayers felt like a singular, powerful wave of devotion, sweeping across their city...and their home within it.

Fardeen felt the door creak ever so slightly, and he snapped out of his memories from the past. Farzana was trying her best to get a quiet peek of the proceedings inside.

"Shhh!" he hissed at her. "What do you think you're doing?"

"I just thought I coul..."

"No you're not. Either you'll get us into trouble or we'll be sent straight for prayers."

"But I thought..."

"Listen, I know what we'll do."

"What?"

"We'll go up to the roof and wait for *bhai*."

The roof of the haveli was a character unto itself; its brick and distressed cement eccentricity home to many a cherished memory. In the infancy of their marriage, Feroz and Afreen used to sneak away and sleep up there during early summer and early winter alike. Wrapped in an atmosphere of romance, those early days and nights had probably been the most carefree of their lives. But then the children had happened, and life had suddenly taken over, as it often does. As the children had grown a bit older though, the roof had been recast in a new avatar—as the location for the occasional board-game or late night pyjama parties. There were two old couches that stood facing each other, right in the centre. Their dark maroon fabric had weathered over time and dissolved into various shades of red and cerise, an unabashed depiction of pink. Whenever it rained, a large tarpaulin was dragged out from the storeroom on the third floor and hung casually over them. And there they would stand during the monsoons, like two old beggars trying their best to make do with whatever fate had left them with.

As Fardeen reached the roof, Farzana's hand clenched tightly in his, it dawned on him that they weren't supposed to be up there. The children were never allowed to be up there without an adult around, as the barrier that ran around the roof was barely a couple of feet high, and a fairly flimsy one at that. But he sensed his sister was getting restless, and he didn't want her to cause any commotion and get both of them into trouble. Truth be known, young Fardeen was feeling a bit restless himself, wondering why his brother had chosen to betray them and sneak away on such an important day.

On the roof, his thoughts drifted immediately towards Fazal Bhai. That same year, when spring had arrived, Fazal had taught him the instantly giddy art of kite-flying. They had flown kites all through spring, Fazal never shy of displaying his dexterity with his pack of blue kites, while Fardeen had had to take extreme care of his bunch of three green ones. He had struggled with the art at first, his arms not yet strong enough to tackle the winds when they arose fiercely, his mind too fickle to grasp the virtues of patience. But then, after a while, something magical had happened. Under Fazal's close supervision, he had begun to realise that kite-flying wasn't about strength, or even experience...it was about far more magical things in this world, like fortune, and perhaps, maybe even happiness.

They would fly kites all day long, Shaan and Shaukat always close at hand to watch over things. Sometimes, their father would come up to join them, and then the wonder gates would truly fly open! Feroz was quite brilliant with the art of coaxing turn and swing, a certain melody if you will, out of the kites. In his hands, they would soar well into the skies, disappearing into the hearts of errant clouds at times, and be lost in the infinite oceans of blue above.

There were many casualties that spring—Fardeen had either damaged or lost his three kites, while Fazal had managed to get himself into all sorts of tangles with the neighbourhood boys during their kite wars, and had been left with just one by the time spring was done. There had been some epic kite wars that season, with boys and girls congregating on roofs of all shapes and heights, flooding the skies with colour and the distinct whiff of freedom. Some of the warfare between the teenage boys and girls would be of the decidedly romantic kind, the crossing of kites a sort of foreplay in their infant flirtation. A couple of delinquent kites had even broken and landed on the Ali Khan roof, and upon inspection, had been found to bear the messages 'I love you Amjad' and 'How about a film sometime?' respectively, leading to much mirth among the brothers. Sets of boys would go at it hard though, hell-bent on cutting the other's line and usurping the other's kite, almost claiming a small slice of the sky as their own. For Fardeen, that spring had been a wellspring of discovery and emotion, bringing him ever closer to his elder brother, bringing him ever closer to the skies over Lucknow.

As he thought about Fazal, Fardeen wandered across to the edge of the roof that looked out into the east, on to the street beneath and the rest of Lucknow, further afield. What a day to be up here. He knew he shouldn't, but he felt he must. Amidst the fond recollections of the spring he'd shared with his brother, brewed a touch of resentment. How could he have abandoned him on a day like today? To go and play cricket with the gully kids, no less! And shouldn't he have taken him along, knowing fully well that he was getting stronger at the game by the day, now fully capable of striking a ball till it rolled into the Mahmood's compound? Hard to understand. Oh, wait a second. He couldn't have sneaked off for an early morning show at the Umrao movie hall, could he? Did they even show films at such an early hour? The long winter break would soon end as well, come the beginning of the new year, and then they wouldn't get to spend so much time together.

He walked as close to the brink of the roof as he could and crouched down on his haunches, with the crumbling outer brick fence acting as a back support. Farzana was engaged in a game of marbles that the boys kept up on the roof. Not knowing the intricacies of the game, she was more content with polishing each marble with her *kurta* till the sun sparkled like gold on its surface. The children, over the course of just an hour, had managed to turn their white pyjamas into crumpled rags encrusted with dirt, even discarding their *chappals* for the joy of being bare-footed.

Fardeen got up and peered over the decrepit brick fence outlining to see what the street below was up to. The usual, nothing too remarkable to see there—fruit-seller laying out his cart, homes swinging into their daily routines, a cyclist almost falling off his bicycle in trying to evade an oncoming motorbike, and oh hello, that little brown dog who had chased Shaukat for nearly a mile the other day. Everything seemed…

The shriek, sudden as it was, tore through the skies and the relative stillness of the Lucknow morning. Fardeen froze with fear, and turned around slowly. But Farzana was right there. She seemed scared, but she was right there where he'd left her. Fardeen ran and grabbed her by the hand, and together they ran downstairs, bypassing the third floor to the second level to find out what had happened. From the balcony, the view wasn't of much help. Fardeen could make out a large green object moving through the crowd below, but he couldn't figure out what it was. Again, he grabbed

Farzana's hand and they rushed, barefoot, down the rickety wooden stairs of their old, heaving haveli, down to the first floor.

As they rushed towards the balcony in front of their bedroom, Fardeen realised that they'd left their mattresses out that morning, just lying there. Boy, there was sure to be some trouble if someone were to ever find out. But they had a purpose to serve now. Fardeen pulled the end of his sister's mattress on to the end of his, and stood up to examine the scene below. Farzana followed closely behind, clutching on to the fold of his *kurta* for dear life. In the courtyard, Fardeen saw a couple of his elderly cousins and the imams from their mosque joining his father and his uncles in carrying a thin rectangular box covered with a large green cloth. The cloth struck Fardeen's fancy immediately. It was a beautiful shade of green, the same shade his mum sometimes wore when there was a wedding or another important event. In fact, wasn't it exactly the same green as her *dupatta* today?

The fringes of the cloth, as they fell down over the sides of whatever the men were carrying, looked distinctly like gold fabric patterns, or that's what they appeared to be anyway. As this entire party moved through the courtyard, the others made way on either side, like an ocean being parted into two. The imams were chanting prayers from the Quran, which the others were repeating. Well some were, the others were just crying these great, big tears, the kind with which your whole body shakes.

"Great; one more Eid custom I had no idea about," muttered Fardeen, jotting it down in his mental diary for later. He looked closely at the cloth, stared deep into what lay beneath. At that very moment, a sudden gust of wind entered the courtyard and rushed through the cloth, lifting it unexpectedly, leaving just a small space exposed at one corner. Fardeen stared. His eyes were gripped by what lay within that diagonal opening. It was the limp, lifeless face of his brother Fazal. Lying peacefully, held by his cousins and relatives, held by the mosque elders, held by his father.

Fardeen stared at the face and the body which was seven inches taller than his, buried under the majestic folds of the green shroud. A strange reverie of thoughts began to unfold in his mind. He thought of kites reaching far into the sky, of laughter shared under big oak trees. He thought of the letter he had found in his mother's storage room. He thought about the name Vikas, and what that name meant in the general scheme of things. He saw his father motion for a relative to come and take his place in the procession. As Feroz Ali Khan left, he reached out for his wife and held on to her arms, tightly. He saw his mother, her beautiful face as still as the skies when the days turn to dusk. He had no way of knowing what it meant to hold on, slowly, to a large, gnawing sorrow, before simply letting go. He thought about Eid, and about when it wasn't Eid. He felt Farzana behind him, too scared to watch what was going on below. He stared at his parents, now bound together as one. Instinctively, they looked up at him. He saw the marks around their eyes, one above the right eyebrow, one beneath the left eyelash, by now smothered in a state of liquid, far away from everyone else's eyes.

Once upon a Mystic Sky

It was Thursday. As he had done every Thursday, for the past 19 years, Mehfil Hussain Zaidi began readying himself for devotion. This evening though, things seemed different. He felt it in his heart, a strange and fickle meandering that refused to subside. He sensed it was coming.

Mehfil had felt it emerging at the beginning of the day itself, when he woke at dawn. An emotion he might have dismissed as wistfulness had only grown in potency and urgency as the day had progressed. So much so, by the time evening prayers had abated, he was nearly overcome by a pain he could no longer bear.

As dusk began to tread softly around Delhi's old neighbourhoods, casting its dark orange flood and emerging shadows on a district that has been long celebrated through letters, films, and verse, Mehfil stood at the mausoleum's entrance compound and tried to keep his heart pacified. In front of him, the boisterousness of a thriving marketplace and the hustle-bustle of a riotously diverse populace mingled freely with the tombs of old rulers and the haunts of poets from history's fabled pages.

In his eyes, the narrow lane winding its way in front of him was as much a shrine as the tomb where he raised his voice in devotion. He inhaled the scents arising from the *attar* placed on baskets of rose petals, their thick plumes of perfumed essence becoming one with Delhi's night. He stared at the tiny kebab stalls and their perfectly lined skewers of perfectly chargrilled kebabs and watched as their flavours too ascended into the skies. He heard the entire scene vibrate to its own pulsating beat, as cries from the sellers of the silk green *chadors* blended as one with the prayers being offered by the *namazis* behind him in the shrine compound's adjoining mosque. This is Delhi, he thought to himself, where every aroma, every fragrance, every essence, and every prayer has its own space under the skies.

"Sir, is everything alright?" The question shook Mehfil out of his ruminations over the surroundings. It was Akbar.

"Yes, why do you ask?"

"Nothing sir, it's just that you've appeared…well, a little bit restless today."

Mehfil smiled. He had grown quite fond of this young man who had joined the Nizamuddin Dargah's *humnawa*, or qawwali troupe, only a year ago. As guardians, in a sense, of the shrine's hymns and praises of its divine saint, each delivered in ancient verse, each celebrated through sacred prayers, the qawwals or performers were nearly as renowned as the mausoleum complex itself. Every Thursday, their love for Allah and their patron saint would rent the skies of Old Delhi with ecstatic potency, rendered through melodies in the Sufi tradition of spiritual love. Mehfil mused over how Akbar, a new entrant to their fold, had managed to break through ranks of the religiously tight-knit group, to emerge as their tabla player over the past year. He reminisced how he had seen the lad playing on a broken tabla by the side of the road and had been so mesmerised by his god-gifted sense of rhythm and flow that he had beseeched the group to take Akbar in. Mehfil was glad he had stuck with his gut instincts.

"How old are you?" he asked Akbar.

"Sir, I'm 21."

"Twenty-one," Mehfil repeated, trying to remember what it was to be that age. "I'm 55 now, and at times it feels that you're more sensitive than I am." He smiled at the youngster. "Shouldn't you be out chasing after girls or something? Did I ruin your life by pushing you into the qawwali tradition?"

It was Akbar's turn to smile. "Sir, how can you say that? This is what I was born to do: to uphold India's ancient qawwali heritage, to express my love for the *Khwaja* in sacred Urdu verse, to be a part of this proud ritual that has been a part of Delhi's fabric for so long."

Mehfil stared at the young man with deep eyes. "Very true, son." He tried to locate the right words from within the din surrounding the shrine and its mosque. "But, sometimes, love is the most sacred possession of all." He motioned for Akbar to come stand beside him.

"You see this scene in front of us?" Mehfil gestured towards the crowded street and its ever-flowing bazaar. "And you see this mausoleum brimming with sacredness, with its silent tombs presided over by the majesty of the mosque behind us?" he nodded towards Nizamuddin Dargah, their home. "All of this was decreed, all of this is our salvation. We're right in the heart of it all; never forget any of that."

Akbar stayed silent.

There were many thoughts brewing in the old maestro's mind. Soon, Mehfil spoke: "We are blessed to be a spiritual part of the Nizamuddin Dargah. We live in such close spiritual proximity to the world's most revered Sufi saint, Hazrat Khwaja Nizamuddin Auliya, and we are guardians of his mausoleum, the holy shrine that sates our souls and replenishes our beliefs."

Mehfil stared into the sky. The orange wash of dusk had given way to a young night filled with stars, which sparkled with poetic abandon above a December night. It was heading to be one of Delhi's fabled winters. The air lay thick with the promise of the epic. "We are his disciples, yes, but we are also our own disciples and the songs we sing are the foundations of our spiritual path."

Amidst the clamour of the bazaar, Mehfil's words scintillated like diamonds, cutting deep into Akbar's soul.

"This is a special gift Allah has bestowed us with. We lose ourselves in our ecstatic melodies, and the audience is swept along with us; we evoke love for Allah and Hazrat Ali through our verses and songs, and the crowd feels the divine arising within them; we find a deep spiritual connection with Khwaja Nizamuddin and bind the faithful into an impregnable bond as well." Mehfil paused to take it all in, before concluding with the vast ocean of emptiness swirling within his eyes. "But then Akbar, what of love…?"

Akbar was silent. He knew this man he had grown to revere was suffering a spiritual crisis of sorts. "Forgive me sir, but wasn't it Khwaja Nizamuddin Auliya himself who believed that along with *aql*, or wisdom, and *ilm*, knowledge, a saint and a devotee needs to have *ishq* in his soul? Isn't this, in the end, about love?"

"Well, that is the basic tenet of Sufism itself," replied Mehfil. "Truth and divine love through direct personal experience—that much is sacred. Our qawwali tradition is indivisibly linked to the Sufi tradition; mystic and melodic in every sense…" he paused, struggling with the torment within his heart. "And yet, what about…"

"What about…?" Akbar beseeched him.

"What about the divine love that has a more, well, a more earthly origin…?"

In winter, though the mausoleum complex began to get crowded from 5 in the evening, the qawwali performances only began at 9. While the dargah had played host to some exceptionally talented qawwals over the years, there was one family that had stood out: the

Nizami Khusros—Chand Nizami, Shadab Nizami, and their group of qawwals—who had carried the sorrows and the passions of seven centuries of ecstatic devotion in their songs. Mehfil Hussain Zaidi performed often with the Nizami brothers, sometimes playing the harmonium, sometimes accompanying them on backing vocals, but on other occasions leading the qawwals as their solo chief. Such was the case that evening, and he had discerned what was about to transpire was beyond his control.

The Nizamuddin Dargah was packed to the rafters by the time the appointed hour was at hand. An ocean of people, a microcosm of India really, had packed into the shrine's open courtyard and settled themselves under a carpet of stars: a humanity-affirming melange of Hindus, Muslims, Sikhs, Christians, Buddhists, and other faiths; a sizeable portion of foreigners, some carrying a deep faith and love for India within their souls, a few simply curious about what all the fuss was about; the religious and the rebellious, the sacred and the sensual, the fragrant and the forgotten—it really was as though India itself had been encapsulated within one courtyard. And a secular India, a sensual India at that, sometimes swaying under the weight of its own complex cultural fabric, but somehow always regaining the essence of what it was to be, undeniably, India.

Mehfil meditated on the tomb as he prepared to go on, his gaze fixated on its lattice screens populated with red threads that millions of devotees had tied with a special prayer for their wishes to be granted. In his heart, all those wishes and hushed desires had somehow accumulated themselves, merged as one, and silently entered his heart with crushing velocity. He stared at the dargah's beautiful marble arches, their curves a stinging reminder of the delicateness of a woman. He placed his hand on his heart, trying to soothe the madness that resonated within, before stepping into the courtyard to take his place on the small stage.

Amongst the restive crowd, mired in anonymity, sat a woman. She sat towards the back of the courtyard, nicely nestled within the throng. She watched as Mehfil walked on to the stage and set about to make himself feel at ease. Her eyes followed the lines on his evocative face tinged with distinction, once undeniably handsome and now, at 55, a mellow, attractive reservoir of stories, memories, dreams, and repentances. She noticed every little detail on him, from the green amulet containing a particularly resonant verse from the Quran and the flowing streaks of grey that populated his beard, to the similarly hued hair, which peeked out from beneath a white prayer cap, and his crisp white *kurta* that trembled lightly in Delhi's December chill. She sensed that the night was going to be different; it was as though she had identified a certain mood in Mehfil's eyes.

Mehfil began with the soft repeated intonations of *Allah Hu*, trying to establish the mood for the evening. Gradually, the qawwali *humnawa* walked on to the stage and began to take their places. The qawwali party consisted of eight men; two accompanying singers, one harmonium player, one dholak player, a chorus of three men for the background vocals, and Akbar on the tabla. Since Mehfil was a celebrated harmonium player himself, he had the instrument for company as well. Everyone was in place, as they sat cross-legged on the ground in two rows. His side singers and the other harmonium player flanked Mehfil while the chorus joined Akbar and the remaining percussionists in shaping the second row. The atmosphere bristled with a raw, electric energy. Mehfil, at last, let the ravaged beasts inside his heart out for a walk.

In the qawwali tradition of Khwaja Nizamuddin Auliya's Chishtiya Sufi order, he began gently, with a soft instrumental prelude, a backdrop to his meditations. During the long *alap*, when the singer is meant to improvise the central notes in the raga of the song to be played, Mehfil made an unprecedented deviation and focussed his entire attention on the word *ishq*, creating a nearly indecipherable version of the word that still gave its identity away.

This relentless obsession on love was unheard of, and some of his troupe members eyed him nervously, but kept along with him. Gradually, he moved towards a few preambular verses allied to the main song thematically, before blossoming into the song proper. His side singers, meant to accompany him from the preamble itself and poised to pitch themselves into the heart of the fray by repeating each of the initial verses, were left speechless, unable to commit themselves to the drama unfolding until Mehfil had reached the main song and they had some time to familiarise themselves with his fascinations.

The problem was that Mehfil Hussain Zaidi was concentrating, purely and deeply, on love. And while Sufi devotion has love as its very heart, this is predominantly a divine love that soars in faith and quest, whereas Mehfil's adorations were, pointedly, centred on a woman. And by the looks of it, a very *specific* woman.

Having begun gently, and as is the norm with qawwalis, the song had built up steadily through high energy, sowing the seeds for a Trojan invasion of sorts, before exploding in an ecstatic, pulsating celebration into the hearts, minds, and souls of the singer, musicians, and audience alike. In Mehfil's final refrain— *tere honton ki zubaan…ishq hai / tere khwahishon ka nishaan…ishq hai,* alluding to the language of a woman's lips and the mark of a woman's desires as love—the sentiment was repeated endlessly with Mehfil's rising passions and his sacred connection to this woman of his imaginations inducing a trance-like state in him, and by extension, his qawwali party and a large portion of the crowd. He swirled, he beseeched, he implored, he caressed, he repented, he rebelled, he sacrificed, he soared…every syllable, every intonation reflected in the pathos of his dark eyes, every moment a catalyst in the unburdening of the sorrows that weighed deep on his heart.

And so the songs flowed, each lasting roughly half an hour, each culminating in a frenzied, hypnotic coming together of the soul, spirit, spirituality...and that beast called memory. The qawwalis, be it during the *hamd*—the song in praise of Allah, or the *naat*—a song in praise of the Prophet Muhammad, or the *manaqib*—the songs in praise of Khwaja Nizamuddin, focussed much of their ardour on a love that though divinely sacred on the surface, hinted at a deeper wound within. This was an ecstasy of the soul that lay mired in the sorrows of the heart.

Playing behind him on the tabla, Akbar knew that Mehfil wasn't devoting himself to Allah or to the Prophet or to the *Imam* or to *Khwaja*. He was devoting himself to a woman. Submerged within the crowd swaying beneath the swirl of hypnotism, deep within the throes of a devoted throng, who knew not the origins of their evening's consecration, one specific woman knew it too.

Each song lay united by the thread of tabla, dholak, and meditative clapping; each member immersed in the singing of the refrains, each main verse a memento of a storied lineage. Mehfil's *humnawa*, though shaken at first, had caught on to their leader's besieged heart and had begun matching him step for step. They would improvise, they would adhere; they would soar, they would retreat; they would break out into repeated chants in praise of the higher power, they would sit quietly in the wake of a spiritual awakening, all in adherence to Mehfil's meandering heart. As the songs simmered with passion and trembled with rising tempo, the singers abstained from trying to outdo one another through vocal acrobatics, allowing Mehfil's wrenched laments to ring out pure and true.

Mehfil filled his songs with lyrics that only he knew by heart, sprinkling them with vocal and tonal improvisations befitting the qawwali. His side singers allowed him to settle into his space while they took time to acquaint themselves with his words before wading in, repeatedly, whenever the chorus came around, becoming spiritual cousins to the percussive hymns of the tabla with their unrelenting claps.

During Mehfil's profound ruminations on that eternally sacred trilogy—love, loss, and longing—his reflective repetition of chosen words began to blur into incomprehensible chants, their only purpose being to elevate him to a state of hypnotic trance, and to take his players and the audience along with him. He ended each song without warning, abruptly, sensing that any further elevation of the soul could prove almost fatal. His heart lay transformed, unburdened by its secrets; his body lay trembling in the wake of *fana*—the state of spiritual enlightenment that every Sufi craves for.

Mehfil ended the night with a ghazal—the song of love. Freed from the yoke of slight secrecy, his passions arose like a newly released bird into an epic Delhi night. Weaving delicate poetry with the exquisite agonies of a man bereft of his lover, he caressed the audience into a state of near bliss. They swayed with him, they mouthed the choruses with him, they wept with him, and they soared with him; a sea of humanity bound together by this sacred, secular Indian tradition of melody.

Mehfil's intoxication reflected in his eyes, his yearning reflected in his arms as they reached for the sky. Lost in his world, he even threw in a couple of sudden verses in the *kafi* poetic tradition of Punjab and an especially haunting *munadjaat* from Jalaluddin Rumi. With the ease of a master at the top of his game, he deftly married his pining for this woman and his inebriation over the craving for alcohol, following the traditional qawwali theme, into a more sacred yearning for a union with the Divine, ending his performance on a note of something resembling divine joy.

Finally, Mehfil Hussain Zaidi felt a sense of calm. The audience staggered to their feet and eventually left, many carrying a prayer for Mehfil's celestial voice on their lips. Some stayed behind to step inside the shrine and pray. The atmosphere bristled with beauty. The troupe had finished their performance against the backdrop of Amir Khusro's tomb on the left, Begum Jehan Ara's tomb on the right, and the Jamaat Khana Masjid in the centre; Mehfil felt the presence of the fabled Indian Urdu poet, the fallen Mughal princess, and the mosque invade his soul as one solitary, noiseless creature. Ahead of him, towards the back of the courtyard, stood a woman whose eyes betrayed the fact that she knew. She knew that each and every word sung that night had been about her.

As the woman walked towards him, Mehfil felt as though every measured step of hers was a revelation from the past. He tried to remember whether he had seen her before. How was he supposed to know, with that delicately embroidered shawl draped over her hair and covering most of her face? But those eyes, those eyes burning with the essence of a dark Delhi night, didn't he know those eyes? Amidst the crowds, between Thursday night performances, between 19 years of anguished ecstasy, had he missed her eyes as she'd passed before his own?

"Mehfil," the woman spoke his name, as she stepped onto the slightly elevated performance area. With the utterance of his name, she unfurled the shawl and it responded with a cascading motion, duly coming to rest around her shoulders. And then Mehfil knew.

"Zubeida," he gasped.

She spoke softly. "I've been here at the dargah every Thursday night for the past three years, ever since that first night I chanced upon your voice haunting the skies as I passed by the shrine on my way home. Right away, I knew it was you. I knew that destiny was having its way with us again." She looked up at the sky as the moon, unafraid to expose its fragility, earlier camouflaged by a rebel group of clouds, emerged into the night and began to cast its essence on to the shrine. "Soon, I got to know from some of the qawwali regulars that you had been performing here for close to two decades."

Mehfil was silent. He was too stunned with what was happening, but slowly began to gather himself. "You were on your way home? Does that mean you live nearby? Have we kept missing each other out on the street or during prayers at the mosque or here in the shrine for 19 years?"

"No," Zubeida replied. "I only moved to Delhi three years ago and almost immediately chanced upon your singing. Before that my life, its waves and troughs, its fleeting joys and lasting melancholy, were all lived out in Allahabad. As for before *that*, well, I suppose you know…"

"Allahabad," Mehfil repeated to himself, trying to ascertain the broken pieces of a life that lay scattered before his eyes. He was lost in the relevance of the moment, stilled by life and the emotions that brewed within. But he knew he had to speak. He had, after all, waited 19 years for this moment.

"Ever since I began performing here at the dargah, I've had the strange suspicion that you will come walking into my life once again. With every passing year, the strength of that feeling has lessened, but never completely left me. Every night, I've contemplated on the relevance of belonging to such a sacred piece of earth. Inayat Khan's tomb lies around the corner. Humayun himself lies buried not far from us, enclosed within an edifice that matches the Taj in beauty and passion. Our beloved Mirza Ghalib, whose poetry sewn from stars and tears still flows through this country's soul, lies in peace right beside us. Every night, I've contemplated on them before heading out to perform or to pray, every night I've bowed my head to Ghalib's poetry, every night I've prayed to

Amir Khusro's romance-laden heart, that one day, you will come walking through the door…" Mehfil trailed away, the echoes of a thousand past regrets colouring his thoughts.

"Today, those songs were for me, weren't they?" Zubeida asked him, her voice filled with a gentleness he knew well. From the way she said it, Mehfil knew she wasn't asking out of conceit but out of an appreciation for what she had witnessed earlier that night.

"Zubeida," Mehfil replied, taking her hands into his, "everything was for you." She didn't snatch her hands away, as he had feared, but left them in his, assuredly.

"I know why you left suddenly all those years ago…what has it been now, nearly 22 year?" Mehfil stayed silent, but his face had turned white. He deferred for Zubeida to continue.

"I know how your father forced you into marriage with Sultana from the Hassan family. My second cousin Alisha was in school with Sultana, she told me everything. It broke my heart and my will to live, there's no other way to say this. And then there was the…well anyway, there was this large emptiness left by you. All my thoughts were with you. How was I supposed to fill that once again?" Zubeida's anguish danced around in her eyes. "But human beings are miraculous creatures in a sense, every wound heals itself. The only caveat, of course, is that some take a few minutes, while others take years…" Zubeida glided her hands away from his as she finished.

Outside the dargah, the Nizamuddin West Bazaar was in full flow, with Muslim vendors in the thick of lively exchanges with potential customers and the food stalls redolent with both the delicious flavour and the equally delightful fervour of their *lazeez* kebabs. Inside the shrine complex though, a regretful stillness hung over the air.

"You probably know this," Mehfil finally broke the silence, "of how Delhi's Sufi saint, Amir Khusro Dehlavi of the Chisti order, is believed to have fused Indian and Persian influences and traditions in creating the qawwali. His is a legacy that has endured for well over 700 years now. Sometimes I meditate on his divine sadness and his ecstatic portrayals of longing that is reflected in many of his verses. It leaves me broken, desperate for the earth. And then I think of the sadness I must have caused you, and it leaves me equally staggered. I kept up with your life through little snippets I would get from time to time, surreptitiously of course. I knew you had never married, and yet, there were so many things I never had the chance to know."

This time, unprovoked, it was Zubeida who slid her hands into Mehfil's. "But sadness was never mine alone to bear, was it? I know how Sultana succumbed to a tragic illness just a year or two after you two had been married. People thought you had run away. Only now I know that it was then that you moved here to the dargah; maybe repentance was at the heart of it?"

Mehfil nodded his head in silence before speaking. "We were never in love, Sultana and I, yet there was such pain in seeing her leave this earth, someone so young. I felt a life of divine piety was the only path ahead of me. I couldn't rush back to you, of course. I knew the only things you would feel for me at that stage were hatred and contempt..."

Zubeida immediately placed her finger on his lips to hush him. She suddenly realised that aside from the few faithful who were headed towards the mosque, Mehfil's troupe was still in the vicinity, some gathering their instruments, some engaged in conversation at the northern end of the complex. A few of them were staring at the two of them. But they said nothing and they kept their speculations decent. They knew their leader to be an honest man, character and a life of poetry dipped in penance often his only anchors to this earth. They knew that the night's performance had been a cathartic purging of ghosts from the past; or had it, perhaps, been a remarkable resurgence of the soul, a lover's divine invocation for things to come…

"You musn't think that way," Zubeida finally spoke. "In this *mehfil-e-sama*, every Thursday night for the past three years, week after week, I've felt the cumulative melancholy of our combined past hovering over us, like an unwelcome halo. Every week, I've felt the purified surge of Khwaja Nizamuddin and his Chistiya order. I've felt your love for God invoked in your prayer and in your longing. I've felt the purity of our Sufi heritage. But only tonight, only tonight have I truly felt what I've been yearning to feel for so long. Only tonight have I felt the desire to reveal myself to you."

Mehfil reached for her face to wipe the tears gathering around her eyes laden with wistfulness and a drop of nostalgia. "But why did you wait all this while to disclose yourself to me? Wait, you needn't answer that. There was too much that had passed between us. I just wish I could erase the years we've lost with a single prayer. I only wish I hadn't left you feeling so hopelessly empty all those years ago, I just wish I had left you with something to hold on to."

"But you did," whispered Zubeida. "You did."

As Mehfil followed the trajectory of her eyes, he realised that she was staring at a young man absorbed in the task of cleaning and calibrating his instrument. She was looking at Akbar. Mehfil trembled as he took a step back. For the first time, he realised that the eyes, the nose, the smile, and the demeanour he was staring at were his. They were *his*.

In shock, he blurted out, "Did you bring him…"

"No," Zubeida cut short his speculation. "It was sometime last year at the dargah that I noticed a new musician, the young man on tabla. I just knew. A mother always knows. Someone here told me that he had been inducted into your troupe for his prodigious skills. I knew then that it was a divine decree, that we were all meant to have been brought back together, our destinies merged to the revered verses of qawwali, our lives but soft yellow flames in the house of the celestial."

Mehfil hadn't stopped trembling. "I, I still don't understand."

"Mehfil," Zubeida addressed him with compassion flooding through her eyes. "The boy is ours. I had to give him away when I had him. I didn't want him growing up under the yoke of sorrow. Over the years, I came to know of how the family that had taken him had caused him many hardships and forced him to run away. I searched for him, with a wild anxiety gnawing at my heart. I had given up all hope of ever seeing him again or even finding him alive for that matter. But then this dargah, your voice, that face…"

Mehfil turned his gaze away from the young man towards Zubeida. At the age of 52, she was even more beautiful than he had ever known her to be—graceful, compassionate—with eyes that danced in their own sorrowful reverie, framed by hair that flowed in exquisite clouds.

"Sir," Akbar broke his trance. "Do excuse me, but the maulvi is about to recite the night's prayers in the shrine and would like you to be present." He turned to Zubeida. "I am so sorry, but you aren't allowed to enter, as you may probably know." He smiled shyly.

"Akbar," Mehfil whispered. "Please inform the maulvi that I will be saying my prayers with the lady tonight, out here in the courtyard." He felt his eyes transfixed by Akbar's face and tried to fathom the fortunes that had gathered at his door that night. "And Akbar, you will join us as well."

As Zubeida took a few steps and stood beside Mehfil, Akbar wore a look of surprise. Seeing them together though, he felt a strange compulsion to be a part of them; to be a part of something he felt was far stronger than him.

Having informed the maulvi, he went and stood beside Zubeida and the three of them knelt down, facing the shrine of Khwaja

Nizamuddin. They uttered their reverences in silence, as the centuries-old calligraphy and detailed floral motifs on the walls of the shrine sparkled under the incandescence of the moon. They paid their respects with gravitas, as large cloth fans swept over the heads of the faithful gathered inside the mausoleum. Mehfil thanked the saint for dissolving his sorrows, accepting his repentances, and flooding his life with blessings he had never known to be his. It had been 19 years coming.

One Deep Sleep

B etween sleep and rise, life is utter disarray.
Unsure, whether it's meant to be active or passive, the body goes into a robotic lockdown, unable to react, receive, or contribute anything substantial. The mind's an entirely different affair. Swimming in that perpetual ocean between dreams and dawn, it stays cocooned in its newfound limbo to such an extent, you'd think the two had been inseparable friends since childhood. Insomnia, whether you'd been guilty of inviting it in or not, had found you. Like it had found Michiko Abe.

Her bed resembled an ocean of madness with the countless creases and folds on her sheets playing the waves; testament to a slumber destined never to arrive, stark evidence of desperate attempts to find some sort of solace, something, anything, any angle, any structure, that one elusive spot on the bed where sleep lay.

Michiko gave up finally and stretched out wearily for a small calendar lying on her nightstand. She turned on her bedside lamp and took a look at her phone. She jotted down '3:17 am' under that date in April, before studying the pattern of the beast that had suddenly forced itself into her life over the past few days: 2:10 am; 1:57 am; 4:38 am; 3:14 am; 3:50 am; 3:07 am; 4:12 am… She flung the calendar away, disgusted by the role it was playing in her perpetual nightmare.

Michiko lay staring at the ceiling for a while, playing with the lights that reflected, sprang, and shone from the city outside, in through her window, on to her roof and the walls: subdued hues and striking neon; reds, blues, and yellows of varying intensity; some from cars, some from the skies, some from life as it danced along to its own middle-of-the-night tune.

Michiko wondered about the people whose lives sprang to life at that hour, trying to form some sort of an emotional bond with the rest of the outcasts, the ones whom sleep forgot: the night crawlers, chasing the night in one ecstasy-fuelled drive that dragged them from loft parties to underground dungeons, from karaoke bars to sex-crazed raves; the nightshift employees, their entire lives an absurd oddity that flew in the face of a majority of humanity, living their lives in reverse as it were, harbouring the same thoughts about sunshine as the rest of the world did about the dark; and then the criminals of course, for whom the cover of darkness was a clarion call to action of the nefarious kind, disposing off their sins in the various dark crevices of Tokyo.

Michiko walked up to her large bedroom window to look out at all these people, to see if even one of them was looking back at her. Tokyo was adrift in its dreams, but in its inimitably polite fashion, it had left a few lights on so that those ruled by the whims of unlikely hours could continue with whatever it was that inflicted their minds.

Michiko blocked out the lingering street lights, hotel facades, apartment windows, and stubborn neon billboards, bathing her city in a darkness of her own, willing the moon to come and comfort her in her hour of need. Her large window masked the small, though cosy dimensions of her room. As the window stood there, breathless, staring at a Tokyo of a thousand broken dreams, she felt a strange affinity with its relationship to the city—that of being an outsider, true, but a keen observer nonetheless.

Michiko stood there all night and then curled up by the edge of the window-sill as dawn's lazy light broke through the eastern sky.

Her thoughts turned at once to her brotherhood of the sleepless, as she wondered what effect this event would have on them. Would their bodies be blown to smithereens as with vampires, unable to withstand the fury of light, or would they immediately be lulled into a sleep of the day, the darkness having freed them from the clutches of insomnia? But Michiko had no time to wait and examine dawn's effect on her own body. It was time for work.

Tokyo, you're smashed up. You're a mad undercurrent of deference and defiance. You're a culture steeped in the nuances of the ancient and immersed in the flood of spiritual religion. But you have to try and coexist with the relentless onslaught of technology at its fiercest. And you're forced to coexist too, aren't you, with the large population of the disenfranchised and the lonely, all my brothers and sisters, struggling to raise their souls in outrageous rebellion against the boundaries of the past. How else would I explain all the oddities so peculiar to you?

Random thoughts washed through Michiko's mind as she walked towards work, an alien in her own nation. Each land is foreign in its own way, but none more than a land you were born and raised in, but left behind only to return a lifetime later, with much water under the bridge—a truth that struck especially hard in a Tokyo whose, at times, robotic rhythm and shroud of anonymity, could be ominously discomforting for even the most desolate of human beings.

Though Michiko's absence from Tokyo hadn't been longer than 12 years or so, that span had taken her from early youth to a full-blooded young woman about to step into her 30s. She had been happy to come back to Japan after all this time, having graduated from an American university, having lived in New York for a few years and then in Chicago for a couple more. Which is about the time the investment firm she was with had decided to strengthen its Tokyo operations and offered her a fairly substantial career leap to go be part of a core Japan-based team trying to assimilate itself into the soul of a country that had only recently recovered from the relentless ravages of nature at its fiercest.

Michiko thought about how she liked being back home, though the Tokyo of the present held very few memories for her. Her mother had died when she was 17, and she had moved to the States shortly thereafter. Her father was a distant figure in her life who lived in the coastal port settlement of Nagoya with his second wife and their three children. But despite these upheavals and enforced loneliness, she'd picked up the pieces of her life and blossomed into a deeply sensitive, genuinely soulful being.

Being home amongst her people was an oddly reassuring feeling, offset by the jarring lonely anonymity of present-day Tokyo. Life in the city was a constant flow of contradictions. Even minor experiences arrived heightened by the truly alien nature of the land and its assortment of characters.

Michiko found herself holding on to the few friends she'd made since her return and a few more from the past she'd managed to reconnect with—courtesy the mangled magic of modern-day social media. These people formed a reliable dose of reality in a Tokyo that was only too happy to be intoxicatingly, undeniably unreal.

And then the insomnia had been triggered, which she'd brushed away at first as a hangover of too many late nights spent liaising with America at work. But now it was close to a month, and she simply couldn't get her head around it.

In her state of sleepless limbo, as she walked around like a zombie at work, seemingly devoid of the core human sensations of touch, smell, and feel, she suddenly found herself in familiar company—one amongst a million faceless humans, hurrying on their way to a life of labour—one familiar soul in the streaming river of anonymity that swept through the city.

At Goldcrest Blue, situated in the thick of the city's thriving business district of Akasaka, many plans were afoot. A few recent lucrative deals regarding some of Tokyo's wealthiest citizens had to be closed for good. An initial foray into South Korea was on the agenda too, and some members from the Hong Kong team had to be assimilated into their new home amidst the Japanese work culture of astonishingly reliable late hours. The minutiae of global investment patterns were being set with the conglomerate looking to rise into the ranks of the big boys through some timely moves.

As the 17-strong Tokyo team gathered in the tastefully done, main conference room, everyone's head was buzzing with ideas, figures, concerns, and dilemmas. Not Michiko Abe's though. She stared at them wistfully. She recognised the fact that her mind was nothing but a blur, her brain trying hard to reconfigure the imbalance that had crept into her life, trying with all its might to spark some movement into her lifeless being.

As she sat motionless through the morning's briefing session, her condition, as it had for the past month, remained relatively unnoticed by most. Not only were the investment bankers too rushed to stop and weigh their colleague's emotional frame of mind, her friends in turn wrote off her state as simple tiredness. No one really thought of delving any deeper within her to understand what was wrong.

No one, save one.

Satoru Nakada was a simple, likeable young man whose shy nature seemed at odds with the cutthroat world of global investment. But he was one of Goldcrest's most prized possessions, slicing through the vagaries of the global scenario, the Japanese market in particular, with startlingly accurate assessments. Such had become Satoru's penchant for striking future investment patterns, squarely on the head, that despite having been at Goldcrest for just over a year, he had become an integral part of the core think-tank, often sitting at high-level meetings with the firm's global leadership, at times if only for the good luck he brought to proceedings. But despite this slightly exalted position, Satoru remained endearingly indifferent to the world of movers and shakers at large. On many an occasion, it appeared as though he was striding through the plush confines of their offices, unaware of anyone at all, lost in the beauty of his own little inner world, pretty much at peace with whatever was going on in there, without ever being cold or thoughtless, sometimes not actually noticing anyone around him.

But Satoru noticed Michiko. And he immediately sensed what was wrong. After the morning's meeting was done with, he walked up to her.

"Oh hey, Satoru," mumbled a mildly surprised Michiko. "What's up?"

Satoru hesitated for a while before letting go of his reply. "It… it…it only gets worse, you know."

"Sorry?"

"The insomnia. It…it only gets worse."

An exaggerated echo of 'He knows' hissed through Michiko's mind. Though embarrassed at having finally been caught out, she felt quite relieved that someone had actually been observant enough to pick up what had been wrong with her these past few days. As she thought which direction to take next, Satoru stepped in.

"But it *could* get better, you know."

Hearing the sudden sense of secrecy in his voice, Michiko burst out laughing.

"Oh right. And here's where you pull my leg and make up some old Japanese legend that cures me in a second, right?"

Satoru smiled. "No, it's not that ancient, actually. Anyway, I know what it feels like. Just wanted to see if I could help."

"You've had sleepless night too?"

"I didn't sleep a wink for a couple of months. I thought I was going to go mad. You don't really know whether you're coming or going. I mean, your entire life decides to start living out in reverse slow-motion."

Michiko wasn't laughing anymore. This was all too familiar. And all too real. She fixed in firmly on his words, reassured that here was a human who had been through the hell she was in, and had, by the look of things, come out of it really well. Mostly it was about a sense of connection, the sensation that she wasn't alone in this strange time-zone of the mind.

"I remember walking down the late-night streets, counting cars as they drove by in a rush," continued Satoru. "I was so desperate for some sense of reality, that I would stop people on the streets and try to strike up a conversation with them. Anything to make me feel like a real human being…"

As his thoughts trailed away, Michiko wondered why she hadn't bothered taking the time to get to know him before. Behind those dark-rimmed frames and genuinely couldn't-care-less hair, he was a nice-looking man. He seemed thoughtful. He went about his day at Goldcrest with a refreshingly light attitude. And there was just a little something special about him, which she couldn't quite place. She returned to the matter at hand.

"I've tried everything. At times I think the internet just feeds off people's problems! You go in there with one small question, and suddenly you're bombarded with more stuff than you'd bargained for. At the end of your research, you feel more stressed out and worried than before you hit 'enter'," she smiled, drowsily. "I've tried them all: warm water bath before bed, warm glass of milk before bed, incense treatment, ginseng, the works. As you can tell by my appearance, none of it's worked yet."

Michiko paused to gather herself. "So how did you get out of it? What remedy were you talking about earlier?"

Satoru looked around him, to see if anyone was listening. Again Michiko was struck by the sense of secrecy, but this time, she gave him complete attention as he drew his chair over right up to hers.

"Please try to keep an open mind. Sometimes this works, sometimes it doesn't. And while I'm no expert on it, I think your attitude decides a lot of things too. Just remember, not everything in this world can be explained."

He took out his wallet and silently slid a slim card out of the card slots. Even when almost blocked out amongst a crowd of anonymously banal corporate business cards, it stood out. It was slimmer than most, crisper than most. Not a crease or tear, though every other card was frayed at the edges. And then there was the, for lack of a more appropriate term, aura around it. Michiko knew there was no denying it. The card carried with it a soft, mellow glow.

As she took the card in her hands, she was taken aback by how decidedly plain it was when actually held up close: just a plain white card, with frugal words in the form of a single telephone number and a silent permission to 'Call Anytime. Day or Night.', on the back. As Michiko flipped the card over to its front, the appearance of two stark words, poised in black, stared out at her with alarming stillness from the top-left corner: Doctor Dream.

Michiko gave in to the frustrating predictability of it all. She didn't fight the sleeplessness or the desperation of nonstop tiredness. This is it from here on in, she reconciled herself. This is how my life is going to play out. A waking memory. Lost to everyone but the edgier fringes of Tokyo, deep in the death of night. Lost to everyone but the silent rumblings of my own distorted mind. She lifted her head from the pillow and looked at the clock. 3:13 am. Yeah, that sounded about right. Now there was nothing more to it but to come up to her only friend in this misery, the large window, and stare out at an unforgiving Tokyo. But as she rose, she found her eyes hooked on to the card Satoru had slipped her earlier that morning.

On seeing the words 'Doctor Dream', she'd been quick to dismiss any thoughts of entertaining that route. What the hell was Satoru leading her into? Midnight acupuncture sessions? Mystic Zen eccentricity picked out of some long-forsaken manga classic? Some sort of a weird sex ritual perpetuated by Tokyo's underground crime lords, executed in the deepest, darkest crevices of the city?

Nah! Doctor Dream was just going to have to wait before he added another patient to his roster. She'd been polite enough while thanking Satoru for his help, assuring him that she'd fight her apprehensions and give it a try. But they both knew it would be a bridge too far for her intelligent mind to cross.

So why the hell was she here, at well past 3 at night, staring away at the card, actually contemplating giving the good doctor a call? Michiko knew that boredom, exhaustion, frustration, and most compellingly, curiosity had to be at the heart of it. She took the card up to the window and stared at it, its stark letters illuminated by a comfortingly familiar Tokyo Blue. 'Call Anytime. Day or Night.' And so she picked up her mobile.

As she dialled, myriad thoughts flew through Michiko's mind. What would be the first voice on the other line? A sexy female voice, surely. Doctor Dream's 'Private Secretary', no less. Or maybe, a man speaking in an ancient dialect. The one thing she knew was that if the voice at the other end turned out to be an automated one, she would switch off and tear the card up straightaway.

"Hello."

The sudden, crisp nature of the voice shook Michiko out of her internal conversation.

"H…hello."

"Yes."

"Ma…may I speak with Doctor Dream?"

"This is Doctor Dream."

"Oh, hello. My name is Michiko Abe."

"Yes."

"I've been having a problem. And a friend of min…"

"You can't sleep."

"Sorry?"

"You can't sleep. That is what everyone is here for."

"Oh, of course."

"That's okay. Everything will be alright."

"Thank you. Don't you need to know what my symptoms are?"

"I know them already. Everything will be alright."

Just like that, the voice at the other end was gone. For a minute, Michiko struggled to figure out what had just happened. An imagined picture of the man lingered before her eyes like a dream. She saw someone in a crisp black suit, back turned towards the world, speaking silently and assuredly into the phone; his cabin, a stylishly decorated ode to minimalism, stunning in its charcoal grey and steel aloofness. She saw him having liberal specks of grey and white in his hair, brushed back rather suavely, as he went about dispensing his doses of treatment upon the world. Michiko laughed aloud at the curiousness of it all, deciding firmly that despite the undeniable allure of the anonymous exchange, this was clearly a farce; yet another "trendy" fad sweeping its way through Tokyo's restless heart. To end the matter, she tore the card and threw it out the window, watching the pieces float and dive as they merged with the city's neon fabric.

✺

All of the next day, Michiko diligently avoided Satoru. Neither did she want to explain the curious exchange to him, nor did she want to, unwittingly, give him a piece of her mind for leading her down that strange alley. She simply trudged her way through work, eyes half-asleep, before taking the metro back home. Michiko walked up the stairs to her apartment, in that auto-daze that had now become part of her, when she saw a small parcel lying at her front door. It resembled a brown doggy bag.

She picked it up to examine it. Though tiny and non-descript, there seemed to be something very prim and proper about the bag. There was a small note pasted on one side that had the words: 'Take as required' in printed letters. On the other side was a name embossed as a watermark on to the paper, visible very faintly: Doctor Dream. Michiko panicked. Her mind rushed back to the previous night and began playing out the conversation she had had. No, she was certain; she certainly had not given out her address to the doctor.

She looked all around her, suddenly stricken by the thought that she was probably being watched. No, not a soul in the hallway. Just a CCTV camera, which was clearly the property of the building.

Michiko opened the door to her apartment and hesitantly took the packet in with her. The packet's contents turned out to be one single strip of small round tablets, 28 in all. And the doctor's card. Well that's some clever, persistent marketing, Michiko thought. Either this guy really knows how to push his product, or he somehow *has* managed to fix some cameras in here, she told herself dryly, taking one suspicious glance all around the apartment before shoving everything off the kitchen slab.

As darkness and sleep began to spread their conspiratorial arms around Tokyo, there was no waking up at a strange hour for Michiko. She decided she simply wouldn't sleep at all. She would keep herself awake—one more experiment to add to her long list—to see whether staying up all night wasn't actually *better* than having to wake up groggy in the dead of the night and face the world in that state.

She switched off all the lights, put on some soft wordless melodies, an uninterrupted 5-hour playlist on her iPod, consisting of deep, hypnotic lounge. She lay back on her bed, and began to distil the constantly changing stream of reflected light on her ceiling into a single stream of thought: wakefulness.

Resistance proved futile, though. She gave up after a few hours, exhausted by the effort it took to keep the game afloat. She reached for the alarm clock. The irony of it struck her in the face. 3:16 am. So much for changing things around.

Michiko arose and set about making herself a cup of coffee to take to her normal resting-spot: the windowsill. She turned on all the lamps, large and small, in her living room, trying valiantly to wage war with the darkness that was now hers to keep. She decided to crash in the living room for a while and drew the wide curtains apart, revealing another large window, but without a sill.

Her apartment, accented by the soft glow of the lamps and frequently intruded upon by the random city lights, looked pretty. She flung back on the couch, folding her knees to her side, finding some solace in the instant gratification of hot coffee.

This is such a pretty apartment, Michiko admitted to herself. Small, yes you are, longing for some more human warmth, yes you are, but pretty nonetheless.

It actually wasn't all that small by Tokyo standards. Her living room was large enough for her to have imparted a certain personality to it. There were three large black-and-white photographs, framed in black, neatly placed in line beside one another, on the main wall that ran alongside the front door. They were snapshots from her favourite, New York—one, an iconic Times Square scene with the cabs whizzing past and people parading by just as fast; the other, an overhead long-shot of Central Park where the beauty of the trees, the pervading arrogance of the Upper East Side, and the appearance of an unsteady flight of clouds was overshadowed by a flock of pigeons in the foreground as they fluttered and soared in a frenzy.

Finally, the third was that of a slightly more intimate scene from a café. The image had been captured from the outside, and focussed through the glass on a couple lost in each other, oblivious to the mad rush of a city that never stopped moving ahead, beautifully reflected on the window. Each photograph was a cherished New York feeling, textured just a bit, and an instant flashback to a city Michiko knew she would never stop loving.

There was a photograph of a 15-year-old Michiko with her mother, taken barely a couple of years before her mother passed away. She wondered whether she was going to end up looking just like her mother as she grew older, and decided that that would be a good thing.

Rikona Abe was of medium height, with short silver hair that swept across her forehead in a diagonal. She had a sweet smile, evident in the photograph. Her shy nature and vulnerable countenance had only begun to grow on Michiko after her death, as the young girl slowly began to blossom into just the sort of woman her mother would have admired.

In the photograph of them together, Rikona had her hands clasped behind her back, and Michiko smiled as she marvelled at the sense of politeness on display; such deference, even with or possibly because of a loved one.

There was a single photograph of her with her father, taken when she was much younger. She couldn't quite place why it still held a place in her home, in spite of the lack of connection with that man. As she stared at his side-swept silver hair, square jaw, and rugged features, she deliberated on her parents and the two of them in those first years of love, a beautiful couple no doubt, so oblivious to the disconnection, detachment, and rancour that would follow a few years down the road.

There were other things in the room she was less conflicted about. A pair of twin bonsais that she cherished, gifted to her by a dear friend; multicoloured vases from Amsterdam that were strewn on a table, brought over by a colleague; a large scroll filled with beautiful Urdu letterings, a poem by the Indian lyricist Sahir Ludhianvi, gifted to her by a friend at NYU. Next to it, having been disdainfully swept away earlier, lay Doctor Dream's package.

Softened by a barrage of nostalgia, sorrow, hope, and that relentless little devil, curiosity, Michiko walked over to the package, removed the strip and popped a tablet. Just like that. No obsessing over it or dissecting the pros and cons. It was something that felt right. It was something she needed to do.

She walked back to her room and sat on the sill, knees huddled up to her chin, her gaze swaying between Tokyo on the outside and her own little home.

You're pretty too, Michiko reassured her living space. Your grey walls and your manga art, your splash of pink...and your cute... cute...pillows, your wa...ll l...amps and Ze...Zen...

The garden had a small stream running beside it. She bent down with cupped hands, eager to quench her thirst. There, her reflection shone brighter and clearer than it ever had before, and every single element beneath the water, be it rocks, pebbles, or tiny fish, radiated with a light that pierced through the heart.

After having her fill of the fresh water, she noticed how the stream flowed in a downward curve. Only when she traced its course for a little while, did she realise that she was on the top of a mountain, with the garden at its very peak, and with the stream originating right where she was. She watched it descend blissfully into a far-away valley of flowers and foliage below.

As she looked around her, individual branches from some of the shrubs and trees in her private Zen garden transformed suddenly into blindingly white flashes of snow, leaving the garden a half-green, half-white vision of mist. Soon, many other elements began evolving into pure snow—rocks along a pathway, mystic Buddhist carvings on bark, three fleeting sparrows in mid-flight— each a motionless masterpiece in white. As she continued to explore this new kingdom sprinkled with enchantment, enveloped by awe, she noticed that her little stream was, quite magically, not being left untouched either.

Rivulets of water within the stream were slowly freezing into ice, as were half the fish, now simply majestic onlookers to their living, breathing brethren, who splashed and swam about in their incandescent reds, yellows, and greens.

As she bent down even further towards the water, intent on identifying each and every change, her reflection rose before her like a mirage. She gasped, unable to move. She hadn't been left out either. Her face, hair, skin, and body were now resplendent in white, an unimaginable dalliance of snow, purity, and ice.

As the picture developed and framed out further, she understood things clearly. The garden, the stream, and her body were a homogenous snow-capped peak, together crowning an entity she had taken a while to recognise. This was Mount Fukushima, immortalised in verse and celebrated through the centuries. This was Mount Fukushima, frozen in winter. And she, of the snow-graced hair and the ice-dappled eyes, was now its undisputed princess.

When Michiko awoke, the sun was streaming in bright and clear, stroking her warmly on the face. She found herself on the windowsill, where she'd crawled up and slept through the entire night. She felt her body for the obvious aches and pains of having slept in such an awkward position. But instead of any irritations, there was just one unfiltered, unadulterated sensation coursing through her. It was an awareness she hadn't experienced in a long time, in fact, not ever: crystal-clear freshness.

There was no denying it. She had fallen asleep as the Michiko Abe with weary eyes and a heavy heart, and had awoken with such a new lease of life, it were as though intense doses of rejuvenation, purification, and cleansing had been injected directly into her body. This was no time to question how or why, this was no time to consider the ramifications of the pill she had taken the night before, certainly not the time to begin questioning the way she was feeling. This was a time to accept. And rejoice.

As she was leaving for work later that morning, Michiko decided to stand before her window for a couple of minutes and have a morning chat with Tokyo for a change: Tokyo, you gorgeous thing. Thank you for standing by me, thank you for all those lonely nights. But I have a feeling things are about to change.

Before leaving the apartment for work, she spotted the package lying on the kitchen slab. She examined it for a while, uttering a silent thank you, and wondered what sort of ginseng-like magic had gone into those tablets. Placing the packet inside the drawer of an antique Japanese shelf tower she'd picked up during a weekend trip to Osaka, she walked out into the world with a smile on her face and the sparkle of hope in her eyes.

The insomniac experience is such, the first elusive sleep is placed in hallowed territory. It seems like a miraculous ship over a distant horizon for the long-shipwrecked. Though earlier her colleagues had been quick to dismiss her battle with sleeplessness by putting it down to work-related exhaustion, some missing the signs entirely, that morning almost everyone had instantly picked up the change in her.

She seemed to glide across the richly furnished corridors of Goldcrest Blue, with a lightness of redemption that refused to leave her being. The guessworks were off the mark, yet again. They ranged from speculations of a new boyfriend, a salary raise, even a 'warm glow of being pregnant' to one forthright fellow who simply put her newfound happiness down to an instance of great sex the previous night.

As Michiko dismissed all of them with a good-natured laugh, she wondered about that last remark; what sort of reflection was it on her? For the previous few weeks, the public perception was that she probably hadn't got any?

Michiko had eyes only for Satoru that morning. One look at her, and he knew.

"Ah, you slept last night!" he exulted.

"You bet!" replied Michiko, with equal enthusiasm.

"And, how was it?"

"Oh God, forget the fact that I was sleeping after so long, it was probably the best sleep I've ever had in my life."

"I'm really happy for you."

"I'm happy for me too, can't you tell?"

Satoru smiled as he nodded. "Yes, it's written all over your face."

"I really can't remember the last time I enjoyed such beautiful sleep," she said contentedly. "This Doctor Dream of yours is really something, isn't he?"

Michiko paused for a second, and took his hand in hers, giving it a tight squeeze.

"Satoru, I really can't thank you enough. From the bottom of my heart, thank you for saving my life. I don't know who this man is, or how he does the things he does. All I know is that if it wasn't for you, I'd be lost and without hope. I mean it. Thank you."

"It's my pleasure. I'm so glad I could help someone like you."

"Someone like me?"

Satoru fumbled with his words. "Yes, you know I, I…I mean, someone so nice and so different."

Michiko felt a sudden wave of something she'd never felt for her colleague. She was unsure whether it was fondness or attraction or just a temporary flirtation. But she allowed the feeling to seep in, not wanting to nip it in the bud.

"That's so nice of you. You're really different too."

Satoru seized the moment, albeit with gentle hesitation. "Michiko, I wanted to know…It's just, you know, really simple… Would you, I mean, will you, have a coffee with me this evening?"

Any day in the past, and the answer would've been a foregone conclusion. But this was a new morning for Michiko, a new day in many respects, and she didn't have to think twice about her reply. "Yes, I would love to," she said softly, giving him a bright smile in the bargain.

After deciding on the place for that evening, both of them started to head back to their workspaces, when a thought struck her.

"Oh, I should probably call the doctor and thank him, shouldn't I?"

"Actually, I don't think he cares about those things. There's no need to thank him. He already knows," Satoru shrugged, as though the doctor and his miracles were matter-of-fact occurrences, like picking up bread from the grocery.

Satoru's life began to unfold before Michiko's eyes that evening, revealing things that not too many people knew. For one, he was a trained violinist, who often performed live as part of a quartet. He was a voracious reader too, and contrary to everything his personality seemed to point towards, he was addicted to trashy pulp fiction. In the same vein, he also owned a large collection of Japanese and foreign B-grade films, and appeared to know each scene and dialogue from a majority of them by heart.

His penchant for fragrances was another standout, a talent that had led some of Japan's top perfumeries and a couple of international houses to arrive at his door, seeking the services of his distinguished nose. But the thing about him that surprised Michiko the most was that he too, not unlike her, came from a fractured family.

She'd always assumed that people who seemed as centred and uncomplicated as Satoru owed that sense of clarity to a happy, supportive family. But he had disowned his when he'd turned 24, shattered by the shameless greed his parents and two elder siblings had shown over the acquisitions from a Will left by an unknown great uncle.

So here he was, an orphan of sorts, an unexpected kindred insomniac who'd unearthed the gift of sleep. He was braving Tokyo and all its follies by himself, just like her. And he was now sitting across from her sipping coffee at a pavement café in one of the normally bustling Shibuya district's quieter acres.

Michiko felt close to him, warmed by the presence of a man who had suddenly acquired a pretty special place in her life. Under the gaze of an ochre sky, filled with promise and swaying leaves, they spoke of families and familiarity, they spoke of the special beauty that comes from being anonymous in a large city, of regrets and aspirations, of dislikes and delights. And most of all, they spoke of Tokyo. Michiko was aware of the fact that their conversation had the easy flow of two people who'd known each other for years, confident that their words would not be held up to scrutiny, or worse, judgment.

"I'd always thought I'd end up someplace more poetic," Satoru confided. "But I've found out over these past few years that Tokyo can be a pretty poetic place, in its own crazy way."

Michiko laughed. "Yeah, I guess you could say it has its own crazy poetry going on. I love it here, really. I never thought I'd abandon New York, at least in my heart. But now, both these cities live side by side, without punching each other out!"

"Wow, New York. Must've been quite special, huh?"

"Oh yeah, a glorious city with glorious people," she looked away, chasing New York in her eyes.

"Maybe I'll go there someday."

"Why someday? You must try and go there now, like this year or something."

"Really?"

"Absolutely. And guess what?"

"What?"

"You'll have an expert tour guide with you when that happens." Satoru smiled at the prospect. "That would be fantastic."

"But Tokyo, I don't know, it has its own special things. And I think…" she trailed away.

"Yes?" Satoru prodded.

"Well, I think the more I get to know of it, the more special it gets."

She moved her hand towards his, cradling it softly. Satoru, though shy at first, slowly placed his other hand on top of hers.

"I don't think Tokyo has ever felt more special to me."

By the time they left the café, it was around 9. Within no time, as they walked hand in hand, the slow serenity of their earlier address slipped into the loud frenzy of Shibuya's throbbing heart. Tokyo seemed to have slipped off its morning mask of placidity and taken on an altogether new avatar for the night. But for the two young colleagues, slowly coming to terms with the first pure waves of affinity and new possibilities, the madding crowds didn't feel like intruders at all but more like a cheering party, happy to be part of their freshly-brewed connection.

Over the next couple of months, like a flower rescued from the harshness of winter by the unexpected arrival of summer, Michiko blossomed into herself. She felt healthier and happier. After those endless pale days, there was a visible flush to her face. She had started seeing Satoru and, in the process, had begun discovering new things about herself and new things about her city.

In a touch of serendipity, Japan's fabled blossoms were in full bloom too, bathing many parts of the city, its outer suburbs, its distant mountains, and farther afield, its beautiful scattered towns in clouds of mystical pink and white.

The couple had started putting their newfound companionship to good use, exploring hidden facets, poetic nooks, and interesting detours in and around Tokyo that they previously wouldn't have thought of engaging in by themselves. As a consequence, their friend circles, both as individuals and as a couple, had begun to rise.

At Goldcrest Blue, the new companionship was greeted with equal parts of happiness and disbelief. They certainly weren't two people who appeared to be a perfect fit, at least from the outside. But Michiko and Satoru dismissed the naysayers and their nagging doubts, embracing this fresh lease that had dropped in quite unexpectedly into their lives. They began to take art classes, started reading regularly, and would make it a point to explore, at least, one new place every weekend—a bar, a jazz club, an underground dance party, whatever appealed to them on impulse.

One weekend in June, the two decided to subvert Tokyo's manic tendencies and go back in time with the *chaji*. Satoru had always felt that the centuries-old Japanese tea-pouring and tea-drinking ceremony was nothing short of an art form. Thus, the spark for an ancient teahouse was his idea. He'd found out about their address through a fanatic tea-drinking friend of his, whose primary hobby was to scour Tokyo's older neighbourhoods, suburbs, streets, and outlying villages in search of the perfect cup. It was he who'd pointed Satoru towards En, a small teahouse in the Gion neighbourhood of the city.

En had cultivated a cult following for itself by guiding many through one of Japan's foremost cultural practices with care and precision. Its high-rise neighbours, adjacent old homes, surrounding industrial buildings, and a nearby small store, selling predictable Buddhist artefacts, deepened the sense of surrealism at play.

In the midst of this curious melange, En had managed to create the smallest square piece of nirvana possible. Michiko and Satoru decided to skip the elaborate three-course meal known as *cha-kaiseki*, relaxing, instead, in En's small but meticulous garden, peopled with perfectly curated bonsai, while their tea and its rituals fermented in preparation.

Back within their individual tearoom, the preparation turned out to be no ordinary affair. The sparse Zen leanings of their wooden home invited them in through sliding doors and welcomed them to floor-level arrangements. Michiko fell in love instantly and sat down with folded legs on the floor, as was the custom, to partake in a ceremony that could only ever be Japanese.

An old lady in a kimono took the two of them through each step of the process, a tea-drinking gathering bathed in ceremony and custom, characterised by patience and respect towards the revered tea leaves; each slow movement a firm commitment to the journey, each savoured sip an aromatic manna for the senses. *Koi cha* demanded the presence of 13 individual items of utensils and inch-perfect arrangements.

After the near meditative exercise of the tea leaves, hot water, and tea bowls being brewed, poured, and handled with skilful exactness in front of their eyes, Michiko and Satoru were left to relish the rare flavour of their tea.

"This is very much a spiritual world I'm in," Michiko realised, with the water meant to represent the *yin* and the fire in the hearth signifying the *yang*. "I have just received a life lesson in a cup of tea, a memory to carry with me forever," she confessed silently.

The two of them were well in their elements in this atmosphere of serenity. After their hostess had left them to tend to the other patrons in the house, settled within the dispersed closed chambers separated by sliding wooden doors they began discussing life as it had unfolded those past few months.

"This feels right, finally," Michiko confided. "My job, my health, my Tokyo...you. After a long time, everything feels right."

"I know," replied Satoru. "Thank you."

"For what?"

"For making me very happy, that's all."

"Shouldn't I be thanking you? I mean, everything started changing after you told me about Doctor Dream. Without that happening, who knows, I might still have been a waking zombie, slowly developing a taste for human flesh."

As they laughed, a knock on the door ushered the arrival of a delicately small Japanese pot, filled with an essence that glowed with the most remarkable golden fluid.

"Pure honey," informed their hostess. "Please, you drink," she instructed, as she poured a precise amount of the fragrant liquid into their pot of tea.

After she had left, Satoru returned to their conversation.

"You really don't have to thank me at all. Anyway, it's not like Doctor Dream is a secret or anything."

A puzzled look came over Michiko's face. "What do you mean?"

"I mean sure it's not like his presence is public knowledge that gets advertised on newspapers and billboards and all that, but quite a few people know about him." He paused to take a large sip of his tea, relishing its strong aroma. "I mean, you need to be a certain kind of person who likes certain kinds of things, who moves around in certain kind of places with a certain kind of crowd...but no, definitely, you'd be surprised that it's not our little secret." He smiled and resumed his tea.

An intrigued Michiko needed more information, though. "Wow, I had no idea. I actually did think it was our little secret, so this is a bit disappointing to hear." She pondered over it for a while. "But I suppose it's fair. The more people that know about him, the better. If he can work that kind of magic, all of Tokyo should know about him!"

"Well let's not go about making him a pop-star, shall we?" rebutted Satoru. "You should keep his information as close to you as possible, only let it out if someone very close and trusted to you is really going through something bad in their life."

"Hmm," Michiko nodded.

"And anyway, the amount of people knowing him would actually still be quite small. It's just that there are a few more like him, and I guess each one of them would be known by a certain set of people, so that's what I was talking about."

As Satoru resumed with his tea, Michiko was left having to sift through all this new information that was coming her way.

"There's more like him?"

"Sure. I'm not an expert or anything, but each one of them deals with a certain problem or condition or ailment." He thought about it for a while. "Or just deals with a certain need, if I've understood things correctly. I guess you could say, each is a specialist in his own field," he grinned.

"But what I'd like to kn—"

Her query was interrupted by Satoru's mobile phone. He looked at the number and groaned. "Great, it's Suzuki," he winced, referring to Hidetoshi Suzuki, their MD at Goldcrest and a man notorious for having no respect for trivialities such as time and holidays.

"On a Sunday?" winced Michiko. "God, this man!"

"I think I'll step out into the garden and take this, who knows how long it might take," Satoru said, rising from his seat on the ground as he slid open their cabin's door. "Please go ahead with your tea, I'll try and finish this as quickly as possible."

All by herself now, Michiko began to study the environment she was in. En wasn't lavish by any means, following the Japanese aesthetic of Zen minimalism. But then, it wasn't meant to be. In their room, there was nothing to distract her save for an alcove known as *tokonoma*, containing a *kakemono* scroll painting revealing the theme of the ceremony etched in Buddhist scripture.

Japanese blossoms and spiritual haiku painted in broad brushstrokes of black, interspersed by thin black accents, complemented by strong flourishes of red paint from time to time, emphasised the central theme. Her eyes fell on a book Satoru had brought with him that day. It was the same one he'd been carrying around with him for over a week now. Though she'd never examined it up close, she'd seen it in his cabin at work as well. She wondered whether it was something important to him or whether he was just a painfully slow reader. She also wondered why she hadn't bothered to ask him about the book and whether it would be worth her while to have a go at it too. Up close, she realised it was Herman Hesse's seminal classic, *Siddhartha*. She'd heard of the book in snatches of conversation. It was certainly a firm favourite with many of the college students back in New York.

She began to read the synopsis, leading on to an initial paragraph or two. Hmm, maybe a bit too deep for Satoru? she smiled. Maybe just a bit too deep for me, come to think of it. As she closed the book shut to slip it back into place, something fell out. It was one of the most beautiful bookmarks she had ever seen—a rich tapestry of red and gold, with the Japanese symbol for wisdom sketched out at the centre of the piece, flanked on either side by two intricately inked Buddhist monasteries. Michiko gazed at it in wonder before turning to the back, where she came upon a hand-written message:

This is for you, as is the book it comes with. I hope you read it in good health and good time. I don't know how and why I fell in love with you, so suddenly; I just did. I've stopped trying to explain it to myself and have decided to just accept it. I know you're in love with me as well, I see it in your eyes. I saw it last week when you took me to the En teahouse and we spoke of our lives; our yesterdays, our days to come. We are both trying to build our lives and we both bear sadness from the past, so I don't mind that we keep taking things slow. I treasure your warmth on the sparse but precious evenings we spend together; I treasure your presence every few weeks, when I drop in to Goldcrest with the Imperia data. I know we were meant to be together. We will be. Someday. All my love, Suki.

Michiko's eyes blazed as they caught sight of the tiny emblem Suki had sketched at the bottom of the message; a tiny rose with an accompanying date. It felt as though her eyes would scorch through the paper. The date pointed to a time two weeks earlier. Michiko placed the bookmark within the pages and put the book back on the table, her mind aflutter, and yet, numbed. This wasn't something old, something from the past. This was a fresh wound, its blood and guts spilling out into her current address—a teahouse that itself felt like a treachery. She knew this person. She knew this Suki. It was Suki Endo, an executive analyst with Three Twigs Consultancy, the firm helping Goldcrest weigh the pros and cons of a possible partnership with Imperia—another regional player in the investment stakes.

Satoru returned, ready to resume his tea and their conversation. "Sorry, just the usual. I think he sometimes just forgets that it's Sunday. To Suzuki, I think every morning must seem like it's Monday morning at work," he chuckled. "Sorry, what were we talking about?"

"I have to leave," Michiko replied, and arose from the floor.

"Er, sorry, what…you have to…what, right now…?" a confused Satoru blurted out.

"Yes."

"Oh. Okay. Is there some work?"

"No, not really."

"Suzuki didn't call you as well to tell you about Tuesday morning's trip, did he?"

"No he didn't. The tea was really nice. Have a nice day."

"I'm sorry Michiko, I don't understand."

"I want to give you time to complete that," she said, pointing to the book on the table. "And I want to give you time to complete that bookmark," she concluded, as she slid the wooden door of their cabin open and left.

Satoru didn't stir from his place for the next few minutes, his heart seemingly as crushed as fallen blossoms beneath the feet of marching pilgrims. With his face buried in his hands he contemplated on what had just happened. He dried away a few tears and stared at the bookmark, felled by its beautiful design. He wondered how he could have been so stupid to carry it with him while meeting a woman he was clearly getting increasingly attached to. He wondered why he had been so confused and so weak to let things get to where they had. He thought about Suki and his feelings for her; about whether she actually meant anything to him or whether she was simply a detour with no address, waiting to be dissolved.

He thought about Michiko and how her arrival had changed everything, causing her to become, slowly, the stronger object of his heart's affections. Sobered by the reality of what had just taken place, as it gradually sank in, and the comforting aroma of the hot Japanese tea now settled within him, Satoru realised that the situation was beyond him.

Knowing the sort of woman Michiko was, he knew that trying to weave stories around his folly, attempting foolish ways to win her heart back, or, most relevantly, dismissing her reaction to his indiscretions, would only deepen the hole he had dug himself in.

Knowing the sort of man he was, he understood that false bravado and forced charm were clearly both beyond him. Satoru decided then and there that he would have to let go of this. There would be no point in chasing after it, no point in taking what little was left of their relationship by way of memories and making it even worse. He could always hope for the best, that Michiko would someday forgive his cheating heart and return closer to him of her own accord. Or, perhaps, wake up the next morning and realise she had been too rushed in her judgement. But for now, all this was mere conjecture, none of which was in his hands really. He would need to let go for now.

Over the course of the next couple of months, Michiko began to distance Satoru from her life. At work, she tried to manoeuvre meetings, timings, and discussions in such a manner that any personal contact between them was reduced to the minimum. Outside office, there was absolutely no contact at all. She tried to detach herself from memories of their time together, from each moment when they had shared a special connection, especially the ones where she'd found herself being drawn to his odd charm.

Sometimes, on that rare occasion, when they would find themselves together at a meeting, or pass each other in the hallways, she would think about how strange it was in a way that she had felt so attached and attracted towards this man who wasn't even her type; someone none of her close friends and colleagues would've marked as a natural match for her.

And yet, without noticing it, thoughts of how she had found herself longing for his company and had slowly begun accepting the fact that there was something special and indefinable between them would creep up. Whenever such deliberations raised their heads, she would quickly conjure up a picture of the bookmark in her mind and just like that, they'd be gone.

Soon, she managed to increase her friend circle considerably by making a concerted effort. She began forcing herself to step out to attend all social gatherings, even when her mind felt it wouldn't be the right fit for her. She began saying yes to all social requests, whether from friends or colleagues or social media contacts, eager to open up her mind about Tokyo and its people while simultaneously blocking out unwelcome remembrances from the past.

Before she knew it, mere colleagues from work had graduated to becoming genuine friends, something that gladdened her immensely. Through all these new dimensions that opened up in her life, Michiko was also starting to learn that Satoru had been bang on about one thing—that Doctor Dream was not the only one out there. Through a mixture of drunken revelations, hushed conversations, and intimate confessions, it had become clear to her that there really was a secret network of doctors absorbed within Tokyo's fabric; not known to one and all of course, still confined to just the privileged few, but a network nonetheless.

Michiko began diving right in. The modus operandi for all these purveyors of life-solutions remained much the same; a single card, a single ominous number, a single anonymous voice on the phone, who, as though a deep illusion, appeared to be the same man over and over again, the same parcel at the doorstep, and voila, job done! Michiko began tenderly enough, still unsure of what exactly she was getting into, but soon, emboldened by the results and egged on by her closed circle of confidantes, she had become a seasoned doctor aficionado.

Every weekend now, she would be burning up dance floors at Tokyo's hottest clubs and bars in Roppongi, her clumsy feet of yore now having been transformed thanks to Doctor Dance. Her previous aversion to extreme sports and the like had been kicked out the door thanks to Doctor Dare, resulting in indoor rock-climbing sessions and further emboldened by weekend surfing trips to Japan's coastal surf hotspot of Shonan Beach.

Even her slightly prudent sexual mores of old had been given a makeover, thanks to the magical touch of Doctor Delight. It had become a vivid new world for her, textured with psychedelic dreams and soaked in the elixir of multicolour escapades, one in which every new experience brought with it a whole different prism of characters and memories.

Tokyo itself opened up to her like she never would've imagined, right from the galleries and bars in the Ginza district, the old pleasure quarters and temples of Asakusa and the street markets torn from yesterday's pages in Ueno, to the bizarre attractions of Harajuku and the late night drinking sessions in Aoyama. So much so, that in the span of the past few months, Michiko felt as though she had gone through many lifetimes. Satoru was all but a forgotten memory. But as with the strangest of memories, he was destined to resurface, whether she liked it or not.

The continuously churning cycles of the global economic crisis had taken a fair toll on Goldcrest Blue. The firm had been hit particularly hard by mounting losses in their stronghold, Japan. One Monday, the entire staff was called into the large conference room for a high-level emergency meeting. Suzuki was at his belligerent best, berating employees left, right, and centre for not being able to predict financial mood swings with pinpoint accuracy. His most unreasonable tirade was reserved for a most surprising nominee.

"You've been awful these past few months!" he thundered. People stared wide-eyed at the target of his accusations: Satoru.

"Not only have you not been able to see what's coming, but you've shown zero leadership skills in dealing with these currents twists and turns," Suzuki continued. Satoru himself had been blinded by the fury, amazed when he'd raised his eyes to see that the flowing diatribe was being directed at him.

"I was thinking of grooming you to take on a senior managerial role one day. But with this sort of performance, how the hell can I trust you to even take care of yourself?"

Satoru, as was his wont, took all of this in with a stoic reverence, his face now showing neither a glimmer of anger nor a glint of hurt.

"Firms like Avalon and Shinzo-McFarley are managing to pull themselves out of the current mess because of the people they have on board. But with people like you, I really don't see any future for Goldcrest," he fumed as he banged his fist on the conference table and left, leaving behind a stunned audience and a silent, crestfallen Satoru.

Everyone in that room knew that true to his irrational nature and sadistic streak, Suzuki had gotten things horribly wrong. Not only was Goldcrest Blue on the verge of some crucial dealings and acquisitions that would lead the way in steering their ship out of troubled waters, but it was also common knowledge that Satoru had been the one saving grace, in the worst of times, and the one leading this vanguard action against recent fortunes. Many whispered amongst themselves as they began proceeding out of the conference room, knowing that a mixture of greed, immaturity, and perhaps even jealousy lay at the heart of Suzuki's behaviour.

Hideaki Nakamura, VP of Operations, came over to Satoru as he was leaving.

"I'm sorry, son," he comforted the young man, placing a gentle hand on his shoulder. Satoru looked up at him with eyes of deference and bowed.

On the other end of the table, standing diagonally across from him, Michiko had viewed the entire scene unfold before her, with eyes bathed in compassion. There was one strong, unexpected emotion surging within her. Empathy. Within the short space of five minutes, all the bitterness from the past had dissolved and she suddenly found herself both angry with Suzuki, for his mindless rant, while being swept by a wave of reconnection towards Satoru. She watched silently as he picked up his phone and notepad from the table, and left the room.

❀

The next morning, Michiko arrived at work with all thoughts from the previous day still resonating through her mind.

"That Suzuki is such a dick, isn't he?" she said to Alison, a Britisher who'd been with Goldcrest for a year, but had only just relocated to Japan a month ago.

"A proper dick!" agreed Alison. "Did you see the way he went after that poor guy?"

"Satoru."

"Yeah, Satoru. That was terrible."

"I know."

"And the fellow just took it all, I don't think he even said a word."

"That's just who he is."

"Yeah, I suppose. But still, you'd th…"

"We went out for a while."

"Who?"

"Satoru and I, we went out together for a short while."

"What?! Gosh, no way. You and *him*?"

Michiko fumbled around with a pendant she was wearing, trying to sort out her thoughts, as much for herself as for Alison.

"He's a lovely guy, if you get to know him. I don't know, it happened without even thinking much about it. He's...he's a really interesting guy."

Alison thought about it for a while. "Yeah, I mean, I don't know him very well at all. I just thought he was this reserved, slightly weird guy, who's brilliant at his job."

"He's not weird at all," Michiko shot back, surprising herself with the show of loyalty. "We struck a real connection. There's so much about him one doesn't know."

Michiko went on to tell Alison about their dates and tried to paint a picture of Satoru, explaining how she and Satoru had formed a bond of sorts. When Alison inquired about why they'd broken up, she told her about the revelatory incident at the teahouse, and how she'd shut him out of her life over the past few months.

"But yesterday...I don't know...yesterday I had this sudden sensation that maybe I've been too harsh with him. I don't know what it was, one minute I couldn't care less whether he was in the room or not, and the next minute I was feeling this strange attachment to him all over again."

"So what're you going to do?" asked Alison.

"We'll see," Michiko replied, bringing her game with the pendant to an end.

Later that afternoon, when Michiko was heading down for lunch to a sushi bar just up their street, she saw Satoru standing in front of a window in the smaller meeting room. The sun streamed in and rested on his face. She was about to leave him to his desolation, when she changed her mind and walked in.

"Hi," she said, a bit hesitantly.

Satoru turned around and offered a weak smile. "Hi."

Quietly, he turned back around towards the window, his future at Goldcrest as well as his current personal situation seemingly lost amidst the craziness of Tokyo's streets.

Michiko came up beside him and looked out towards the same

city, trying to rescue his thoughts from the streets. "I'm sorry," she offered, simply.

"What for?"

"For what happened yesterday. It was extremely rude and wrong of him to go off on you like that, in front of everyone."

"It's okay. I wasn't the only one having to face his words."

"Yes, but he was harshest towards you. Besides, many of the others deserved it, and more! But not you. I know you must be worried about your job, but…"

"I'm not. What's meant to happen will happen." He was silent for a moment. "I'm quite confident about my skills here."

Michiko perked up at this flash of poise from Satoru. "And you should be! You're one of the best in the business," she smiled.

"Thank you. I'm sorry too."

Michiko didn't reply.

"I'm sorry for what I did to you. I wasn't brave enough to tell you. It was a complicated thing with Suki. I didn't think it would turn out the way it did. I shouldn't have let it. Anyway, that's over now. I'm sorry—for lying to you, for failing you…for letting down our friendship. Very sorry."

Michiko chose not to say anything for a while.

"Maybe I was too impulsive in the way I dealt with it. I mean, I know people sometimes get themselves into situations they never intended to; I've been there myself. I hope Suki's fine as well. I actually wanted to have a chat with her after that day at the teahouse. But then I figured it was your mess. You needed to sort it out."

"I have, I promise. I hope one day you will forgive me."

As they stood silent together for a while, each trying to figure out the best way to take the conversation forward, Satoru felt a hand slip into his. After his initial surprise had died away, he clasped the hand and gave it a squeeze; as much out of relief, as affection.

Michiko slipped her hand out, and began to walk away.

Compassion leading towards forgiveness, distance giving way to fondness, and with a spontaneous wave of love having washed over her without much warning, Michiko began seeing Satoru again. Their steps were a bit hesitant at first, each taking their time to regain the sense of balance and restore the connection that they'd once shared. But as one month gradually dissolved into two, they found themselves back in much the same happy place that they'd once shared, discovering Tokyo on fun weekend detours, sharing long conversations over cups of tea, each revealing more layers to the other.

Michiko's rebirth since their break-up in the form of a much larger, crazier friend circle and her fresh lease of life, courtesy the occasional dip into the menagerie of good doctors, began to rub off on Satoru as well. He began to open himself up further. He began to make a conscious effort in becoming more of a social being, be it through willingly joining Michiko in her new adventures or through accepting her wider network of cohorts and their activities with ease, if not enthusiasm. Michiko's friends, including colleagues whom she'd gotten closer to at Goldcrest, started to see Satoru in a new light themselves, pleased that the generally affable young man was adding more facets to his personality and becoming more like the sort of man that seemed a genuine fit for their friend.

When Michiko contemplated on all that was happening, she knew that this was now a serious relationship. As befitting one, the couple decided to take a break and head away from Tokyo for a week. They chose the island of Miyakojima in the Okinawa Prefecture and headed straight for Sunayama Beach, with long stretches of white sands cradled by beautiful waters, which became bitingly cold during Japan's unforgiving winters. In every way, the address appeared to be a fitting companion to the romance-laden filters of young love.

After checking into their guesthouse with dusk well on its way, they took a stroll on its soft sands, hand in hand. Michiko was in a content place.

"Everything is just where it needs to be," she confessed to Satoru, stroking his palm as they walked, barefoot. "I'm happier, I'm healthier, I'm in love," she glowed. "And best of all, I haven't had a single bad night's sleep in nearly six months!"

Satoru nodded. "I hope you haven't been overdoing that pill though. I know you've given a few of those doctors a try. Please don't start depending on them, because once you get hooked on to them, there's no getting out of it. I've heard some shocking stories."

"That's not going to happen to me, or to you," Michiko said, firmly. As her sentence lingered around her, she raised another thought, this time with a bit more trepidation. "Actually we've never really discussed your relationship with the doctors, I hope none of those shocking stories are yours."

Satoru dismissed her misgivings. "Me? Never. They're meant to be used in small doses, that's all there is," he concluded as his mind got swallowed in the enormity of the advancing waves.

Michiko regained her air of assurance. "Exactly. We know what we want out of them. We go to them when we need urgent help, when we need to balance ourselves. When we need something more out of our lives. But once we're on our way, we certainly don't depend on them to make our lives happier or more fulfilling. I'm happy right now, and no doctor has anything to do with it," she affirmed.

"I'm happy too. I thought I'd lost you."

"I'm right here," she reassured him. She took his hand and gave it a tight squeeze.

"Thank God. These last few months have been the best moments of my life. I never felt I would be able to experience this kind of happiness, or find a woman like you. And now you've happened to me, twice over."

Michiko smiled at the thought. "This is true, it really is. This is what counts."

Satoru kept silent. He watched the waves in the sea rise and collapse away as they came crashing on to the shore, their increasing fervour finding unlikely reflection in his own silent thoughts.

"I've always wanted something genuine, someone genuine in my life," Michiko continued. "That's the only way to find true happiness, to find someone who loves you for who you are, someone who's real."

Satoru stayed silent, his mind and his thoughts now entirely one with the waves, rising and colliding in a fierce dance of to and fro.

"Later tonight, I thought we'd…oh look!" Michiko stopped her sentence midway. "Candy floss!"

Satoru turned in the direction, where he saw a small stand, out on the beach, closer to the road, selling impossibly coloured pink and white floss.

"Why don't you go get some?" he suggested. "I'll just stay here for a while."

Michiko laughed as she ran towards the cart, her feet leaving a trail of sand bursts in the wind, each a charm-filled companion to her state of mind.

Satoru watched her run for a while and then turned back towards the endless sea. There were very few people out on the beach. While the cold weather was no more than a few weeks away, there was already an appreciable nip in the air. Just a couple of weeks more, he surmised, before biting winds descend and not a soul is left on these sands.

As he stared at the horizon, miles off into the distance, and the turmoil of the waves much closer home, he reached into his trouser pocket for his wallet. From the inside jacket of the wallet, he pulled out a card and stared at it, his eyes refusing to blink. The words stood crisp and clear, stubbornly refusing to be swept away by the onslaught of the waves.

Doctor Delusion.

He stared at the words some more. Harder. He closed his eyes, staring even deeper with eyes closed, before opening them up again. But the words were still there. Stark, dark.

Doctor Delusion.

Michiko crashed into him, giving him a big hug from behind. She wrapped her arms, bearing candy, around his waist, quite purposely getting a melange of bright white and shocking pink onto his shirt. Her sudden action caused the card to go flying out of his hands and be dragged away by the breeze for a while, before falling into the waves. As she giggled mischievously, Satoru placed his hands on hers and held her tight. Her laughter flooded the air, while in Satoru's gaze, the reflection of the drowning card seemed to deepen, soon smothered by the wellspring of sadness in his eyes.

In Symphonies We Flow

Life, in all its red-blooded bliss of ache, skin, soul, and sky is brief; wouldn't you know...

And tonight, the night refuses to be anything but brutally young. Photographs keep washing on to the shore, and dreams keep playing truant with the light within your eyes.

As pupils blossom and in seeps the ocean's silent sonata, you see an ancient wooden home by the waves, keeping time to the rebellious tides. You sense three stilled notes of pure, amazing grace. You uncover atonement in knowing that someone, somewhere is thinking of you at a café by the sea; wanting to be held in your arms, wanting your shoulder to rest her head on, wanting your lyrics to make up her song. That's all there is. And you try and figure out the dots and the lines that lead to something resembling a picture; an image filtered through the rapidness of time, tide, man, and myth.

Were you destined to play the rebel to karma's near-perfect script? Was it decreed that for this act, you be the joker of the pack; a Capricorn dissident wreaking disorder with the beautifully aged tarot cards? You cast such aspersions aside as you drink some wine and you smoke some moonlight and you try and keep innocence alive. It's nothing. It's everything. The ocean saves its best for last.

❋

Beyond me, like an ancient sacred snake, winds the mighty Bosphorus. It is early morning now, and a soft layer of mist rises above the water. No life here in Istanbul is left untouched by the maiden's majestic sweep. These are two different halves of the world, being unified by a cadence that sometimes flows in shades of pure blue, as it is doing now, or in billowing clouds of ink black, or, as when dusk is at its doorstep, in striking palettes of golden red, or, most thrillingly, as when the night is thick and filled with the moon's romantic essence, in streaks of giddy silver.

I step on to Galata Bridge, taking the lower passage, and walk, keeping step with the shores as they flank different customs, different communities, different relationships, and even, as it feels at times, different eras. Beneath the onslaught, there are boats coming in with the day's first catch and small ferries waiting to transport an anxious working-class horde to any of the city's distant villages and tourist hotspots.

As the fishermen dock their precariously tiny vessels, one of them offers me a smoke. I accept gladly, and inhale the dark essence of dawn, nicotine, and rancidness. My senses are alive to every heartbeat. My ears are privy to every secret. Small makeshift cafés have already begun grilling the fish and handing them out in hastily wrapped paper.

I'm reminded of yesterday at dawn, of biting into the ethnic chaos of the Eminonu ferry docks, out by the banks of the old peninsula, opening my arms to some of the most spectacular views in all of Istanbul. Yesterday's fare was the fried fish sandwiches, delivered to me by a young fisherman with a toothless grin. Basit was sailor, commander, and head chef of the good boat Ayda, a garish, illuminated wonder that rocked ever so steadily on the water even as its chieftain set about his delicacies. Akin to this morning, I sat for a while on a red plastic chair, while the dock and its coterie of pickle sellers, corn men, and leather-goods salesmen set about readying themselves for the day ahead.

Today, with every savoured bite, with every protracted drag, with every inhalation of dawn, always and forever, the revered hush of the water's sacred flow fills my mind. Ahmet and I bond over the silent language of the wisps of our unified smoke. I sense from his eyes and the scars that mark his face and the soft trembles that accost him from time to time that here is a man whose past lies littered with loves lost, hopes crushed, and addresses forgotten. But in his sea-worn smile and the glint that often infuses his eyes, I also see the bliss of a life lived in tune to the strange vagaries of the sea. Even at this early hour, Istanbul lies afflicted with a symphonic cacophony of hooting cars, streets waking up to the surge of the day, wailing calls to prayer, the equally wailing replies from a wealth of seagulls, and, as always, those haunting sermons from the far-away dissonance of water traffic. I try and map out a course. I try and gauge the direction of the wind. I try and imagine myself as being one with the city—exotic, erotic, multi-ethnic-hypnotic—one amongst its 19 million, an anonymous speck in a wild confluence of colour and texture. In the distance, a few larger ships have come into view. Everything lies spread out before me—from Golden Horns to Blue Mosques, from Turkish disco to the heart's libretto, from ancient rites to cosmopolitan rhymes, from mystic savants to misfit miscreants—a rich cauldron of everything my heart could have ever hoped for. And yet the Bosphorus flows…

OVERTURE

Light, with the weight of embers, sparkle, glimmer, and hope is brief; wouldn't you know…

Blink of an eye, eye of a storm, storm in a cup. The Native Americans have this staggering superstition wherein if someone takes a photograph of you, you lose a little bit of your soul in the process. Flash. Burn. Gone.

These shadows must have been taking photographs of her since the day she turned 17, because this vacancy doesn't seem forced or instantaneous. It bears the marks of many a painstaking year, it bears the soul of a masterpiece in progress. The days are already slowing, and I'd be better off not knowing. There are familial windows around every unfamiliar street corner, some with torn, ragged corners, holding years of family secrets within the horizons of wood. Others are freshly painted, all glistening and new to the world. No sense of history. No tinge of mystery. Tomorrow will be an unanchored new story.

Enough with windows, I wonder what's behind these doors. And so I walk these streets of dawn, where shadows, rooftops, darkness, and dampness reveal more than words ever could, and as I walk I drink some wine and I smoke some moonlight and I try and keep innocence alive. It's nothing. It's everything. The ocean saves its best for last.

❄

The streets of Galata, Beyoglu, Cihangir, Taksim, Nisantasi, and a bevy of neighbourhoods whose names flow like poetry, together with their bewildering assortment of side streets, intimate pathways, and accidental arteries throb under afternoon's steady gaze. I harbour a near perverse addiction to Istanbul's old, forgotten streets, those in which you find ravaged men drinking cay and reminiscing sadly over their youthful conquests or the ones in which forlorn women stare down at you from the windows, silently cursing you for having intruded on their melancholic lives and claiming a small slice of it as your own.

I walk, shielded from the sun by shops and buildings and trees and pillars, each a vital piece in a maze without any real escape. My heart skips to an ancient beat, as apartment buildings greet me with stories ancient and fragrant. The stylish newer ones, with their

European wrought-iron flourishes and beckoning al-fresco terraces, hint at a romance yet to fully bloom.

But it is the old symphonies that consume me. A strange and familiar sadness has overcome me under its gaze, numbing me as much to the restlessness of youth out on Taksim Square as to the stylishly bohemian fallacies of chance encounters and Turkish coffee parlours out on Beyoglu. The strange and familiar sadness I speak of was in full view a few days ago as well, when Mehdi, Dilara, and Aydin, my lifelong Turkish connections, had taken me out for coffee.

"I'd like to step inside a fabled Turkish coffee-house, a place painted in nostalgia," I had told them. And so we headed towards Kadikoy Market, where on Serasker Caddesi stands a place steeped in yesterday. At Fazıl Bey, the smell of freshly roasted coffee beans lives with the simplicity of small gracious cups.

As music, interspersed by crackling of the record player and silences, played softly, we dipped into the gentle chocolate textures of their house favourites, before venturing on to the unexpected pine flavouring of the *damla sakızlı* and winter-battling *salep*. As we discussed the vagaries of our lives in the company of centuries-old wood, I felt it creep up to me. It revealed itself quite gently through the black-and-white frames that had nearly seeped into the walls, before confidently taking a seat at our table and becoming a breathing part of our conversation: that sadness, that longing, that inexplicable *yearning*.

But today it is here in Beyoglu, traversing the mystic climb of Istiklal Caddesi, flanked by homes and lives and memories and regrets to which I have no access. My heart is on the verge of exploding into a million poignant pieces. Every outer visage carries a certain art to it, regardless of whether the home is a French-style villa, presiding over majestic views, or a tiny, anonymous apartment in a tiny, anonymous tenement, brimming with decline and mediocrity.

I ruminate on the buildings. I ruminate on their tragic histories. I ruminate on the sad lives they harbour, their shapeless squalor, their bleeding hearts. I ruminate on the painful contradictions of having so much style and hedonistic elegance in the same square address. I ruminate on the pointlessness of their tomorrows. I ruminate on the harsh realities in their eyes. And I come to accept the fact that I can no longer move, anchored to this earth by a regal connection to its very core, horrified and attracted by the profound truths of these lives placed before my eyes.

What to say of human beings who haven't set foot outside the places in which they were born, who have stubbornly refused to accede to the world and its myriad pleasures all through their lives? Is theirs a quality to be admired? This principled stance of having no interest in the world and the mysteries it holds, being content instead with the piece of earth they were born into and bequeathed? Or is theirs a fate to be bemoaned? Just sad lives bereft of fragrance and courage, coloured in a relentless, monotonous shade of monochrome? And are all our lives, rich or poor, intrepid or insipid, poetic or robotic, bound, in the end, by the select few human experiences that no one is destined to escape?

These questions haunt me: I crave for their stories. I ache for their secrets. I'm engulfed by these unknown names and faces, stilled by the cumulative profundity of births, deaths, ecstasies, epiphanies, childhoods, celebrations, failures, fathers, mothers, sons, daughters, rivers, homes, shops, the first crush, that last dance, the enraptured kiss, that transient romance, those moments of silence, these flowing parades of loud crowds—the cumulative profundity of life, in a manner of speaking. And yet the Bosphorus flows…

❈

ADAGIO

Lies, in their comfort zone of habit and habitual dependency, are brief; wouldn't you know...

There's a broken radio playing an old Jeff Buckley song somewhere out there tonight, a song that isn't his to own by right, but one he's been bequeathed, thanks to his tender collage of diffusion, delicacy, and divinity:

I drink much more than I ought to drink, because it brings me back you.

Its plaintive notes and that slightly odd time signature are giving birth to forgotten black-and-white portraits from days long lost. I can hear it if I put my ears to the ground. There's a swirl of clouds coming together gracefully, forming an erotic portrait of a woman's thigh somewhere in this soon-to-be ink-dipped sky. I can see it if I close my eyes. There's a parade of mystic mermaids making their Chanel-clad way down a boulevard of destined disappointment. I can smell the excitable anguish on their lips, drunk in their own repentance, scared by the thought of what might happen when the ingénue roles dry up.

Sweet Chardonnay, there's nothing in her way; forego it for something that'll crush the pain away. They dance, yet the despair persists, so they drink some wine and they smoke some moonlight and they try and keep innocence alive. It's nothing. It's everything. The ocean saves its best for last.

❋

Evening has settled over Istanbul, thick with the scent of *narghile* bubbling through glamorous oriental cisterns, redolent with the aroma of a strikingly sensual city that bristles with the embers of Byzantine, oscillates between the fragrances of the Ottomans, and wrestles with its Muslim identity in a decidedly cosmopolitan European visage. There is squalor and there is glamour; there is poetry and there is savagery; there are the millions of tourists, there are the handfuls of purists; there is a brutal synergy, there is a mystic symphony.

I have come to realise that my attack of sadness from earlier today in the afternoon hasn't been such a bad thing after all. It has only served to bring me closer to this fascinating conundrum of a city. I have recalled how the Turkish writer Orhan Pamuk speaks about the overpowering melancholy that grips him and envelops his city in a blanket of haze that drifts from rooftops and chimneys and homes where the light lingers with a soft sadness well into the night before gradually becoming one with the sky that hangs over Istanbul; a shroud, a veil, a second skin, a heavenly sin. It's a Turkish term called *hüzün*. I hope I'm pronouncing it correctly for you. Pamuk dissects it as a communal melancholy of sorts, as opposed to an individual sadness, wherein the entire populace of the city finds itself united by an inexplicable sorrow, one bred from the striking inevitability of their own lives, one nourished by the embers of a fallen empire struggling to come to terms with the harshness of its sudden reality.

Of course, all this flies in the face of the millions of tourists who are here, eager to tick off Hagia Sophia, Grand Bazaar, and Bosphorus Cruise from their lists. It flies in the face of the excitement that pervades the outer layers of the city as well, because this is an inner sadness, a poetic sadness, an invisible aura that leaves neither pristine Islamic minaret nor dazzling high-rise; neither the buried embers of the old wooden *yalis*, the seashore houses that once used to preside over the Bosphorus' course, nor the rolling hills that nestle the city in their grasp; neither the neighbourhoods with no name, nor the throbbing coastal hotspots redolent with bliss and ecstasy—it leaves none of these untouched by its spell.

Has my recognition and realisation of this *hüzün* brought me closer to Istanbul? In coming to terms with the sad, bitter truth of Istanbul, have I now been freed from the yoke of preconceived notions; free to delve within its inner silences? In viewing this communal melancholy with my eyes, as it weaves and flows through homes, lives, loves, yesterdays, maybes, tomorrows, how comes, what ifs, have I finally found some sort of secret key to deciphering this maiden's compelling flow?

But I've stopped at this, confident in the thought that having recognised the scent of *hüzün* and having come to peace with it, I am now much more attuned to the wild, scattered heart of this city. Also, perhaps I am now more attuned to the wild, scattered heart beating within *her*. And yet the Bosphorus flows…

ARIA

Love, forged through breath and brocade, forged in fire and the gentle art of forgetting, is brief; wouldn't you know…

All the rage of a scathing tempest, and just as suddenly, all the tragic submissiveness of a washed-up actress. You're a prisoner to its constant whims and fancies, wrapped unwittingly in the deep sleep of a possession that comes laced with three sweet drops of poison.

Boats arrive, boats depart; love affairs lie dappled like a carpet of stars. Here's a fragmented horizon, make of it what you will. Nothing will injure you more than this, this temptation to swim across miles of stillness to the lighthouse that glistens beyond the earth's rim, sending those carefully orchestrated beams of hope and life to storytellers stranded at sea, only to come crashing against the rocks, betrayed by the very rays that once nourished your faith. As it leads, so it deceives; as it transcends, so it bereaves. So near and yet so far; a fistful of sky to a last sip of stars. And thus are fables stitched and legends sown, growing heavier each year under the unbearable weight of water. These sailors know better than to grieve for the lost, so they drink some wine and they smoke some moonlight and they try and keep innocence alive. It's nothing. It's everything. The ocean saves its best for last.

✳

I'm running wild through Istanbul's streets, spurred on by the intoxication of the night, urged to give every last bit of my heart to a city that dabbles in poetry and delivers with ecstasy. Am I chasing after the ghost of Flaubert, he who loved so mercilessly, only to perish to an assailant as inelegant as syphilis? Am I enraptured by the essence of Rumi, weaving sacred verses of Sufi and 'save me' in a bid to decipher a truth most divine, a truth that would next lead him onward to India? Am I matching steps with Julien Viaud, whose oriental obsessions lie entrenched in the hilltop café that overlooks the Eyup Sultan Mosque and bears but his nom de plume, Pierre Loti?

Great men have faltered at the hands of Istanbul, and yet, a few great men have soared under its wings too. The greatness of a few is what I crave. And the greatness of ourselves is what we craved last night, Leyla and I, as we made love to the frantic ebb and flow of the Bosphorus. Last night, ours was a love built on urgency and potency, desperate to quench every last drop of its thirst, lest it be swallowed by the city's greedy melancholy.

Tonight, as they did last night, her flowing wisps of dark black hair are having their way with me; flicking my lips as she throws her head back in hushed, rhythmic moans; brushing against my face like wayward feathers in an unexpected breeze; and unfurling onto me in a violent pool of melody when we are in ardour's deepest throes. Our cries and whispers and scratches and movements are like a melodic counterpoint to the traffic and the murmurs and the distant echoes of ships and the even further laments of seagulls.

We've stepped out onto Leyla's small balcony now, our naked bodies still flush with the fragrance of recent love, with only a thin blanket for company. Lives, millions of lives, lie scattered before us—across undulating rooftops and sloping cobblestone streets, across dimly lit homes and brightly scented candelabrum, across a capital that once presided over four empires spanning 16 centuries and those seven encircling hills that have enraptured poets since time immemorial.

Leyla wants to know what my plans are for the next few days. But what am I to tell her? I, who hadn't even planned to fall so deeply within her. We met a week ago when my Istanbullu friends threw a small party for me at their charming apartment. But wasn't I to have left already? A week has come and passed. This was meant to be a detour, not an epiphany.

As Leyla guides my hands and wraps them around her delectable waist, the skies are assaulted by a blissfully orchestrated performance of the day's final prayer. From our balcony, we perceive the prayers, being set to a celestial domino effect of sorts, cascading from one mosque to the next, creating a divine dance that has soon engulfed the entire city.

"Why do you think you've stayed on in my city?" Leyla asks me.

"I wasn't expecting to be so moved," I tell her, "and I wasn't expecting you." She turns around to face me and rises on her toes to kiss me, deeply. "Can we chase the night?" I ask her. She winks, and we're off.

On Necati Bey Caddesi in Beyoglu, the heady blend of densely textured tobacco, ancient lamps, and strong coffee at Katmerler is just the tonic for our restless hearts. We don't even mind the roaring football fans in here tonight. Leyla's done with her melon-flavoured shisha, and we've moved on to Karabatak, where solemn churches and a busy whorehouse look down upon us from either side. Here, seated on old cane chairs in the heaving quarter of Karakoy, Leyla and I must talk to one another in the presence of bygone European grandeur and the remnants of a fairly authentic Ottoman essence.

Quaint poster-art bearing 'Meinl Kaffee' looks me in the eye, jostling for attention with the antique Islamic motifs on the tiles. Herr Meinl's legacy is strong, potent, and perfectly brewed. Leyla is telling me about her childhood, spent in a small wooden yali just off the shores, where she and her two older brothers would pretend they were pirates out to plunder the seas. Theirs was one of the few Bosphorus-gracing wooden mansions still standing in the eighties, before it too came crumbling down into the earth in a hypnotic dance of fire, blaze, smoke, and finally, forgotten ashes. There is something in her voice. It's not just nostalgia, it's not just sadness, but a sense of *impermanence*, as though she's telling me about the childhood of some other girl from her imagination.

I find out that Leyla has done her masters in philosophy from Galataseray University. Is she going to get bored of my illiteracy, I wonder? I find out that she wants to discover India, that she wants to get to the heart of its mysteries and spiritual proclivities, that she wants to spend two or three months there, not as a tourist, but as a philosopher trying to determine her own truths.

I tell her a little bit about my own life, about wanting to become a poet, journalist, writer, and documentarian at various points in my life, and how words have somehow always been at the heart of it. I tell her that when she arrives in India, perhaps we should meet. I tell her what I think of Istanbul, at least what I can fathom of it. I tell her what I think of her. At least what I can fathom of her. We fall into a slow, beautiful hush. It is close to midnight, and our final stop for the night is going to be the Marmara Pera Hotel, whose rooftop plays home to the exquisite flavours of Mikla.

I can see the Golden Horn shimmering in the distance, and all 360 degrees of Istanbul embrace me with the fervour of a long-lost friend. We have some delicious finger food on our high-table, and a bottle of deep Shiraz for company. Set darkly against her perfectly almond-shaped face, Leyla's eyes are full of sparkle. We talk, we laugh, we slow dance with the intimacy of a familiar couple. We hold on to each other's bodies with the trembling audacity of two passionate strangers.

The night is slipping away, our hearts are but minor specks in its wake. And yet the Bosphorus flows…

❧

FINALE VE CADENZA

Lust, inflamed by a heady tango of touch, breath, sweat, kisses, and promises, is brief; wouldn't you know…

Wrapped in the cruel crush of destiny's wayward arms, days flew by like letters thrown out of a car headed nowhere on a windy evening. June, July, August. Three months. Might just have been three months too many, back when summer was all impassioned pain and scathing glory.

Whisper a name. Carve it into the skin of a tree. Memorise to heart the way you feel right now. Pick something to go with it. A song, a smell, a word. Anything really, to keep you chained to the dangerous attraction of now. Nostalgia riddles the night, nostalgia soaked in the futility of fractals, nostalgia marked along the contours of skin, within the deliberation of moans, along the nuances of curve and smell and soak and drip, nostalgia memorised through the tone of laughter and the echo of scream. Whatever resonates must, some day, surely culminate; be it in declarations, be it in simple conversation devoid of blame or overt romanticism, or be it the final swirl of a poet's conclusion to a thought. It overwhelms us, this thought, so we drink some wine and we smoke some moonlight and we try and keep innocence alive. It's nothing. It's everything. The ocean saves its best for last.

✳

It has now been over two weeks since I landed in Istanbul. Within my recognition of Istanbul's lingering melancholy, within my realisation of my own *hüzün* and the place it holds within the city's fractured sorrows, within my grasp of what is to become of Leyla and me, I am at peace.

The two of us have been hedonistic flower-children, only too willing to dissolve within the fragrance of lasting *narghile* smoke, only too happy to lose ourselves in the wild confluence of breathlessness and nostalgia that is this city's calling card. We've made the Cihangir quarter our home, delving into its leafy, literary nooks with curiosity and emerging with a cradle of memories: Susam Café with its air of friendliness, those potent Aegean Mojitos, and a living-room-like vibe that opens out to a street-side terrace of unrelenting drama; Smyrna, and its laidback ambience replete with the literati and an outdoor space blooming with plane trees; Cukurcuma 49 and its split-level eccentricities that come laced with Turkish-style pizzas and an artisanal house wine bottled on the Aegean shores of Bozcaada; or better yet, 5.Kat, where flame-haired actress Yasemin Alkaya presides over a boudoir-bliss essence draped in deep red velvet and staggering Bosphorus views that come at us from full-length windows.

We crave more, and it is more we shall have. We cherish the rich essence of Turkish wine by the waterfront at Incirli Saraphane. We get loudly, stupidly drunk over the fermented semolina and cinnamon madness of Boza at Vefa Bozacisi. We immerse ourselves in the old-school opulence of Kybele Café in Sultanahmet and have deep conversations with the spirit of Alphonse de Lamartine at Desde Café, right at the very top of breathtaking Camlica.

Whether at dawn after an all-nighter or later in the morning, breakfast is just the one address though, no options necessary. Ada Bosphorus, which Leyla informs me was earlier known as Van Kahvalti Evi, tempers my insatiable craving for the maiden while satisfying both our cravings for warmly traditional Turkish breakfasts. My senses are aflutter at the explosions of colour, history, and artistry with which they're being assaulted. The night instigates its own alchemy, whether it's the domed passageways and carpet-covered stone walls and ethereal mosaic lamps at the 18th-century *madrasah* tea gardens of Corlulu Alipasa Medresesi, or the old brick walls and cezve-accented coffee of Ethem Tezcakar Kahveci near the Grand Bazaar; whether it's the heady confluence of Turkish rock, late-night backgammon marathons, unexpected troubadours, and shapely puffs of smoke that accents Kucuk Parmakkapi Sokak in Istiklal Caddesi, or the worthy combination of ice-cold Efes Pilsen, coma-inducing *baklava,* and sesame-blessed *simit* bread on cobblestone-streets…

Leyla and I hold on to one another, tightly, dreamily, lest each moment pass us by. Mehdi, Dilara, and Aydin come join us in Galata, and we go browsing through vintage book stores where the smell of old paper merges with the faint whiff of embedded regret on the owners' distant faces. We step inside small, incredibly atmospheric art shops and galleries where portraits of Rumi swirling to the tune of his own calligraphic etchings merge seamlessly into the lost stares of dusky maidens from the Pasha's harem.

My head is spinning, my heart is thumping. I want it all. I want it now. I want all this happiness and all this anxiousness and all this ecstasy and all this melancholy to be dissolved within my intrepid body. Is no one else aware of this, this all-encompassing melancholy? Has no one been unable to unearth the finality of his or her existence?

Such an achingly cool city, and yet, its *hüzün.* This is a poetic sorrow, as it flows along the seven-kilometre stretch of the Theodosian Walls, from the Sea of Marmara to the Golden Horn. This is a nostalgic sorrow, as it flows through the narrow streets and the silently poignant *yalis* in the Bosphorus villages of

Arnavutkoy. This is a ravaged sorrow, as it flows between delicious cocktails and divine sunrises at Zelda Zonk. This is an evocative sorrow, ideally suited to the bevy of *narghile* cafés that lie fragrant with the scent of rosewater and rose-accented smoke in Tophane. This is a tempestuous sorrow, reconciled to its destiny within the intricate mosaics and exquisite apartments in the harem quarter of the Topkapi Palace, and within the glitzy ostentatiousness of the Dolmabahce Palace. This is an inevitable sorrow, left to wander through the mystic blue essence of the Rustem Pasha Mosque and the almost elegiac courtyard of the Yavuz Selim Camii in Fatih. And this is a drunken sorrow, stumbling its way past the talking parrot and the silent nostalgia of days gone by in Buyuk Londra on Mesrutiyet Caddesi, past soft jazz views of the Golden Horn at Le Fumoir on Serdar-I Ekrem Street, past the sweeping views from L'tera Bar on Yenicars Caddesi. But most compellingly of all, this is a divine sorrow. And nowhere is it more potent than when I'm by the Bosphorus' side, as I am now, on the banks of Ortakoy village, staring out at the immensity of 'the First Bridge' and the divinity of the neo-Baroque Ortakoy Mosque.

"You should stay on a while longer," Leyla tells me. We're standing hand in hand.

"Everything's moving too quickly," I tell her. "Istanbul is moving too rapidly for me. What if everything were to just disappear?" I ask her.

Young men sell baked potato *kumpir* on rickety streets. Why don't I stay on for a while, I ask myself. Why am I so afraid of Istanbul's veiled sorrows? Why am I consumed by the sudden thought of losing Leyla, when we haven't even had the chance to find each other to begin with? Can't Leyla and I just be, allowing our desires and destinies to write their own script? These questions escape my mouth and hover around Leyla for a while, before drifting towards the Bosphorus and being swallowed in its vastness. Yes, yes, I'm aware that yet she flows. As she always has, as she always will. Only now, she carries the added texture of two lovers and their secret needs wrapped within her waves, engulfed within her reflections. The city rises hazily in the distance beyond us— blissful, hectic, its melancholy indelible as ever. Dreams and hopes and fears and regrets and expectancies and ecstasies rent the sky in a technicoloured dream.

Leyla grasps my hand just a little bit tighter. The wind is fierce. Our hearts are full. It's like Istanbul has come to an unexpected, unrequited standstill. And yet the Bosphorus flows...

The Thousandth Bridge

Echoes of the Past

It was only after the devastating drought of 2002 had dried up the river, that Azadeh Razool began paying attention to the bridges. Before then, in her still-formative mind, they were simply a means to an end. They helped her get across. They helped her get back. And that was all she required of them, really. She admired their beauty, to be sure, and she understood their cultural significance to Isfahan. But as you do with a prodigiously gifted member of your immediate family, she was perhaps just a little too blasé about their majestic profundity, as culpable of taking their beauty for granted as she was of her own latent artistic brilliance.

It took the drought for her to realise the importance of the only remnants that still stood over where the river had once flowed. It took the drought to bring about an outpouring of artistic grief. It was only then, at 19, that the inconspicuous pencil and dark ink and brushstrokes, bearing a rare cadence, began to blossom, her solitary means of quelling the suffocation of a deep, irreparable loss.

Zaindeh Rud, *the river that gives continuous life*, had betrayed the very essence of its name, leaving once-flourishing fields bereft of their primary source of irrigation, leaving once free-spirited children and couples gasping for its grassy banks and reflective waters.

"It is as though I have lost a lover," the old owner of a teahouse nestled within the grottos of one of the bridges had betrayed to her with sad eyes. "I can still hear her voice, I can still sense her soul… but she is no more."

As Azadeh thought about those tears of his and remembered the simmering sadness of the days that had brought about a tumultuous epiphany within her, she noticed the reporter walking towards her.

She recognised Ali Majidi from the small photograph that accompanied his articles every Thursday and Sunday in the cultural section of the *Persian Parade*. After a brief exchange, Ali got down to business straight away.

"Azadeh Khanum, in any discussion on Iran's best young artists, your name is spoken of highly. How do you feel about having the spotlight shine on you?"

Azadeh smiled and poured herself a cup of tea, from a blue teapot encrusted with Persian motifs woven in painstakingly considered shapes and patterns.

"That's very kind of you, *Aga*. But in all humility, I do not think myself worthy of such adulation."

"Some of our greatest living artists have spoken about you in glowing terms. Your modesty is not justified."

"This is all I know how to do. If it is true that I have some sign of rarity within me, then I owe it all to the blessings from above."

"Well, I think what has caught the imagination of so many people is this specific project you have undertaken for the last 12 years or so, in fact, your only major project from the time you began painting seriously. Could you tell our readers a little bit about it?"

Azadeh gathered her thoughts. The small teahouse exuded a sense of warmth that managed to defy November's audacious chill. Its interiors of dark wood and rugs entwined with remnants of opulence, and spaces infused with the lingering evidence of rich Persian teas made her feel at home.

"Well, it is the Thousand Bridges project," she began. "Isfahan is known as the city of a thousand bridges, even if that may just be a symbolic signature. But its soul, its fragrance, its past, its enigma, they are all tied within the confluence of a thousand bridges. There may only be 11 bridges standing in Isfahan today, but I reinterpret and reimagine them, producing nearly 100 unique renditions of each bridge. These renditions are given birth by my memories of conversations from childhood or from pieces of literature or from some of the rare etchings in our archives; sometimes, just from a longing of what might have been. It is the bridges that are my passion. They are what I paint."

Ali was capturing every word of hers with his recorder. As she spoke, she saw him constantly reaching for a few errant strands of grey hair that kept falling across his face. As he kept brushing them aside, she wondered whether this tic of his was born out of necessity or vanity. But his questions were well-defined, and she was enjoying the casual flow of the conversation.

"*Khanum*," Ali continued, "it was the cataclysmic drought that gave birth to your project, didn't it?"

Azadeh had known the question would eventually arise. "Yes," she replied. "The Thousand Bridges project is my ode to the beauty that once flowed. When the drought hit us and the Zaindeh Rud dried up almost immediately, I remember the blank looks on people's faces as they stood by its ravaged banks and stared into nothing. They were inconsolable. The drought hit the southern part of our land and large parts of Afghanistan, but here we were, in the heart of Iran, equally vulnerable to nature's whims."

As she paused to take a sip from her tea, teeming with fragrance, Azadeh took the opportunity to gather her thoughts as well.

"Someone asked me at that time, of what use are bridges now, when we can simply walk across these rocky plains and dried-up riverbed to the other side. That statement hit me very hard. I wanted to show people that the bridges most certainly held significance in the life of Isfahan, if for nothing else, just to remind us of what once was."

"A homage of sorts," Ali suggested.

"If the river doesn't exist, does Isfahan have no meaning anymore? Without the river, are our lives meant to be lived in one endless parade of melancholia over the past? This isn't simply homage. If you'll allow me this indulgence, it is also meant to be a harbinger of hope."

"You do paint other things too, of course?"

Azadeh laughed, and her uninhibited laughter filled the spaces of the teahouse, causing the other patrons to smile as well.

"Yes, I do," she replied. "But whatever else I embark on, the bridges and this project are always brewing in my heart."

"We will get to some of the special ones in a while," Ali commented, "but what people are quite curious about is…"

"I know," Azadeh interrupted him. "They want to know why I haven't painted the Si-o-seh pol yet."

Ali smiled. "Well, it *is* Isfahan's most famous, and arguable, most beautiful bridge."

"For precisely those reasons," Azadeh replied. "I've always felt some kind of sacred bond with the Si-o-seh pol, and wanted to save it for last. There is also a sense of intimidation when dealing with it—those mystic 33 arches, its haunting Safavid architectural legacy, its bricks and stones from many centuries ago…" she sipped from her tea. "I needed to save it for last."

"Last?" Ali questioned with an inquiring look.

"Yes. I'm glad to tell you that I have now completed 900 paintings of ten of Isfahan's bridges. And I shall be devoting the final 100 paintings to Si-o-seh."

"Oh," Ali exulted. "How brilliant. This will be a revelation for our readers. And when will you commence with the final passage of your project?"

"I want to give myself two or three weeks to study the bridge, to examine it in silence. I need to prepare myself for this, this final passage as you call it," she concluded with a smile.

Over the remainder of the interview, Azadeh went on to tell Ali about varied aspects of her art and the Thousand Bridges project. She spoke about some of her cultural influences, as varied as the echoes of Persian classical vocalist, Jalal al-Din Taj Esfahani, which haunted her frequently, and Tar soloist, Jalil Shahnaz, all the way to the footprints left behind by the director, Asghar Farhadi, and her childhood memories of watching Iranian actress and princess, Soraya Esfandiary-Bakhtiari. She spoke of her admiration for Freydoon Rassouli's fusion-art rebelliousness and her love for Hoseein Mosaverolmolki's miniaturist perfections; she spoke of studying Javad Rostam Shirazi's artistry while at the Art University of Esfahan and losing herself in the intricacies of Mahmoud Farshchian's miniatures.

None of this was as revealing to Ali as when she spoke, with some trepidation, of being orphaned at the age of nine. "My mother died a few months after I was born, due to some complications suffered while giving birth," she revealed to him through scarcely concealed regret over a relationship she had never known. "And my father had perished when I was nine, his persistent love for the bottle finally getting the better of him."

Ali felt a sharp tinge of sadness pierce through the years of cultivated objectivity as he heard Azadeh give him the singular gist of her life since that day: of how across unfamiliar relatives and cruel aunts to running away from foster homes and finally finding her place on this earth, art had become the healing and the hope, allowing her to make her life in Isfahan, allowing her to free herself from the yokes of the past; eventually blessing her with the gift of Isfahan's most revered remnants through the special project of hers.

At the end of the conversation, Ali thanked her with warmth in his voice. He was pleased, he had a lot of information at hand. But he was genuinely moved by the path that Azadeh's life had taken. "If you weren't recognised already, I think this feature piece might just take you there," he smiled. "A photographer from the *Persian Parade* will be here in Isfahan sometime tomorrow to take a few photographs, if you don't mind. As for me, I best be off, back to Tehran. *Khanum*, it has been a pleasure," he tipped an imaginary hat, "and an honour. *Khoda Hafiz.*"

"My pleasure, Ali Aga," replied Azadeh with a smile. "I hope to have another conversation with you when the thousandth bridge is complete. *Khoda Hafiz.*"

AN AGELESS FRAGRANCE

Maryam came striding into the coffee shop with her customary flourish. Even under the enforced piety of long sleeves, covered legs and the stark black hijab, freedom wasn't a distant concept, style even less so. As her flirtatious black kaftan rose and flowed with her gliding steps, it revealed flashes of temerity—courtesy a pair of striking red stilettos picked up during last summer's European jaunt and her unhesitant steps in a pair of perfectly-fitted black jeans. Equally cultivated were the brief glimpses of burgundy-rich hair, ever so prone to peeking out from beneath the fringes of a headscarf given to unexpected bursts of naughtiness. Maryam sighted Azadeh sitting in a corner of the café and beamed a bright 'Hello!'

As she neared her, Azadeh noticed that Maryam was waving a folded newspaper with all the customary drama of an ingénue. She knew what to expect. Three days earlier, 'The Passion of a Thousand

Bridges' by Ali Majidi had appeared in the Thursday edition of the *Persian Parade*, and created quite the buzz in Isfahan's artistic and social circles. Azadeh had been pleased with the article. She felt that Ali had captured her passion and the journey of her life thus far with objectivity that came sprinkled with a fair amount of grace.

"Oh, you beautiful thing!" Maryam exclaimed as she descended upon Azadeh with a tight hug.

"I take it you've read the piece?" Azadeh replied with a wink.

"Piece? Is that what you would call it? It's the main feature of the *Persian Parade*'s cultural section. Surely even you understand the relevance of that."

Azadeh smiled. Despite being so far removed from her in terms of personality and background, Maryam had been her best friend since their days in the Art University of Esfahan. They had bonded over their shared love for art with a certain striking resonance, unhinged from time and sometimes, even context.

The traditional Persian café where they had decided to meet was part of the bazaar in Naqsh-e Jahan Square. As Azadeh looked out on the vast public square that once played host to games of polo marked with passion, equally passionate flirtations, and the odd public execution, her thoughts were consumed by the past. Maryam understood the faraway look in her friend's eyes.

"Really Azadeh," she sighed with exasperation. "There are families picnicking out on the main lawns, young people everywhere, young lovers staring deep into each other's eyes, the sounds of plans and laughter, and you still seem lost in yesterday."

"I can't help myself," Azadeh replied with a gentle shrug. "Don't you see it? The fine river sand that used to accent the plaza, the acrobats weaving and flowing through the crowds, the marketplace with its aromatic textures of Indian spices and Chinese silks, the sun reflecting wildly off the Venetian glassware—I can see them as though they were right in front of my eyes."

Maryam rested her face in her palm, and looked at her friend with endearing resignation. "No wonder we can't find a boy for you. The fools that we are, we keep searching for someone from the present. We should actually be looking out for some guy from the 1600s."

The two women burst out laughing.

"I'm sorry," Azadeh offered. "We're surrounded by the bustle of the bazaar, its formidable arch and vaulted ceiling sheltering a loud collage of conversations from the past; we're sipping coffee under the shadows of the Imam and Sheikh Lotfollah Mosque; Ali Qapu Palace lies so close to us, its spiralling stairs keep swirling within my mind, Reza Abbasi's wall motifs leap out at me in dreams; it's hard not to be swept away in all their yesterdays."

Maryam sighed once more. "Artists, I can handle. But an artist and a poet is too difficult a proposition, even for me."

The women laughed heartily again.

"But I am hugely proud of you," Maryam resumed. "Given your early life, to find such colour and snatches of beauty in life is something I just can't..."

Azadeh slipped her hand across the table and cradled Maryam's hand. "Thank you, *jaan*. I won't pretend it's easy. Some days, I find myself almost crippled by a simple sadness that keeps me chained to myself. Thankfully, that emotion doesn't last for too long."

They had ordered for a *dizi*—the complex Persian broth in which lamb, vegetables, and bread demanded to be beaten by a mallet before being consumed. Between spoonfuls, Maryam interrogated Azadeh further.

"So was he handsome?"

"Was 'who' handsome?"

"Who? Ali Majidi of course!"

"Maryam, trust you to turn an interview into some sort of date."

"Gosh, he's got the silver fox thing going, doesn't he? If he was interviewing me, I'd have…"

"Maryam!" Azadeh hushed. "You really will get us into trouble one of these days."

"Oh come on, things are so much better now. Mahmoudajinad's evil yoke doesn't hang around our necks any longer, remember? I mean, just look out of the window. The hijabs are getting riskier, the stilettos are getting higher. And look," she pointed in a particular direction, "girls and boys walking together, some hand in hand, with love clearly in the air. Could you have imagined this a short while ago? And we aren't even Tehran, we're oh-so-timid Isfahan."

"Things have gotten much better," Azadeh agreed. "And you can feel a fresh sense of freedom in the air." She looked out towards the group of girls and boys who were strolling along Naqsh-e Jahan. "But don't forget *jaan*, things can change at any minute."

After their meal and coffee, Azadeh and Maryam decided to take a walk along Chahar Bagh Boulevard. It was nearly five in the evening, and dusk had begun to settle around Isfahan's spaces, both old and new. It cast the same beauty, without prejudice, on the forgotten visages of a city once as cosmopolitan as Paris and on the houses of furtive hardliners waiting to seize their occasion; on palaces and mosques once crowned with striking blue-mosaicked domes and on the nuclear-research facility that now loomed ominously in the distance; on the decrepit embers of mansions that once sparkled with poetry, and on the ever-expanding suburbs that now heaved with the fallout of three million people; on graceful pavilions that once lingered for miles, to the neon-bright shops of chicness that had long ago replaced them. Dusk's essence was impartial, save for the fact that its mystic glow brought a vastly different reaction from the two eras it was dealing with.

Azadeh was slightly wary of heading towards Chahar Bagh because she knew she'd be swept up again in the fragile poignancy of a past she could only imagine in shapeless wisps of air. Maryam would surely have another good-natured go at her. She smiled to herself at her friend's restlessness, one that filled her abstract paintings with a manic sense of disorder and her relationships with an equal amount of tumult. Once on Chahar Bagh Boulevard, there was no escaping it: those mystic appearances of a canal dissecting the perfectly manicured main avenue, that prosperous outpouring of chinar trees, the onyx basins heady with the fragrance of freshly-cut roses, all as existent to Azadeh as the friend walking by her side. As they munched on *pulaki*—a coin-like Esfahani candy—and *gaz*—Isfahan's fabled nougat-like melange of angebin sap, almond shavings, saffron, pistachio, and rose water—Maryam gave Azadeh her final verdict on the interview.

"*Jaan*," she intoned, in that lullaby-like tendency of hers, "I think this interview is your first step towards greatness. I mean, we've known it all along. It's only a matter of time before the whole of Iran does as well. And then, the world!"

Azadeh smiled. "Greatness is such a big word, no?" After a moment's reflection, she continued, "But as long as we're dabbling in greatness, I think you should know that your abstracts have a profound impact on people as well. You're blessed with something special. If only you could..."

"Stop chasing after men?" Maryam interrupted her with a laugh. "And if only I wasn't born so bloody rich. Maybe I would be more serious about my work," she concluded with a customary matter-of-factness.

It was dark by now and Isfahan had descended into the depths of its winter chill. Both women had flung on thick woollen overcoats and slipped on gloves as well.

"So it's time for Si-o-seh pol, isn't it?" Maryam asked, breaking the temporary silence that had ensued with the onset of darkness.

"It's time," Azadeh confirmed.

"What a journey this has been, the Thousand Bridges."

"I still have a 100 paintings to go. Going by the past, I'll probably devote all of the coming year to it."

Maryam beamed at her friend. "Your passion is incredible. You'll start after a while?"

"Yes, maybe three weeks. I need some time to meditate on this journey and equip myself for the task at hand."

Maryam squeezed her friend's hand. They continued to walk up and down Chahar Bagh, firmly wrapped in its echoes of yesterday, in an Isfahan sustained by its remembrances of what once was.

RUINS OF PARADISE

Azadeh awoke the next morning at just after seven. As she rubbed her eyes, she felt November all around her as it seeped through her windows, circled around her bed, and even had the gumption to invade her thick quilt and embrace her in its affectionate chill.

Azadeh looked around her. She loved her little apartment. She had loved it from the moment she'd first set eyes on it as a 21-year-old. After the indifferent walls of those random relatives, the vicious roofs of failed foster homes, and the cruel anonymity of myriad hostels and dormitories, her home on Sonbolestan Alley—just off Ebn-e Sina in the Shohada neighbourhood—was nothing short of paradise. She had been renting it from the day she'd begun making money from her art, at first selling a few traditional Persian motifs, slowly moving on to a fairly steady diet of commissioned work from a precious handful of loyal clients, all subservient to her overpowering passion, but naturally.

Azadeh had often pondered the reasons for her prolific artistic output. She was well aware of the anguished existence of the pained artist, often struggling for years to complete that perfect collection. She had only been able to come up with lucidity as a reasonable enough explanation: when it came to commissioned work or art created for sale, there was a freedom because her passions and heart were not consumed by it, of that she was clear; and with the Thousand Bridges, she was equally clear that the paintings here would never be restrained by fear or thought or preconceived notions—that they would be allowed to fly in different directions, through different mediums, bearing no allegiance to a single style of thought. Which is why she'd completed some of the smaller renditions of the bridges, the ones splashed abstractly on 21 x 21 canvasses, in as little as a day.

Over a hot cup of tea, Azadeh watched the sun's diffused rays play around with her apartment, accented in sparse, elegant touches. A few odd keepsakes from childhood—a couple of nearly faded remnants of a mother she had never known and a father she would just as soon not have; Maryam's gifts collected religiously from places far and exotic; some dreamily-sketched charcoals of a man and a woman lost in the hazy dissonance of their realities; the oddly attractive smell of paints and the freshly brewed liveliness of tea—all lay submerged within a sweeping wash of fragile sepia. Azadeh's world, now that she examined it, was an ode to nostalgia. This apartment felt like home, it smelt like home. Even some of its neglected spaces had their role to play, collecting unspoken feelings and lost words and discarded ideas within their quiet folds.

Old Mrs Hossein, her landlady who occupied the entire ground floor beneath her, felt like home too. Azadeh knew that the widow had a particular fondness for her, one almost certainly accentuated by the lack of warmth from her own children long-since settled in distant Australia. Mrs Hossein was never short of a bright smile or a gentle hug, making sure her uncommon tenant from above always joined her for some tea and *dizi* at least once a week.

As Azadeh left home, she yelled out a 'Goodbye, Mrs Hossein' from the entrance, unsure whether the old lady was at home or off for breakfast at her sister's. A five-minute walk later, in Shohada itself, she stopped for a while, as she always did, in front of Bekhradi Historical House. Examining the traditional Persian *khane sonnati*, crafted in the Safavid style, with its two-gardened courtyard, she felt that familiar calm, eerie in its stillness.

She kept walking, towards a recent gem she'd uncovered within a crumbling maze of Isfahan's forgotten backstreets. It was an old mansion, only recently subjected to the trials of renovation. It had been built in the traditional Persian style: rooms on two opposite sides, a reception area depicted with lavishness, and a beautiful central courtyard flanked by a solitary entrance. A fireplace of ancient vigour crackled with stories of the past, sadness writ large on its once proud curves; the courtyard lay consumed with dust flakes and the lazy chatter of men barely at work.

Even in its ruined state, Azadeh felt the glories of what once was. She sensed the mansion's spiritual affinity with Shah Abbas I, when Isfahan's Safavid splendour had risen to the summit of its glory. It was a time of cruelty and extravagance, it was a time of showmanship and sacredness, it was a time of paradisiacal gardens and secular ambitions, it was a time of Shiite emergence and a soon-to-be-lost cadence, and standing in front of the mansion's courtyard, Azadeh couldn't help but let out a sigh.

She took a couple of steps inside the courtyard. At that exact instant, two of the workers appeared in front of her holding a mirror, bordered by an aged golden frame. They stopped before her to await their orders on where to place the mirror. As Azadeh stared into it, she was struck by the suddenness of herself...porcelain pure in November's morning air. Framed by melancholic signatures that manifested themselves in forlorn roses and a potpourri of thorns on the mirror's four corners, Azadeh felt she had been transported to another time. In this past, she stood with her hijab aflutter in the breeze, her strikingly precise face and large eyes bereft of the excessive make-up and explicit flourishes that many modern-day Iranian women excelled in. She stood there, still, till a soft voice brought her away from the past.

"My, aren't you beautiful."

Azadeh turned to see a woman who must've been in her early sixties. She had thick, grey hair that bobbed and flowed in harmony with her lilting phrases. She wore jeans and a thick woollen sweater that was graced at the edges with pearls.

"Oh, I'm so…so sorry," Azadeh stuttered.

"Don't be," the woman replied. "I would stare at myself too, if I were so beautiful," she laughed abundantly.

"Actually, it wasn't me," Azadeh countered shyly, "it was the mirror and the frame; they took me away to some other place."

The woman looked deeply at Azadeh, not saying anything. "Yes, the past has a way of overcoming us, doesn't it?" she commented after an instant.

"You have such a beautiful home," Azadeh expressed.

"Oh, it isn't mine. Well, it is now. It's been passed down from a never-ending stream of relatives and ancestors, each of whom has done their bit in leaving it a crumbled, sorry shadow of its regal self. And now, once all the glory has faded, it has fallen on me to inherit it and try and make something of it."

Azadeh smiled. "I didn't introduce myself. I am Azadeh Razool. And I still think you have a beautiful home, it is filled with an inexplicable character."

"I'm Saba Farashahi," the woman offered in exchange. "And thank you my dear; very few people would have the perception to see through so many layers of decay. I do agree with you. At the moment I'm slightly overwhelmed with all that there is to do, that's all. There is a beautiful soul lurking in there somewhere."

"I wish you all the best with bringing it to life. I'm sure it's in safe hands."

"Yes, I came down from Tehran with the intention of renovating it and turning it into a small boutique hotel. But the more I spend time with it..."

"Yes?"

"Well the more I spend time with it, the more reluctant I am to let go. Maybe a life in Isfahan is what my ancestors have bequeathed to me," she concluded with a smile.

"I'll take your leave now," Azadeh said. "It was very nice meeting you dear."

"You too, my dear," the woman replied. And as Azadeh walked out of the courtyard, Saba offered her an invitation. "You be sure to come back soon, we'll sit and talk over tea." Saba stepped out of the courtyard too and watched her unexpected intruder disappear, this pretty illusion who seemed strangely familiar. Had she not seen her in the newspapers a few days ago?

There was no agenda to the rest of Azadeh's day. She wanted to walk, she wanted to see, she wanted to explore. She needed to keep her mind blank, free of any niggling worries or those strange sorrows that snaked and winded their way through Isfahan's grieving alleys. Today there was no agenda, but tomorrow there would be; because tomorrow she was going to spend some time with her bridges.

A THOUSAND DESIRES

The Abbasi family mansion, in stark contrast to many rich Iranian homes, was a study in restraint over extravagance. It contained riches of unimaginable degree, but nothing screamed out at you. In fact, a rare shyness permeated the mansion's paintings, ornaments, curios, furniture, chandeliers, carpets, ancestral treasures, and coloured glassware of striking effervescence. It was as though all this luxury was careful not to preen its own beauty, lest it faced the dignified wrath of Ghaith Abbasi. The patriarch of the family, Ghaith's 74 years, thus far, had witnessed many a tumultuous phase in both his family's and Isfahan's lives.

His lineage went back several centuries and deserved its own dissertation: the family's earliest origins could be traced back to the time of Persia's prominence itself, when Cyrus the Great had bestowed a religiously tolerant rule of land that swept across an empire. They were there during the time of the Sassanids and their impassioned revival of Zoroastrianism, back when the christened Espoohrans, members of the seven noble Iranian families, presided over its fortunes, and they were there when the Safavid ruler, Shah Abbas the Great, transformed Isfahan into one of the 17th century's most stunning destinations. This golden age of Isfahan, where culture, art, and architecture mingled in a sublime dance, found its resonances in the Abbasi mansion.

In the mansion's basement, Azadeh stood staring at a sublime dance of her own making. This was a basement only by name, not in function. It stood above the ground, bearing the mansion's elevated perch on its shoulders. In its subdued elegance, in the two side windows that allowed morning's romance to pour in, through accommodating sluices, and in its vastness that showcased depth without offering cold anonymity, Azadeh's 900 paintings were at home.

She stood transfixed by them. Overhead lights that ran in delicate fashion across the entire breadth of the room on both its opposing sides complemented the sun's mischief with their pale gold radiance. The paintings were everywhere. After so many years of familiarity, they weren't just comfortable but positively attached to their surroundings. Each of the bridges had their own scattered cluster, neatly managed, yes, and yet rebellious by way of size, form, and the imaginations that had shaped them.

Azadeh's gaze was gripped. Memories were at play, as was a stubborn melancholic resonance, as were the murmurs of the bygone. She saw Shah Abbas and his sons in many of these bridges, framing the Zaindeh Rud to the silent pattern within their hearts. She began to walk amongst her paintings, along their stories, through their 12-year existence and the secrets submerged therein. There was the Pol-e Maarnaan, lying 3 kilometres to the west of Si-o-seh. Its sluices giving way to waterfalls that fell in a hush. Azadeh could still hear Maarnaan's melodic heartbeat echoing through the water as it flowed. Nearly all her paintings of Maarnaan were abundant in their abstractness, as though her brush had wanted to weave a symphony of its own, fully cognisant of the fact that its dexterity would never match that of the water's.

She moved along, slowly, to the Pol-e Khaju cluster. Azadeh loved this bridge deeply. She loved its dark brick essence; she loved the stone dam that stood firm beneath it; she loved its sluice gates that had their own sense of rhythm; and she loved its 24 arches, each a marker of the Khaju's journey. She imagined it linking the Khaju quarter on the north bank with the Zoroastrian quarter of Gabrestan across the Zaindeh. As her eyes scanned the Khaju cluster, Azadeh could hear the delighted screams of children playing by the gardens enriched by its largesse; she could sense the soft whispers of furtive lovers as they basked in the anonymity of its cavernous arches; she could see herself as a child, one of her few memories of childhood happiness, walking with her friends towards the pavilion at the heart of the bridge where Shah Abbas II would sit and wax eloquent on the vistas he had conjured; she could see Shah Abbas himself, resting under the gaze of the symmetrical striped tiles that glistened yellow, and the exquisite paintings of mildly erotic veneer in a bridge he had originally envisaged as his teahouse retreat.

She began to examine a few specific paintings. There were the courtiers, converging towards the upper central deck while commoners strolled along on the bridge's lower level, their movements blurred in an amber wash that swept across the breadth of the painting. She moved her attention to the large canvas of the octagonal pavilion, where a veiled woman stood by its arch, looking out on a world flooded with an inevitability her heart appeared not to bear. Given Khaju's brick essence, most of Azadeh's paintings in this collection had shades of clear red cerise, amber, blush, and wine-coloured marsala coursing through their spaces.

Azadeh's eyes had filled up by now, deluged by all they were witnessing. They settled on a minimalist piece executed in seven free-flowing strokes of grey, dark grey, and yellow, an imagined summation of Khaju's visual and aural perfection. They moved on to another slice of desire, a mystic blue interpretation of the lake created by the closure of the dams of the Allahverdi Khan and Khaju bridges, giving rise to the royal retreat of Sa'adat Abad. And they settled, eventually, on her sparse imagining of Pol-e Khaju under its alternate moniker of Pol-e Baba Rokn Al-Din, in allegiance to a proximate shrine, dappled in illegitimate specks of grey, indigo, green, and deep red.

Azadeh suddenly realised she'd been lost within the Thousand Bridges for nearly an hour and a half. She felt a pang of regret at having neglected her benefactors in such a manner. But they, more than others, would surely understand. She decided to have a quick breeze-through of some of the remaining bridges, to make sure they were, as she'd imagined them, to confirm that they were indeed as she'd painted them.

She began to run her fingers along the Pol-e Joui collection, familiarising herself with their textures once more. The thick surfaces of her oil paints, undulating and riding rebelliously over the canvasses, depicted Joui in its avatar of forsaken wood and a splintered heart, lost in a perpetual state of limbo between the Khaju and Ferdowsi bridges. Was it a finely wrought stone footbridge, was it an exclusive address for the ruler's harem? Her paintings bore no answer, choosing instead to revel in the questions.

She knelt down to smell the essence of Iran's oldest surviving bridge, the Pol-e Shahrestan. On a few canvasses, she had focussed on some of its intricate detailing, believed to have been inspired from Roman architecture. They were works in micro-fantasia, allowing her to merge specific features with the wild embellishments of her mind.

Azadeh ended the intimate journey through the last 12 years of her life by moving towards the centre of her adopted gallery. She closed her eyes. She began to pray, a hymn borne not out of religion or devotion but artistic meditation. In her mind's eye, she sensed the rich, surface oils rising and flowing to a certain silent rhythm. She felt the sparse notes of the rare watercolours in the collection. She intuited the dark, frantic fragrance of charcoal as it burrowed itself within the sadness of a woman's eyes here, perished within the curves of a hollow arch there. All these colours, all these memories, they rose out of their canvasses and danced across her in a symphonic performance where technique and precision lay subservient to intensity and emotion. So many elegant bridges, so many centuries of Isfahani history, so many Turks and Indians and Europeans assimilated within these chosen stories…and at the heart of it all, the Zaindeh Rud—the crux of a once proud empire, flowing with might from the Euphrates to the Oxus. The very soul of a paradisiacal city remembered in verse and perpetuated in prose—its endearing memory, its deepest wound.

Upstairs in the living room, Azadeh found Ghaith and his wife Nisreen waiting for her. "I am so sorry to have kept you waiting," she apologised profusely.

"There are no apologies necessary," Nisreen Abbasi replied. "You've spent 12 years on these paintings, what's two hours here or there?" They burst out laughing.

"But don't forget, there are a 100 paintings still left," Ghaith reminded his wife.

"Yes, she has saved the best for last."

Azadeh sipped on the tea and nibbled on the biscuits laced with almonds and pistachios. Her eyes wandered across to the two paintings that always demanded her attention when she was here. At the heart of the living room, behind the central lounge where Nisreen was seated, was a rendition of the calligraphic inscriptions that were to be found on the Imam Mosque, painted within an intangible mosaic tile that bore the mosque's seven prominent colours. To its left, by the large window that opened out to the porch area was a miniature of the Holy City of Qom that lay roughly a 100 kilometres from Isfahan.

Gathering her thoughts as she ruminated on the painting, Azadeh finally spoke.

"While I was examining the Thousand Bridges below, it struck me hard—this feeling that none of this would have been possible without your…"

"Oh don't you start," Ghaith interjected, "there's no need for that."

"Please allow me to continue," Azadeh responded, in a soft but firm manner. "I really do need to say this. All that I have, when it comes to my art, is because of you two. You have been my confidantes, my guardians, my benefactors…and in many ways, my saviours."

Ghaith and Nisreen looked at each other with the warmth of two parents.

Azadeh continued. "When I first arrived in Isfahan from Qazvin, I had no one here. I only had my art. Due to my blessings, word slowly began to spread. But by that time, I had already been swept up in the passion of the Thousand Bridges. I knew I wasn't going to sell them. But where was I going to keep them? They had already swelled to nearly 400 paintings by then. You remember don't you how they were scattered in my home, friends' homes, the art university's old chambers, an unused wing of the library; I don't think you know this, but I really was desperate by the time you arrived. You really were my angels."

Nisreen smiled. "We had chanced upon that painting of the Hasht Behesht you had done for the Otroch family. My God, how you'd depicted its eight paradises; I fell in love immediately. And when Ghaith got to know of the bridges, well, you know how special a connection he had with it…how could we not have invited you and the bridges within our home?"

Azadeh bowed her head shyly. When she brought it up again, Ghaith was about to speak. She could see that he had emotions welling within his eyes. She watched how they quivered with each word of his.

"As children, we used to take off our shoes and glide barefoot over the cobblestone ledges that ran beside these very bridges. We would sit by the edge and weave dreams to the sound of the river's currents. From accommodating our games of hide and seek, their arches became our only recourse for romantic dalliances. It was a special time, my dear. Everything was sacred, everything was certain. As long as the Zaindeh continued to flow."

As Ghaith wiped away his tears, his wife came and sat beside him and gave him an affectionate squeeze. Azadeh stared at this rare bond of theirs. She wondered whether her father too would have grown old with grace to have such handsome hair and skin indicative of stories and a compassionate smile as Ghaith. She wondered whether her mother would have been like Nisreen at this age, elegant and well-dressed to a fault, a simple necklace of pearls adorning her neck, her hair tied up in those buns of old European flair, her mannerisms a reflection of those classic Persian actresses.

Ghaith recovered himself to speak again. "Whether you're smoking a water-pipe in the old teashops, or you're contemplating a romantic tryst from days long lost, your Thousand Bridges matter. There is no more of the river, which is why they matter…"

✳

Later that evening, Maryam and Azadeh arrived at Si-o-seh. It was Azadeh's favourite time of the day. Dusk to her spelt romance and the possibility of a little magic. Under its tormented showers of deep red and crimson, led by a dance of gold and fuchsia birthed by sunset, and an improbable alchemy of colours in between, her bridges never failed to look anything but timeless.

The two women wore long black overcoats over their denims and tops, once again. But whereas Azadeh's was of a soft woollen texture, Maryam's was of unapologetic leather, picked up from her Milan excursions of the summer. It was complemented by another precious commodity from that trip of hers: long black boots that made her rise three inches above the ground.

"Glad you've chosen a perfect walking attire," Azadeh grinned.

"Aren't they gorgeous," Maryam exulted. "Right, so it's time for Si-o-seh…"

"Yes it is," Azadeh replied. "Though I'm just as happy calling it Allahverdi Khan Bridge, as it was named."

As they approached it from a distance, the bridge stretched out before them like a maiden, a maiden touched with aloneness, only too aware of her untouchable beauty.

"But yours is a beauty that now lies ravaged," Azadeh thought to herself, "consumed by your own proud legacy, humbled by the cruelties of time."

Her inner dialogue gathered momentum as their steps quickened pace:

212

"Why is yours such a fate, oh Allahverdi, to be the abiding remnant of a sad city that once rivalled Paris and London in terms of cosmopolitan beauty? Why should you alone bear the burden of the haunting loss that flows through the heart of every Isfahani? Why must these memories of Zaindeh Rud accost our souls every day, and why must you bear witness to these withered riverbeds where her waters once so generously flowed?"

They were nearly at the bridge, but Azadeh's thoughts showed no intention of ending.

"Here you stand, a thousand feet long, bearing these 33 arches along your elevated sides. Where you once linked the Chahar Bagh between the royal precinct of Dawlat-khana and the Meydan, where you once bridged the palace retreat of Hazar Jarib with the southern suburbs, now you simply bridge memory with reality. Where you once breathed life into the Armenian neighbourhood of Jolfa, now you simply breathe sighs over romances of the past. And yet, why is it I love you so…"

Maryam didn't say a word during her friend's conversation with herself. She knew Azadeh all too well. She recognised her frequent artistic ruminations and knew better than to intrude on her. It was only when they'd stepped on to the bridge that she spoke.

"No wonder Eskandar Beg Torkaman, all to awake to its exalted nature, called it the sublime bridge."

Azadeh awoke from her ponderings and smiled.

"Are you going to go about this one the same way as the others?" Maryam wanted to know.

Azadeh nodded her head. "For the most part, yes. Many of my paintings will be done from the bridge—focussing on a particular detail, looking out at the views, these pedestrian promenades by the sides, the shaded pavilions under the archways—bringing the bridge up close and personal to the viewer. A few will be painted with my easel at some distance from the bridge, looking on to it from various angles. Some will be imaginings of the past, of what it must have meant to watch the Zaindeh Rud flow through its arched pavilions, of courtiers and their conversations, of King Abbas lost in thought, possibly even a couple of abstract re-imaginings of those erotic paintings that used to hang in the interiors during the 19th century." She paused to take in her subject. "And at the end of it all, hopefully I'll have a 100 paintings."

Maryam smiled at her friend. "If anyone can…"

They walked arm in arm across the Si-o-seh and then back again, as the bridge soon became mired in darkness.

A FEAST OF FRIENDS

Maryam was directing the family chef, out on loan for the night, with her usual aplomb. While delivering orders for the *chelo* kebabs to be cooked with just the right proportion of grilled meats and fragrant saffron rice, she was also being hands-on with the *beryouni*—ensuring the baked mutton and lungs were minced to perfection and that only the required amount of cinnamon was entering the special vessel that perched above the open fire. To go with it, the Persian bread *taftoon* would, but naturally, be warmed and fluffed up just before serving. This was the night after they'd been to the bridge and Maryam wanted to celebrate the journey of the Thousand Bridges with a small feast for a close gathering of friends.

"Not only to all you've achieved, but to these remaining 100 paintings you have yet to conquer. Oh, and let's not forget that insignificant matter with the *Persian Parade* feature. Here's to Azadeh everyone, *salut*."

Everyone raised their glasses, some filled with wine, others, as in Azadeh's case, with sparkling juice.

Maryam's home breathed affluence. It was tucked away in a quiet space on Nezami Street, three bylanes removed from the Khaghani

Street intersection. Her neighbour here, by a short distance, was the Holy Saviour Armenian Cathedral, where she and Azadeh would often go to marvel at the paintings and gilded carvings. Their main fascination with the cathedral was its central dome of blue and gold, where the world's creation and Man's expulsion from Eden were portrayed in stunning murals.

Maryam had grown to become quite attached to her abode. It was a small bungalow that her parents had bought for her when she'd turned 25. She had had no qualms in accepting their generous gift, knowing that in a way it was their way of holding on to her and having some modicum of control over her life, even if only in the littlest manner. She allowed them that privilege, fully aware that she always had the stronger license of giving it up and stepping out on her own if the need arose. Enriched by the family's excessive wealth, its ancestral furniture and keepsakes, Maryam's own rich tastes and her annual holidays undertaken with religious devotion, the bungalow brimmed with abundance.

As Azadeh sat sipping her juice and making idle chit-chat, her eyes kept wandering across to the plush rugs that filled nearly every square space of the bungalow's small, prosperous spaces as they vied for attention with the Azzouni family souvenirs and paintings, nearly always framed in gold curves.

Azadeh's eyes fell upon the cluster of four paintings set in a square formation. These were Maryam's works. Azadeh marvelled at the fluid abstractness of her portraits—Maryam only painted people—and noticed, as she did every time she was here, how Maryam's works were the only ones in the house that were bordered with simple black frames.

I'm going to ask her some day—Azadeh thought to herself—whether the simple black elegance is the true her, and all this other excessiveness simply a mask.

The group sat down for dinner around nine. The bungalow's back garden had just enough space to fit in a large wooden table, which burrowed into the soil, its accompanying chairs, the open fire that had given birth to the *beryouni*, and a statue of stone in one corner of a woman in turquoise pouring a jug of water whose contents had frozen in time.

"I'm glad we're settling into a time when men and women, whether married or unmarried, whether brothers or sisters, whether fathers or daughters, can once again gather like this out in the open and make their affections known without being fearful all the time," said Hafiz, Maryam's elder brother.

"Oh I'm not so sure," replied his wife Zeinab. "I still fear that the moral police is going to leap out of those bushes and drag us away at any time. The new government is slowly bringing about some change, I agree with you, but this is Iran; a certain amount of fear comes with being part of this land."

"Well I keep telling this one," Hafiz replied, pointing towards Maryam, "that she's not in Europe and that she can't be too loud or too proud or too, you know, 'Maryam', whenever she holds one of her parties."

The others laughed.

"Oh my dear, I can only be Maryam," his sister replied with a dramatic flourish.

"Everything on the table is delicious," offered Saba, whom Maryam and Azadeh had known since college. "The *chelo*, the *beryouni*—just perfect. And so is the *fesenjan*," she commented as she helped herself to a second helping of the pomegranate infused chicken and duck casserole.

"Speaking of just perfect, Azadeh I can't wait to see what you do with Allahverdi," Maryam commented.

Azadeh smiled at her friend. "Let's see what the bridge has in store for me."

"Ah, Si-o-seh," sighed Zeinab. "When will you begin, Azadeh Joon?"

Azadeh pondered the question. "Well, initially I thought I would give myself a couple of weeks or so just to acclimatise myself with the bridge and its intricacies. But last evening after Maryam and I had visited it, I felt this urge to…well, to begin right away. So I'm going to start painting from tomorrow morning."

"Oh!" Maryam gushed, as did the others.

"That's wonderful," Hafiz said.

"I think you're on the brink of something special, *Khanum*," mentioned Ahmad.

"You certainly are," concurred his girlfriend Fiza. Both were close friends of Maryam's, and Fiza had even accompanied her on a couple of holidays.

"Azadeh Joon, I always wanted to ask you this," Fiza continued. "Apart from the bridges, what architecture in Isfahan really inspires, what do you find beautiful?"

Azadeh thought about the question for a while. "Atashgah has always held a certain fascination for me," she replied, referring to the Zoroastrian fire temple that perched dramatically atop a rock on the fringes of Isfahan. "I feel many of us have a special connection with the Sheikh Lotfollah Mosque as well, the way Sheikh Bahai designed its untouchable beauty without any minarets. Sometimes Maryam and I like to head up to Kuh-e Soffeh mountain and be inspired by the views…"

"I just go there to get away from all the people," Maryam interjected. "There's three million here now, one day these bridges will just crumble under the weight."

Azadeh held her friend's hand in compassion. "I know the feeling. Whenever I'm overcome, I try to get away to Nain and its edge-of-the-desert romance. Or I'll take a book and head out to the gardens of Kashan, or even just head south to Shiraz for a few days, just to break away from the regularity of things."

"Actually there's one thing that has been on my mind with regards to your paintings," spoke Azad, who had grown up with Hafiz and spent much of his childhood in the Azzouni household.

"I know you referred to this a little bit in your interview, but did you really have to save Si-o-seh for last?" He smiled as he finished his question.

At that moment, Mir Mohammad arrived with the dessert for the evening. He brought with him fereni—a sweet blend of rice flour and milk—and *khoresht-e mast*—a traditional yoghurt stew of lamb, sugar, saffron, and orange zest concocted from boiled orange peels that was always served as a sweet pudding. The head chef bowed to generous praise and even a small bout of applause from the appreciative diners and made his way back into the house.

Azadeh turned towards Azad. "To answer your question, I felt it needed to be so. There is a sacred connection with that bridge that required me to pay it adequate respect. I needed to save it for last."

Between mouthfuls of the traditional yoghurt stew, she considered her thoughts. "I don't know if you've ever felt this, but there is a strange, ominous halo that surrounds the bridge. I'm uncertain whether it is a warning or an invitation. It's almost as though its stories and its tragedies and its myths and its sorrows have all conspired to shield it within this foreboding mask... anyway, I'm being too dramatic. Tomorrow it is. I'll find out what that ominous feeling means, I'll find out what secrets she holds. At the end of the year, I hope to come away with revelation, if not outright salvation."

The others looked at her with a mixture of admiration and wonder.

"Well my salvation for tomorrow consists of heading to a park with Fiza, asking the warden for a carpet and some tea, and then spending the day having a picnic. Not quite high art, but it'll have to suffice," piped in Ahmad.

The others laughed, by now immersed in the night's biting chill, the bonfire's blazing embers, and the satisfaction of a hearty meal.

"I'm off to Dibai House," Maryam stated. "I need some atmosphere in my day, the Old Quarter never disappoints. I'll ask Sufi to request the chef to whip me up a special breakfast, I'll carry my sketchbook and some pencils and I'll sit in the courtyard surrounded by people and the ghosts of the 17th century." She focussed her gaze on Azadeh. "It's about time I began to get a little serious about my paintings as well."

Azadeh beamed at her friend. "One of these days, we'll do the same thing together at the Abbasi Hotel. We'll see whether the Madar Shah Caravanserai has any treats in store for us."

"Oh yes!" Maryam exulted. "And we'll keep a look out for some handsome boys for you. *Joon*, you're 32. I sometimes worry that you'll be an old woman of 65, still painting away at some bridge or the other, living a life without any glimmer of excitement, surrounded not by cats but by these old, forgotten paintings…"

Azadeh laughed as she gave Maryam a light-hearted punch. "I like how this one talks, as though she's a well-settled, fulfilled mother of three."

Amidst loud laughter and playful banter, Maryam walked up to her friend and held her from behind, whispering into her ear: "You be fulfilled. You be content. And know this, the bridges are the most beautiful things I have seen. You go complete your destiny."

The group dispersed after a little while, with hugs and many promises for the future. As they were stepping out of the bungalow's front gate, Zeinab turned around and addressed her sister-in-law: "It's on nights like these, when the weather is beautiful, when the food is delicious, when the company is perfect, when the conversation is memorable, it's on nights like these that I feel Isfahan really is half the world."

Hafiz nodded his head in concurrence. "*Isfahan nesf-e jahan*," he uttered, and the saying hung in the air for a while, before dissolving into the night.

THE FINAL DAWN

Azadeh felt as though she was being flung violently from side to side on a ship mired in tumultuous seas.

'Fade away, silly dream,' she whispered in her sleep. The cataclysmic noise that followed told her it wasn't a dream. She opened her eyes. Her apartment felt odd, as though it had been tilted by 30 degrees. Something didn't feel right. There was another deafening roar. This time she knew it was from the earth. She was wide awake.

She staggered to her feet and struggled towards the window. A bizarre pull of gravity seemed intent on dissuading her, finally relenting at the end and letting go, sending her crashing against the wall. Nursing her bruised arm, she looked out at an Isfahan she did not know. Her anonymous little street, gentle to a fault, was almost unrecognisable.

Dawn had broken, and filtered through the faint embers of the east, Isfahan felt like a curious dream. Azadeh inched her way back towards her bedroom closet and eventually managed to fling her woollen overcoat over her nightdress, together with her boots. She got to her front door and looked back at a stranger. She left the home she had once known. Like a drunkard, who refuses to be pacified, Isfahan continued to shake and swirl, the violence in its tremors tempered by a peculiar meditative cadence to its movements. Azadeh stood by the front door of her building, trying to fathom the hopelessness of all that was.

Thank God old Mrs Hossein was at her sister's, at least she had the warmth of that bond to hold on to. But what now? What of all the screams that had begun renting the air, merged into a farcical duet with the muezzin's cries that had just begun to emanate from the mosque nearby? What of the majority of buildings on her street that lay bruised and broken, their collective veneer of dust and mist creating the impression that they were nothing but an illusion torn from the ancient pages of Safavid history? What of this city and her sorrows, what of her people and their melancholic eyes, what of her sublime architecture and her fabled bridges...her bridges, *her bridges*.

Azadeh froze. And then she began to run. She didn't know why, but it was the only thing she could do. It was her only release, her only escape from the suffocation felt at a deep, irreparable loss—the same kind of loss she had felt tug away at her heart when the Zaindeh Rud had dried up.

She ran through the destruction and the remains, she ran through lives scattered in a hazy confusion of screams and laments, she ran through streets whose names and numbers and identities counted for nothing, and her heart refused to slow down. She ran along the enormous crack that had shattered the ground and ripped right through the heart of Kohne Meydan; she ran through her thoughts of the quaint village of Toudeshk-Cho and its specific stillness that had held her from the first time she'd gone there a decade ago; she ran through her illusions of the central desert of Dasht-e Kavir and its haunting enormity that had the power of always putting things in perspective—and her heart urged her on.

She ran, breathless, through millions of strands of Isfahani carpets that had magically risen into the sky and had begun weaving, flowing, and merging themselves into a calligraphic motif that appeared to spell 'sorrow', she ran, hopeless, through projections of the painstaking miniatures and blue-domed mosques and preciously-tiled mansions that had gathered in an elusive sky, she ran, fearless, through her memories of a Chahar Bagh once kissed by beauty and her dreams of a Gunbad-i Khaki crafted through the romance and the tears of Omar Khayyam himself...until her heart forced her to stop.

This was it, the point from where the Si-o-seh pol usually began to come into view. But what was usual about this dawn? Azadeh's steps softened. She stared off into the distance, her eyes hungry for her bridge and its comforting ominousness. She looked deep within its heart, through dawn's cruel dissonant mist, to find something to hold on to—those arches of 33, that familiar encompassing structure that swept from one side of the banks to another, that promenade with its poetic sadness, those teahouses poised to come to life at just about this time of the day each day—to anything to help cease the unbearable anxiousness within her heart.

From a distance that lived somewhere in yesterday, she heard the same fragile voice of the teahouse owner with those same haunting words uttered 12 years ago. What was it that he had said through those sad eyes? 'It is as though I have lost a lover. I can still hear her voice, I can still sense her soul…but she is no more.'

She stood there silently, frozen at a distance from the Allahverdi Khan Bridge. She said a silent prayer for old Mrs Hossein and the simple home she had nurtured with much love; she uttered a silent wish for Saba Farashahi, lost in the melancholic majesty of her old mansion covered with dust flakes and bleeding the remnants of lost Safavid splendour; she made a fervent wish for Ghaith and Nisreen Abbasi, by now almost certainly, staggering under the broken promises of a thousand broken bridges; she thought of Zeinab and Hafiz…and then she closed her eyes and wrapped her arms around the air in front of her…

Maryam's grace and love for life swelled within her. Azadeh felt a deep sense of peace. She felt at peace about the relationships she had lost as a child and the relationships she had nurtured as a woman. Maryam's warmth pervaded deeper within her soul. She felt strangely assured of the 900 bridges and their benefactors, assured that their destinies had been forged long before any of this. She felt calm about her Isfahan with its fabled sorrows and its forgotten glories and its people whose memories endured well beyond their lives. And she felt Maryam's love, coursing with unshakeable fortitude deeper within her, her truest connection to this earth, the persistent fragrance of her life.

Azadeh opened her eyes. As they began to adjust to dawn's increasingly well-established glow, she looked out into the distance towards Si-o-seh once again. She'd never known her heart to feel this way, strangely unburdened, yet brimming with all the hidden desires of Isfahan. The mist had dissipated. She began to count the pieces of her life. They lay tangled...a chaotic collage of fragments, desires, dreams, dust, and rubble.

Kleptosufi

Whenever she leaves, a fragment of me leaves with her. I've beseeched her time and time again to leave with an 'au revoir' not a 'goodbye', to not leave me with the overwhelming numbness that it's meant to be our last.

"There's no beauty in 'bye'," she always replies, "but 'goodbye'… now that has a melody to it, a story to go with it."

And thus I exist, in this time-frozen limbo, my dreams tethered to Rose Fakhri and the fatal touch; my emotions suspended in ether, my passions for her suspended in an instance.

This moment, this love, comes to rest in me
many beings in one being
In one wheat grain a thousand sheep stacks
Inside the needle's eye
a turning night of stars
There is a light seed grain inside
you fill it with yourself or it dies
I am caught in this curling energy, your hair
whoever is calm and sensible
is insane!

Well past midnight, the breeze begins to rustle through the orchards and the ghosts of Bsharri. Every time the wind brushes past my face, I'm reminded of her hair, cascading past me like forgotten feathers. I yearn, I grasp…slowly, I learn to let go. I try and frame my longing with Rumi's words and couplets, only to have it create a distraction and escape out into the world. And there it roams, in Bsharri's dark skies, dappled with stars and Gibran Khalil Gibran's rebellious wounds.

If there's anything I know of Rose Fakhri and me, it's that our silent passion is too potent to withstand much longer. One of these nights, touch we must. And then everything will be known, once and for all…whether our love is meant to singe through the sorrows that surround our souls, or whether that first touch will be my last.

Tender words we spoke
to one another
are sealed
in the secret vaults of heaven.
One day like rain,
they will fall to earth
and grow green
all over the world.

Soon, the agony of goodbye will have some finality; soon, this dance of dreams and desire will have its conclusion. But for a touch, our hearts are as good as one. But in that first touch lingers destiny, and just as furtively, elegy. Ah, but how unforgettably sweet such death shall be…

My name is Ziad Haddad. I don't know whether this story is worth telling or it isn't, but tell it I will. Hopefully at the end, you will understand why my heart, like my body, has reconciled itself to being in this constant dance of motion and turmoil.

It began when I was nine. There were three or four of us, returning from our prayers at the church. I remember the sky being heavy with clouds. I remember thinking at the time that the clouds, which were close to bursting, must have been filled with too many secrets to hold. The air was thick with cedars and childhood mischief and the faint whiff of distant pines. Strangely it's the pines that to this day remind me of summers past and the mysteries they held. On that evening though, all thought of trees and nature at large were discarded for a far more elusive matter—that of girls—whom my fellow companions were discussing with guarded enthusiasm.

Without warning, my feet began to move in a strange direction. Forward, stop, back again, stop, circle, circle, circle. It started slowly. Before I knew it, the pace had quickened. Soon, my arms had arisen. They had their own rhythms to follow, their own journey to map out. Extend, rise, soar, circle, circle, circle. My friends laughed. To them it must have looked like a game. One of them began to imitate me, well, he tried to anyway. After a while he gave up, he could no longer keep up. You see, by now the quickness in my steps and the power in my arms had increased to such an extent that there was no way he could.

Soon I was circling over boulders and through fields, rich with the smell of olives, wheat, and barley, past bewildered village-folk, who clearly thought me mad.

"That Ziad," I could hear them murmur, "he's clearly lost his marbles. He is completely off his rocker."

But I wasn't; I was trying to understand the pattern of my body, I was trying to come to terms with the movements of my feet and my arms, by now a complex yet fluid singular motion. Though I didn't quite understand what was happening at the time, that was the day the whirling began.

Our little village of Baskinta, high in the north-eastern mountains of Lebanon, was never short of gossip. Be it the old man Ghaith, and the stolen treasure of gold coins he'd supposedly been concealing in his cobweb-saturated cellar for half a decade, or the Sarryeh twins, and their particular fondness for switching lives and identities just to add a little spark to their days, Baskinta was a beehive of conspiracy theories. My own role in this communal drama was that of being the odd child out. I rarely spoke, I rarely played games, I rarely made friends, and the few that I did had, but obviously, included me within their fold out of pity rather than any sort of affinity. "Leave him be," was the usual refrain, "he's probably slow or something."

Naturally, my progression from a 'strange little boy' to the 'boy who danced' sent waves of speculation and odd whispers of trepidation rippling through Baskinta's old streets and cobblestone alleyways. "Now what's with this new gimmick? Is he acting out or has he finally been possessed?"

My parents, thankfully, were a bit more pragmatic in their dissections. "I think he's just expressing himself," offered my father. "Perhaps it's his destiny to become a dancer, though only the good Lord knows how all the relatives will react to that."

"Oh, they'll have to get used to it," replied my feisty mother. "As will the rest of these gossip-mongers. It's a blessing Jibril, to show traces of artistry, and who knows, maybe a little sprinkling of spirituality at such an early age. We've been worried about him for so long, let's just leave him be…"

And leave me be they did. From the time the dazed movements began, to when I turned 19, they would comment sometimes, inquire at others, but they never judged. By that time my affliction had been examined and identified by three village elders, who agreed that it wasn't mad circling after all, but a spiritual whirling, a form of spiritual devotion, followed and practiced by the Mawlawiyya or Mevlevi Sufis.

This revelation had set off another wave of hysteria. The initial diffidence and annoyance of the villagers gave way to a fear of the unknown, of not being able to fathom what they were dealing with. "God, is he now going to unleash some sort of Islamic revolution upon our village?"; "Is he going to drag our sons and daughters along with him?"; "Make sure Wissam, Ghada, and others of that age don't leave the house for the next week."

My father began to research this phenomenon known as the Whirling Dervish, whose fabled steps I appeared to have adopted, with unrestrained passion, without any prior knowledge or any interest.

"Look Zeina," he explained to my mother, "the dervishes belong to the Mawlawiyya Sufi Order, founded by the poet Jalal ad-Din Rumi in the 13th century." He went on to explain: "This book says that the whirling is a practice of *dhikr* or a remembrance of their God by his followers. From what I can make out, this spinning of Ziad's is part of the formal *sama* ceremony, basically his initiation into the Sufi path."

My mother remained silent on receiving this information. When she finally spoke, she had one simple query: "But where did he learn this?" To this question, my father had no answers. I, though, had a simple enough reply in return: "Mother, it just came to me one day."

Secretly, I too had started researching on whirling dervishes and Rumi, thanks to a few large volumes of crumbling books one of my few friends, Omar, had managed to source from Beirut. While I'd never really questioned the spinning and its origins, age had brought with it the desire to seek and to find out what sort of religious ramification it held.

As I began to read more about the dervishes and Sufism, I began to realise that the religious implications of my calling were minimal. This wasn't Islam I was delving into, this wasn't some strict, intolerant doctrine I was binding myself to, but a free-spirited spiritual one, where love, sorrow, and desire appeared to be bound together by a celestial swirl of memories and devotion. This was the path of the Sufi. I was relieved. It appeared that my new calling did not have the propensity to cause my parents much grief, and that their deeply Christian hearts would not have to deal with the unexpected nuisance of a convert within their ranks. When I conveyed this piece of news to them, there was a deep sigh of relief. My spinning was *not*, after all, the early sign of fanaticism.

In Rumi though, I had found a figure in whom my obsession and attraction appeared explicit. This was fanaticism of a different sort. Stepping into my later teens, he was my refuge and my truest friend, welcoming me into the world beyond and guiding me through its many roads with simplicity and beauty. Through the mysteries of his many journeys and the romance of his many words, my spinning was beginning to take on a new meaning.

And then on the 99th day of my 19th year, it happened—the event that would change my life and alter the lives of anyone who came in touch with me.

Before reaching the decaying side-stairs that led to the roof of the Cistercian Chapel, one always passed Karam the Cripple. That was what everyone called him. He'd been that way for close to 60 years, ever since he fell down a hill as a child while climbing to the village of Nebba Sannine.

I was heading up the chapel since its roof afforded me an especially clear view of Mount Sannine, standing proud in its nearly 2,700-metre majesty in the far distance. Once up on the roof and with Jebel Sannine in my eyes, I felt that the whirling was at its purest.

Whirling up the crooked, cobblestone road that led to the chapel's stairs, I brushed past Karam the Cripple that day. I said a bright 'good morning', without missing a step. When I got to the stairs and looked back at him, I was left stunned. Karam the Cripple was standing upright and walking tall with the confidence of an army general. What had just happened? Two old men who were playing a game of cards on the street had witnessed the brief exchange. They were up on their feet, raving like lunatics, "It's a miracle! It's a miracle!" To add to it all, Karam the Cripple was now dancing with the wild, gay abandon of a drunken gypsy, his glee expressed in a few unrestrained Aramaic profanities.

A large crowd gathered quickly, with all the festive fervour of townsfolk about to head to a circus performance. And I was the clown at the heart of it all—the object of their admiration and speculation. Fingers were being pointed at me with awe, whispers were making their way around the crowd like a swarm of bees, and my miraculous touch was being dissected with expert insights.

I sat down on the steps, trying to take in the enormity of what had just happened. For years, the spinning had been a carefree process, something I hadn't initiated and wasn't in control of. It had allowed me to step outside my self-imposed confinement and stride into the world, a way of existing within my silences and yet celebrating them. Knowledge of Rumi, Sufism, and the whirling dervishes had brought with it a keen spiritual understanding of the path I was embarking on, a journey I still had no control over. But now this miracle, what was I to make of this, how was I meant to grasp what it meant?

Over the next few months, it became clear that curing Karam the Cripple was not a one-off incident. Whether I was focussing on it or not, whether I spun through the streets and the hills and the fields of Baskinta with a singular purpose or not, the healings continued. People would stream out onto the lanes and the tiny alleyways around their homes as I danced. Some would come and place themselves directly in my path, in the hope that a tiny brush or a minor touch would cure them of whatever affliction they harboured, be it real or imagined.

It didn't work all the time, not every crippled, terminally ill, wounded, or simply feverish person was cured. The miraculous touch, it seemed, had some conditions to adhere to. The one piece of logic I could figure out was that only people with a certain purity of heart and who had lived their lives with warmth and generosity could be the recipients of the healing.

There was Youssef Khalil, the grocery store owner's son, who had set off for Beirut one weekend to deliver a fresh harvest of potatoes but ended up with severe injuries from yet another of those incomprehensible Israeli bombings. The case of Fatema Nasser's hand injuriy was a touch less dramatic—she'd let a knife slip while cutting tomatoes. With Carol Khoury, a malignant brain tumour, growing ominously for over a year, had vanished with the lightest of touches as I whirled past her, on my way to that grove of stone pines along the narrow road extending east from Baskinta towards Naba'a Sannine.

With some it was cancer, with others just a persistent cough. Some were left stunned at their instant healings, not knowing how to tread this world without the affliction they had carried for so long, others spoke in the language of celebration, wild happiness pouring out through their eyes. The ones who weren't so blessed were left cursing me as I spun and circled my way through Baskinta's narrow secrets and forgotten spaces, forced to come to terms with the undeniable burdens and sins that they had bred. I felt a deep sense of regret towards them, I wished that the healing touch would extend itself to everyone it came across, but I knew by then that my only job on this earth was to dance with the winds, and that which was destined to happen, would happen.

At home, my parents were making what they could of this remarkable evolution in my Sufi spirit. "Jibril," my mother confessed to my father, "at times I'm scared of whatever's happening. But it's a miracle, it can only be a beautiful thing, right?" And then, as she brushed aside her auburn hair, a faint reflection of the once-cascading flow she proudly displayed as a beautiful young woman, now a contained reservoir of her fondest memories, she revealed her core concern: "But he's just my Ziad. He was such a soft, simple little boy. And what are we dealing with now? A saint? A healer? It's a beautiful thing…but he was just my little Ziad…"

My father came up to her and placed his arms around her. As they sat on the divan whose fabric carried the fragrances and memories of four generations of Haddads, they looked into the street, beyond the old wrought-iron railing outside their balcony with its single sprig of bougainvillea. A common street, filled with conversations and remembrances and tragedies too personal to forget.

Watching them from just behind the bedroom door, I sensed my father's eyes turn towards the portrait that hung above the door leading to the balcony. It was them—from a time when photographs only came in that strange monochrome, beautiful colours lying somewhere between dull yellow, a hint of brown, and an unexpected maroon—my mother, the perfect Lebanese beauty, her hair coiffured like a French actress, her eyes dark, her skin unblemished, and her smile, faintly restrained, perhaps under the influence of the photographer's instruction; my father, not the most handsome man in the world, but with an attractive aura that didn't believe in perfect features: his soldier's uniform, crisp; his gaze, photogenic, even when he had to look at the camera at that universally awkward angle; his arms placed with gentle shyness around my mother's waist…

I watched them just sit there for a long while, lost in their selves of yesterday.

When my father finally spoke, his words of reassurance came rooted in Sufism itself. "I've been reading a lot Zeina, you mustn't worry about him too much. The Sufis have always been great mystics. Who knows, perhaps our Ziad is destined for much greater things."

After a pause, he reached for the dark wooden shelf nearby and picked up a large book. He rifled towards a particular page, before continuing: "Ah yes, here, look. This whirling of his, it acts as a mystical journey, man's spiritual ascent through mind and love towards the 'Perfect'. As a follower, he must grow through love, desert his ego, and eventually return from this spiritual journey as a man who is able to love and to be of service to the whole of creation." He put a comforting arm across my mother's shoulders. "See Zeina, that's where he must be headed."

I let a hushed tear drop from my eyes, watching them silently from just behind the doorway. I felt humbled by my father's purity, I felt surrounded by mother's love. I held on to myself. Because I knew at that moment, deep within myself, that our lives would need to withstand a fresh, explosive storm.

My life's greatest upheavals were being plotted in conjunction with some secret cosmic clock that I had no control over. Over the years, news of the man who whirled and healed had spread far and wide across the land, and further beyond Lebanon's borders. But time had brought with it temperance, and the hysteria that had greeted me at 19 had slowly reached more manageable proportions. People had begun to understand that not everyone would be healed, and that they might well be one of the unfortunate ones. They had also learnt to appreciate the fact that I would not dance my way through their fields and their homes every single moment of every single day, and that the whirling would never arise on a whim. They sensed there were far more mysterious forces at play.

I was, meanwhile, absorbing every philosophical and poetic sentiment that complemented the teachings arising from Rumi and Sufism. I delved increasingly into the rich lyrical and literary heritage of my village. In Baskinta's revered sons of Mikhail Naimy, Suleiman Kettaneh, and Abdallah Ghanem, and men of calibre like George Ghanem, Rachid Ayoub, and Amin Maalouf, I had struck gold. I would often take one of their volumes and steal away to an orchard, where I would spend the afternoon under the sway of a gentle breeze and the comforting scent of pines, cedars, firs, and junipers. These sojourns of mine would take me to a number of places in and around Baskinta's fringes, such as Wadi al Karm or further on to Kafr Aqab and Ain el Qabou.

One such afternoon, Mikhail Naimy's *The Book of Mirdad* was my companion as I returned from Dhour el Choueir, another small village not far from ours. I had just left the village and got on to the road that led to Baskinta, when I saw a woman. She was walking up the road with a large sack of vegetables on her back, but it looked to me as if she had the entire weight of the world on her shoulders. She was no more than 50, but she looked 75. I found myself unable to move, transfixed by her and the sorrows on her face that seemed so obvious to me, they might as well have been painted in red.

My feet had begun to stir, and I allowed them to. Soon, I was whirling towards her. She stood still, allowing me to brush past her as I whirled. When I turned back to see her after a while, I was left gasping for breath. It wasn't as though I had healed her afflictions, because there were none as far as I could tell. But she somehow seemed *lighter*. The more I stared at her, the more apparent it became. Her face had been, suddenly, filled with colour. When she smiled at me she looked her age, maybe even younger. There was no denying it; that weight of the world she had been carrying and all the sorrows that had set up home within her had, enigmatically, vanished. I had *stolen* her sorrows away. I had become the *robber* of sorrows, and I watched her as she skipped like a little girl all the way towards Dhour el Choueir.

As I watched her leave, I began to sense a slight tingling in my right forearm. I rubbed it a few times and massaged it, but it remained, like an obstinate relative. The truth dawned on me with slow but certain impact: not only had I stolen away the woman's sorrows as I brushed past her, but I had also welcomed them into myself—all her years of strife and visible regrets and silent melancholy and raging sorrows had been taken away and subsumed within the slight pain that now resided in my forearm. It was the 250th day of my 25th birthday. I knew then, standing there on the narrow dirt road, that the Sufi path that had taken hold of every part of my life and the road it was leading me to had been foreordained for me.

This new power of mine was certainly a less perceptible gift than the healing, and just as well. It allowed me to dissect it, examine it, and try and fathom its significance in the world. Lebanon, under the sway of a history of conflict, under the influence of a bloody civil war that had ravaged my beautiful land, under the shadows of nefarious intentions from neighbouring eyes, and under the clutches of a sectarian soul that regularly erupted and threatened to engulf the nation at any time, was a reservoir of sorrow. I would whirl, and my spiritual journey would bring me in contact with an ocean of grief: a wife grieving over her slain husband, parents grieving over their widowed daughter, a mother inconsolable over the death of an infant, a community of Shias bereaved over a recent slaughter administered by the Hamas…

Lebanon's sorrows were endless, and my work was never done. Sometimes it would seem to me that I had whirled through an entire day, and yet there my country lay, still besieged by the relentless tides of melancholy. But silently, I knew, I was making a difference: I could *feel* it in my body. Every memory of sadness and every lifetime of grief that I stole away ended up immortalised within me. That slight tinge in my right forearm now had a wealth of friends who had marked themselves out all over my body.

The people who were graced by this new power of mine and the people who surrounded them were more often than not left bemused and none the wiser, though this was a far more profound occurrence than that of the healing, sometimes cleansing people right to their spiritual core. And so while the legend of 'Ziad the Healer' persisted, the tome of 'Ziad the Stealer of Sorrows' never quite got embellished in rhyme and verse.

As with most things in my life though, my mother knew. "Jibril," she revealed to my father, "it's quite obvious that his healing has started to become less and less frequent. But there is something new with him. He seems to be leaving people happier, as though their cares never even existed." After a slight pause, arrived the true concern. "But in this process, don't you think his own body has begun to become aggrieved?"

My father nodded sagely. He fell back upon his trusted research of that magical beast called Sufism. He removed a tome that had been gathering dust on his old beloved bookshelf for years. It's as though he knew the pages by heart because he soon came across what he'd been looking for. "Ah, yes. Look, Zeina..." he directed my mother's eyes towards a certain passage. "Rumi writes about the eradication of the established fear-based religious orders of the world. His remedy for this is a love-based doctrine—a human journey free of guilt, fear, and shame. Perhaps, that is where our Ziad has now moved in this spiritual path of his."

I watched from the doorway as a few more pages were ruffled.

"Here we are. Within Sufism, a Sufi's way of life is to love and to be of service to people, to rid them of their ills, to free them from their sorrows." He nurtured his thick grey beard thoughtfully. "This was the next destined stage on his path, Zeina. And even if it means taking on afflictions onto his own body, perhaps it is meant to be the way of a dervish."

My mother looked away from my father. Without looking at her, I could feel a torrent of tears forming in her eyes. My parents had never been afflicted with any major illnesses and had never been in requirement of my healing touch. As I watched them secretively though, I was consumed by the need to touch them and wipe away the sorrows that might have accumulated within them, on account of me. But my feet stood still. My soul remained silent. My breath lingered softly. My heart tempered its beat. And that was when I knew, without the slightest lingering doubt—my path of Sufism, through its ecstasies and its miseries, through its revelations and its condemnations, through its epiphanies and its tragedies, would be one that they were going to have to withstand as well.

At dusk, the village of Hasroun lay spread out before my eyes like a work of art created in chiaroscuro. While dusk's rays were dense and penetrative, the 'Rose of the Mountains' was resplendent in its red-tiled simplicity. All the roofs, whether surrounded by verdure or enraptured by the slowly emerging mist, were a beautiful contrast to dusk's dark intentions.

It had been two years since the new chapter in my spiritual path had presented itself. My body yearned for rest. But a strange restlessness consumed my heart as well, the deafeningly silent scream that told me I wasn't doing enough. In this longing, Hasroun had become a new and cherished addition to my escapes. The Maronite fortress village sat on the edges of a cliff that soared over the Holy Valley, with ravines that echoed in darkness and peaks that infiltrated the clouds framing it on either side. Nearly all its stone facade homes came wreathed with vines, like an old actress holding on to her memories of beauty. For me, the most wonderful thing about Hasroun was the richness of its flowers and fruit trees, nourished by springs that trickled along its alleys.

I had found myself a beautiful apple orchard, undisturbed by people. Under the shade of its trees, kept company by the gentle essence of neighbouring cherries and plums, I tried to find spiritual answers to my inner anguish. Rumi was my only succour, and in this sacred space, his sacredness shone through even crisper through his words.

I would carry along a selection of his volumes at different times, sometimes the *Masnavi*, *Diwan-e Shams-e Tabrizi*, and *Love's Ripening*, at other times *Where Two Oceans Meet*, *A Garden Beyond Paradise*, and the *Rubais*. Slowly, the meditations and the spiritual lessons and the love couplets began to distil my mind and offer me a path out of my delusions. Across several of his books, I began to find and nurture what spoke to me the clearest. A private collection of treasures emerged, ferreted from many volumes, like an orchard-picker picking only those fruits that were ripe with possibility.

This being human is a guest house.
Every morning a new arrival.
A joy, a depression, a meanness,
some momentary awareness comes as an unexpected visitor.
Welcome and entertain them all!
Even if they're a crowd of sorrows,
who violently sweep your house
empty of its furniture,
still, treat each guest honourably.

He may be clearing you out
for some new delight.
The dark thought, the shame, the malice,
meet them at the door laughing,
and invite them in.
Be grateful for whoever comes,
because each has been sent as a guide from beyond.

These pains you feel are messengers. Listen to them.

Brother, stand the pain.
Escape the poison of your impulses.
The sky will bow to your beauty, if you do.
Learn to light the candle. Rise with the sun.
Turn away from the cave of your sleeping.
That way a thorn expands to a rose.

Are you jealous of the ocean's generosity?
Why would you refuse to give
this joy to anyone?
Fish don't hold the sacred liquid in cups!
They swim the huge fluid freedom.

It was the 270th day of my 27th year. That fluid freedom was what I craved for. "Rumi, shine your light on me," I implored in stillness. I would have to learn to withstand the pain. I would have to wait for the sky to bow down to my beauty. I would have to learn to rise with the sun. It was time to leave my homeland. It was time to spread what I had been gifted with, into the world.

The walls, the streets, the roofs, the homes, and the Seljuk mosques of Konya reverberated with quiet stories from yesteryears. In this home of a million souls, there was one soul that seemed to exist on a drifting cloud, looking down upon its tomb that lay encrusted in turquoise and embroidery with amusement. It peered out onto Antalya's wild plains and endless prairies still peopled by the ghosts of the Hittites, the Phrygians, the Lydians, the Persians, the Cappadocians, and the Romans, casting its eye further out onto the rest of Turkey.

After negotiating my way through the heart of this ancient city and the arterial lanes and boulevards emanating from the Alaeddin Mosque, I finally reached Mevlana. His sarcophagus lay shrouded in heavy brocade; his son lay by his side. This was the city he'd come to as a young boy, these were the same streets and homes that bore silent witness as his spiritual wisdom erupted into an ocean. Jalal ad-Din Rumi, my saviour. Jalal ad-Din Rumi, my tormentor.

I wept in silence as I heard a reed flute playing softly inside the mausoleum complex, forming a musical score to the calligraphy that lay etched on the walls. I wept in rapture as drops of sunlight came filtering in through the mausoleum's stained glass windows, bathing its walls and my consecrations in mystic rhythms of opulence. I meditated, I prayed, I cast a silent wish towards his lofty soul, and then I whirled my way back out into the old town. An ardent urgency had gripped my soul.

I whirled through Konya's medieval bazaars, knowing fully well that Rumi might well have begun his ecstatic circling in one of those same bazaars. I whirled across carpet shops caked with dust and memories, across cafés brimming with the salty essence of flatbread and the extravagant textures of Turkish kebabs, across sad roadside stalls accented by the poetic flavour of their rose and tulip stalks. I whirled past a line of goldbeaters, knowing fully well that they might have been ancestors of the same goldbeaters whose rhythmic hammering and chants of Allah had brought Rumi to tears and pushed him onto the path of bliss. I whirled in ecstasy, past crowds of bewildered tourists, past local men with long beards and knowledgeable eyes, past local women bound to their headscarves, a conservatism that ran in the face of everything Rumi's soul held sacred; I whirled in beauty, tapping into the same spirit Mevlana might have held as he danced in front of his followers, reciting his verses and poems in sacred rapture; I danced wild and unfettered, straight into the arms of a giant dervish hall of the Mevlana Cultural Centre, with my eyes closed and my arms soaring high. I heard the large crowd gathered at the hall let out a collective gasp as I, this random intruder, whirled and deposited himself seamlessly within the *dhikr* of Rumi's closest: the traditional *sama* ceremony of the whirling dervishes.

It was December, Turkey's fierce winter chill had enveloped Konya, but I felt Rumi's warmth pervade my essence. I felt the warmth of my compatriot dervishes as they whirled and swayed, their long white robes glittering like diamonds, each of us lost in our own spiritual remembrance and yet unified as one.

Within the *sama*, our mystical journey was a spiritual ascent through mind and love to the 'Perfect', abandoning ego, nurturing love, and reclaiming truth. I danced in abundance, with the singer's *naat* solo, the poetry specifically praising the Prophet, and with the improvisational humming of *taksim*, in free rhythm, its cadence already embedded within me.

My legs moved effortlessly as they never had during the *devr-i-veled*, bowing to my companions in acknowledgment of our divine breath. My fellow *samazens* and I eased into the Four Salams, our left feet forming the pivot to our devotions, our right palms entreating Heaven. We danced in praise of our recognition of God, we whirled in recognition of the existence in his unity, we engulfed ourselves in the ecstasy that comes from total surrender, and we stilled the air around us in calmness brought about by our peaceful hearts assuaged by divine unity. Even as the *dhikr* came to its conclusion with a recitation from the Quran and a prayer by the Sheikh, my soul, my heart, my mind, and my body flapped with restive fervour.

How could I have known that it was the festival in celebration of the Saint I had chanced upon? How was I to know that that day was the anniversary of when Rumi rose into the sky? We danced in melancholy and in ecstasy, we whirled as silent spectators and blessed collaborators. Just as naturally as I had entered, I left. My whirling refused to abate, the rabid urgency within my soul as fierce as ever. I went where my feet took me, back past the same bazaars and the same bearded men and the same covered women and the same befuddled tourists and the same simple cafés...but this time, no one stared at me with astonished or frightened eyes. They had all been made lighter, all of their sorrows that I had felt as I had brushed past each of them had vanished. I knew it because I now carried a small piece of them within me, their grief, their sadness, all of which I had stolen away, captured within those pains that my protesting body had now reconciled itself to.

When I left Lebanon, I'd kissed my mother on the forehead and kissed my father on the cheek. In the dignity of their silences, I had known that their understanding of my Sufi path was perhaps greater than my own. Despite his resilient religious faith, my father had not only accepted my voyage into this path as a child, but had also poured his curiosity and broadminded tendencies towards this storm-riddled ocean called Sufism. My mother had done much the same, but with compassion and affection as her crutches. Without them, this journey might well have ended even before it had begun.

I had left with a small bag made out of jute, carrying only a few volumes of Sufi and some bread. It was to Konya and Turkey where my feet had naturally led me. But that day, as I whirled through Konya's spiritual treasures and beneath Rumi's enraptured gaze,

I knew my feet had only begun their journey. Later that night as I rested my frenzied soul by the side of an old road with a few pieces of bread for company, I read from the *Masnavi* and reflected silently on my expedition through Rumi's letters:

Water that's poured inside will sink the boat
While water underneath keeps it afloat.
Driving wealth from his Heaven to keep it pure
King Solomon preferred the title 'Poor':
That sealed jar in the stormy sea out there
Floats on the waves because it's full of air,
When you've the air of dervishes inside
You'll float above the world and there abide…

Beginning from Konya, the next seven years would turn out to be an epic passage of dance, devotion, sorrows…and sparrows. I sensed it would be my feet and the silent songs within my soul that would lead the way, a course far removed from geographical lines and enforced longitudes. I entered the land of the Arab Emirates and eventually reached the city of Dubai, where I got the feeling that my inquiring message of Sufism would fly in the face of everything I saw. But I soon understood that here too was a collage of human desires and failings, of extremely rich people struggling to find some significance in their lives, and of extremely poor people coming to terms with the loss of their original geography and identity.

I brushed past immigrant labourers wilting under the midday sun, even as the city that had been built upon their shoulders shied away from their non-existent wages and deplorable living conditions; I brushed past anonymous middle-class immigrants whose eyes still sparkled with hopes of their Dubai dreams but whose realities spoke of lonely existences in a city that would never be theirs; and, just as easily, I brushed past rich businessmen whose riches and afflictions now soared nearly as high as some of the gleaming towers in the sky.

I touched an old bearded man who lingered beside the waters of the Creek, his eyes miles away from the existence around him. The old man and the hordes, I drank in their sorrows, but did I end up quenching their thirst for significance, did I end up stealing away their memories as well? This I'll never know. But I kept my heart open, I kept my touch pure, I kept my arms raised, and with its contradictions and its hidden layers of beauty and the songs from its deserts echoing in my mind, I danced my way out of the Emirates.

India filled with me wonder. I knew the significance the land had held for Rumi. I was prepared in a sense, but nothing could have prepared me for the rapture that was to invade my senses. Here I was, a nomadic dervish, adrift in the world, my very title having been birthed through a merging of Persian Avestan and the Vedic Sanskrit *adhrigu*, my very essence having been propagated as much by the Persian dervishes as by the Hindu *sanyasis*.

As always, I allowed my feet to lead the way. I danced past the lives of two brothers who had formed a united front against their past sorrows; I danced among the wretchedly poor and I danced among the gloriously rich; I whirled through streets laced with regret and through those laden with joy; I touched faces, hopes, cultures, identities, and religions that I would travel this whole wide world put together and yet not touch.

In a city next to Bombay, I whirled my way into a young woman's path, only to find that she had already managed to make peace with her sorrows of a loved one who had left the earth. In the wild beauty of Bombay itself, I danced past a young lover who seemed almost oblivious to my touch, consumed as he was by the memories of a woman whose touch had already seeped through his core.

In a north Indian town that lingered in the fables of its regal lineage, I danced through the courtyard of an old Muslim family that had been stricken by grief over the loss of a child, but in whose two remaining caring children I also sensed that special sparkle that made life seem worthwhile. I whirled past mountains thick with the beauty of purity, I swam through the confluence of two of the world's most sacred rivers, I walked on desolate beaches, cradling immeasurable seas; I laughed, I wept, I drank in love, and I drowned myself in beauty bound to the divine…

Finally, I reached Delhi as it lay dappled in mist, with its wide boulevards and its festive markets and its silent tombs all under the sway of a lavish heritage. In the oldest part of the city, I ended up brushing against a fellow mystic, one who celebrated his Sufi saint every night in song, one whose devotion for his *Khwaja's* tomb mirrored my own for mavlana's turquoise resting-spot in Konya. Through his memories and his essence, I learned that togetherness and an abiding love and deep atonement have an equal power in drowning away the lingering effects of a remorseful past. India ended up helping me more than I helped it, it ended up healing me more than I healed it, and it ended up teaching me more than I could ever have bestowed onto its people.

By now though, I had to accept the fact that my body was wilting. The marks and pains that had felt like badges of honour earlier were taking hold of me. My body had begun to stoop, unable to withstand the burdens of human failings. But my spiritual thirst urged me on; I couldn't stop.

I danced onward through desolate deserts and mountain rivers filled with heaven's dew; I danced onward through noisy multitudes and isolated pilgrims; I whirled onward in hunger and with divine fulfilment; I touched islands and I touched millions and I touched strangers and I touched my own soul, in countries and cities that none of my books had ever spoken to me about. My body hurt but I begged for it to be courageous, I knew my journey wasn't done.

In the wondrous country of Japan, I found myself more lost than I had ever been. Its large city, Tokyo, burns with strange lights and echoes the sad whispers of souls lost to the night. Amongst the ocean of people I touched, there was one woman whose identity lay mired in mist and shrouded in untruths, one whose heart itself seemed to be nothing but shards of disillusionment, trying to slowly piece themselves together; and at the Shoganji Zen temple in the hidden village of Ojuki, I came in touch with a shy young man whose deceits and fables had caused his heart to be broken apart into exactly the same pieces as the woman's…shape for shape, edge for edge.

I crossed the ocean that very few men have crossed on a voyage that lasted ten nights and reached the large continent of America. I had never known for certain how my encounters with the thousands of people in the past and how my stealing away of their sorrows and their burdens had left them, whether it had healed their souls and assuaged their minds. Was it memories I was doing away with, were they better off with these memories left alive, was I stealing away a vital part of their existence as human beings? By intruding upon their sufferings, was I tampering with the master plan that had been set for each one of them? I could never tell. At times, I chose not to seek out the answers too hard. My body ached while my inquiries swirled, wilting beneath the enormity of human grief. I simply put my faith in Rumi, raised my right palm to the skies, and marched onward.

As I navigated North America and then willed myself onward to the southern continent, I knew that it was just a matter of time before my body gave way. And yet, my soul wasn't pacified; it egged me onward, back towards Turkey, across the demon-riddled waves of yet another endless ocean.

In Istanbul, I was walking along the old cafés that kissed the Bosphorus' shores when my feet and my arms were drawn towards passion's enduring significance in a world increasingly bereft of such.

In the eyes of two lovers, I found desire at its purest. Brushing past the young woman, I was made aware of her anguish over a lover, who was anchored neither to her nor to the city of her birth; touching the young man, I was made privy to his unquenchable thirst for Istanbul's repentances draped in history and poetry. As I danced through them, I was left breathless by their deep desire for each other, a desire that etched its madness onto Istanbul's forgotten addresses and crowded streets alike.

Leaving Turkey, I reached Iran by foot. I was drawn instantly towards the city of Isfahan. Only upon arriving did I realise that it had been ravaged by a large earthquake. As I danced my way through the rubble of human lives and pieces of broken dreams, my body was fed with the anguish of a city in a grief both isolated yet unified. But I also brushed against the courage and adamancy of the human spirit. While whirling my way along a dried-up riverbed, I spotted a woman standing in the distance, her gaze fixated on something that wasn't even there. There was something artistic, maybe even poetic, about her.

As I brushed past her and tapped into her sorrows, my mind was filled instantly with passionate brushstrokes and a lingering obsession while my body held firm against this new assault. I danced away. I dared not look back to see what effect my touch had brought on her, to see how her brush with this miracle might have affected her memories and her sorrows and her artistry and her poetry. In her body I had sensed profound pain but I had also sensed light. As I danced away, my thoughts of her lingering beauty—those fragile eyes, that fluttering black dress—directed me towards that light.

As I made my way through Iran, people's reactions to me were much the same as they had been across the rest of my journey. Some watched in disbelief, some rose in celebration, others shied away in fright, a few rose in anger, but millions, well millions didn't even see or notice or perceive me at all, wrapped as they were in the affairs of their own little worlds, consumed as they were by their own tragedies of the past and their miseries over an unseen future.

It was at this point that the ominous truth arose again, this time with a conviction that was hard to deny. The slightest touch on the streets, the lightest brush with a stranger drowning in his or her failed desires, the gentlest hint of sadness rendered stolen, and I would breathe my last. The body ached for mercy. The signs were potent and undeniable. Perhaps the endless journey was destined to have an end after all. The epic crossing had run out of earth. It was time to return home.

In this part of the world, the moon lingers with wild eyes. We are back to where I began my story with you. Fully aware that even the softest of touches against any human being on the street would cause my demise, I returned to Lebanon just over two years ago. I thought it best not to head back to Baskinta and be in the presence of so many people who knew me—friends, family, onlookers, strangers, inquisitive noses. So I headed directly for Bsharri, where the first thing I did was write my parents a letter and describe my epic journey to them in detail. We spoke a little while after that, and they accepted my decision to stay away from my village with the grace and intelligence that I'd come to expect from them.

They've come to visit me a few times over the past couple of years, taking care not to be followed or seen by anyone still hoping for a miraculous touch from their 'son in permanent exile'. They look much older now, but their eyes carry the tender comfort of two people having come to accept, perhaps even celebrate, their child's predestined journey on this earth. The fact that they have never been in need of my touch has been a blessing whose significance I've felt even more strongly now, allowing me as it has to hug them and kiss their cheeks with the faith of one who has been seven years gone, without the anxiety of any spiritual repercussions.

No one visits Bsharri. Well, they do, in a literal sense. But in the spiritual sense, I'm free. No one visits Bsharri to seek me out, no one visits Bsharri to run into my path. Part of this might have something to do with the fact that I live in a small, isolated cottage deep in the hills. My days are spent in my little garden and the small orchard that accompanies it. I only step out at night. Here in the birthplace of Gibran Khalil Gibran, the night affords me cover to converse with *Cedrus Libani*, the original cedars of Lebanon. I walk, unannounced and unnoticed, through the 19th century monastery that blends into the rocks, right into the chapel where Gibran's soul rises above his coffin and entreats me into conversations about life and longing; I swirl into the centuries-old cave that births a spring and carries remnants of an old fable regarding the Virgin Mary's compassion towards a Carmelite monk; I dance with the breeze along the Qadisha Valley, with only the northern star for guidance and conversation; I dance in perfectly pleasant weather and I dance through several inches of snow; I take a detour through the elevated village of Bekaa Kafra and past monasteries that breathe the essence of rock and speak in the language of the Lebanese Maronite Order.

My body is much the same; the aches, stings, and afflictions have proven themselves to be lifelong visitors. Even the stoop persists. Some evenings, the breeze carries with it strains of a Lebanese Arabic that still holds allegiance to Aramaic and is spoken with a strong tongue; on other evenings, the words I hear come birthed from the land's Phoenician legacy as the 'House of Ishtar'. Both these accents filter through my thoughts.

There is no one here to stir my soul or agitate my senses. There is no one here to instigate my touch or nourish my desires. No one, except her.

When Rose Fakhri first walked into the orchard that I often frequent on warm nights, I thought her to be an apparition. No one could be this beautiful, and yet, be of this earth. That was my abiding contemplation. It was only when she began to sing, did I know otherwise. Her songs were not leisurely ditties either. They spoke of an orphan girl who had gone through life without the love of a parent, one who had suffered terribly at the hands of violent men over the years, and one whose soul ached for release. We were two prisoners, exiled to the whims of our individual destinies.

She gasped when she first saw me, her private world having been infiltrated. I stayed, not saying a word. Slowly, our mutual silence began to grow comforting; it began to speak in a language with meter and melody. She began visiting the orchard every night, well after Bsharri had closed its eyes. Slowly, words began to emerge. Gradually, lives began to merge. We began to speak, we began to reveal. My apprehensions over her being appalled at the sight of this dishevelled Sufi were laid to rest. From being a young man with short hair that veered between light and dark shades of brown, soft blue eyes that I had inherited from my mother, a slim, tall frame, and a face that appeared pleasant on most days, I had turned into a wild, reclusive dervish whose hair was now much longer, whose skin bristled with the ravages of time, and whose eyes appeared perpetually adrift. None of this mattered to Rose Fakhri though. She walked into my life a year ago, but it took three months for our poetic silence to transform into words.

She met me at the orchard that night, as always, and disarmed me with the simplicity of those first words: "I want to hear your life story." Once I had gathered my breath and my memories,

I recounted the same story to her as I have to you tonight. She listened, rapt.

"The more I think about it, I feel human beings are much like sparrows," I articulated, in a bid to bring about some sort of closure to the journey for myself. "We flutter riotously as one large flock, we fly away in these bizarre patterns and circles in the sky, we fly solo, unrestrained, fed by a hunger to seek and to explain; we try and make lives for ourselves, we try and fend for ourselves, we try and find freedom, happiness, togetherness, love; and what are we at the end of it all but these insignificant specks, under the illusion that we're filling the skies when all we're doing is forming the tiniest of dots on the tiniest square piece of sky imaginable..." I paused to take a breath. "Rumi says that 'beyond our ideas of right and wrong, there is a field. I shall meet you there'...we are only sparrows, sometimes even that 'there' appears elusive, though I know it exists."

When Rose Fakhri spoke after a while, her voice was the melodic soul sister to Bsharri's night breeze. "Sparrows have their place. Sorrows have their place. If anything, your journey is testament to that. I didn't know why I found myself attracted to this orchard and kept returning here, night after night. But now I know. I was meant to hear your story. I was meant to meet you."

With her words, my body trembled under this new, strange affliction. The air between our bodies trembled too, aware of the electricity coursing through its inner spaces, of the strange attraction brewing between these two lost creatures of the night. Our bodies hovered around one another, silently courting fate. This furtive sway of to and fro, this slow dance in recognition of the alchemy brewing beneath Bsharri's conspiratorial skies, flirted with the fringes of possibility. Having heard my entire journey, Rose Fakhri took great care not to brush against me. She too understood though that whatever was happening between us had already been set in motion and that eventually, there would be no turning back.

The nights after that fateful occasion have been a perilous opera of restrained ardour, orchestrated by the fatal predilections of two bleeding hearts. We exchange words and lives and voyages, always fully aware that the ending to this exploration can't be anything but incurable. Ours has been a flirtation of the soul, more than anything. We sway like poetry tossed out in the breeze.

Every night, Rose Fakhri leaves me with 'goodbye', leaving me hanging by the edge of skin and fate. Except for last night, when she inched as close to me as she could. A few errant strands of her mischievous hair flew dangerously close to my face, but neither of us shied away. "Tomorrow night," she whispered, "tomorrow night we shall know."

I see her now, on this night dipped in rose. She arrives, guided by Bsharri's new full moon. The breeze has murder on its mind, howling through the valleys of Qadisha as it scours the land for any human being still awake at this hour. Rose Fakhri's beautifully shaped face appears frozen in time, the depths of her blue eyes brewing that rare sparkle I've come to know and love. And it *is* love, this mystic aura that surrounds us when we are together. It may be a furtive love, it may be a shackled love, but love it is—doused with the whims of destiny, accented by the sensual embers of desire, fed by the innocence of one soul locating its fated mirror image in this world. Her lustrous hair is playful in the winds tonight, as it nearly always is. It is constantly vying for her attentions, compelling her fingers borne through sadness and poetry to lavish their undivided devotions.

I am prepared to die tonight. I know this is how it should end. I know this is how it was probably *meant* to end. She walks up to me, this tender, delicate being who does such sweet justice to her name. She doesn't speak a word but brings her face closer to mine. I close my eyes and take a deep breath. I can feel her breath on mine; I can hear her heart beating wildly, perched on the edge of the cliff that is our lives. Such destined perfection this, this manna of spiritual epiphany, this romance set to the rhythms of a beautiful tragedy. Rose Fakhri's lips touch mine. I prepare to dissolve into ether. I expect my fragile bones to evaporate unto dust.

Except, they don't.

I'm suddenly aware of an incredible lightness. When I open my eyes, I see Rose Fakhri in front of me, her gaze transfixed. My stoop has disappeared. I now understand the lightness within me: all the afflictions I had borne, gathered across my great voyage and a life filled with many horizons, have disappeared. The sorrows still linger, but their presence is both harbinger and harvester of all that which makes this wayward mystic human. My saviour runs her fingers along my skin, meditating on its contours, caressing its specific tendencies. Through her touch, I can sense that time's ravages, etched so indelibly on my skin, have vanished too. I am still a young man, but only now do I sense the profundity of that reality coursing through my blood. My Sufi path has never felt more tangible; Rumi's words have never echoed through my mind with such clarity. I am a Sufi, I am a reservoir of sorrows, I am a catalyst for ardour, I am a vessel for all the happiness in this word, distilled through my body unto diamond drops of dusk.

"It is love," Rose Fakhri whispers, as she kisses me deeply.

In the depths of this kiss, lies bliss. Gibran's poetry floods Bsharri's night skies, Rumi's ecstasies pour through midnight, basking in the glow of this purity between us. "*This* is love," I concur.

And I am no longer bereft of human touch.

Acknowledgements

In bringing this collection to life, I owe deep gratitude to:

Jayant and Rajini Dasgupta, for being the rock in rockstars and the soul in soulful; for nourishing my early years towards an existence dedicated to artistry and creativity; and for continuing to inspire, instigate, and impel me in life and along my literary journey—a journey, impervious to formulaic plans, immersed in the simple pleasure of pursuing the perfect word, engaging with readers and audiences and characters and fellow artists, and going about it with the desire of Hemingway chasing that next drink.

Authors, both ancient and young, who manage(d) to create characters and write words that end up nourishing an endless reservoir of urgency and poetry; the river that keeps on giving.

Niyogi Books, for having the courage to adopt a short story collection at a time when many publishers cowered at the idea.

Readers, wherever in the world they may be, for adamantly persisting with books and stories, especially against an onslaught of everything else.

Salud.